"What, are we enemies now?"

Coolly, Jackie turned. "I'm not sure what you mean. We barely know each other." True, even though when they were together, she honestly felt as if she'd known him forever.

Evidently, he shared that sentiment. "Come on, Jackie. It's just me. What's going on?"

Fine. "You appeared awfully ready to believe that Charla could be a criminal."

"You don't?"

Staring at him, she struggled to find the right way to respond. "I don't know. But ever since I've been back in town, I've learned one bad thing after another about Charla. I mean, I always knew Mom spoiled her, but she wasn't an awful person."

"I know," he agreed. "We're all complicated."

Was that a warning? She narrowed her eyes, unsure how to respond.

Before she could, he leaned in and kissed her. A hard press of his mouth against hers, sending liquid fire right through her veins. Her gasp had her opening her mouth to him and she mentally said, "The hell with it" and kissed him back, right there in the sheriff's department parking lot, for all the world to see.

Dear Reader,

Sometimes it can be difficult to shut down the outside noise. Two things really help me—music and a good book. Whether reading one or writing one, I enjoy getting to know the fictional characters who gradually become real to me. Friends. I cheer them on, worry along with them and finally love that they get the happily-ever-after they deserve. That's the one thing you can always count on in a romance book, right?

Eli and Jackie's story allowed me to once again return to my fictional west-Texas town of Getaway. And again I got to be around horses and cowboys while helping two people not only battle danger but overcome so much in order to forge a new life together. I don't live in west Texas, but for whatever reason, that part of my home state has always drawn me in. I hope you find it as appealing as I do, and I hope you enjoy reading *Finding the Rancher's Son*!

Karen Whiddon

FINDING THE RANCHER'S SON

Karen Whiddon

H HARLEQUIN®

ROMANTIC SUSPENSE™

Recycling programs
for this product may
not exist in your area.

ISBN-13: 978-1-335-75966-5

Finding the Rancher's Son

Harlequin Enterprises ULC
22 Adelaide St. West, 41st Floor
Toronto, Ontario M5H 4E3, Canada
www.Harlequin.com

Printed in U.S.A.

Karen Whiddon started weaving fanciful tales for her younger brothers at the age of eleven. Amid the gorgeous Catskill Mountains, then the majestic Rocky Mountains, she fueled her imagination with the natural beauty surrounding her. Karen now lives in north Texas, writes full-time and volunteers for a boxer dog rescue. She shares her life with her hero of a husband and four to five dogs, depending on if she is fostering. You can email Karen at kwhiddon1@aol.com. Fans can also check out her website, karenwhiddon.com.

Books by Karen Whiddon

Harlequin Romantic Suspense

Colton 911: Chicago
Colton 911: Soldier's Return

The Rancher's Return
The Texan's Return
Wyoming Undercover
The Texas Soldier's Son
Texas Ranch Justice
Snowbound Targets
The Widow's Bodyguard
Texas Sheriff's Deadly Mission
Texas Rancher's Hidden Danger
Finding the Rancher's Son

Visit the Author Profile page at Harlequin.com for more titles.

To all the readers who have emailed me letting me know how much they enjoy the fictional town of Getaway, Texas. Thank you so much. Your kind words mean more than I can express.

Chapter 1

The ranch wasn't difficult to find. In fact, having grown up in Getaway, Texas, Jackie Burkholdt remembered when it had belonged to one of her classmates' parents.

Now it belonged to a man who might have harmed her sister. A large handmade sign near the gate advertised riding lessons and horse boarding as well as training, while a smaller one proclaimed there were fresh eggs for sale.

She rang the bell, waiting impatiently for the faded oak front door to open. When it didn't, she pressed the bell again, and then tried knocking—several sharp raps of her knuckles. Still nothing. Since a brand-spanking-new Ford F-150 sat parked in the driveway, she figured Eli Pitts had to be home. Where else would he be at four in the morning?

Taking a deep breath, she tapped her foot, resisting the urge to kick at the still-closed door. Here in Texas, things moved much more slowly than they did in her adopted home of New York City, but this was ridiculous. How could any man be that difficult to wake up?

Finally, the door creaked open. A tall man, his dark hair thoroughly mussed, peered out at her. "Do you have any idea what time it is?" he croaked. "The sun's not even up yet."

Damn. Looking at him felt like a punch to the gut, he was so ridiculously sexy. Whatever she'd expected upon meeting her sister's ex-husband, it wasn't this, a rugged specimen of pure male beauty.

"Hello?" he said, the annoyance in his tone reflected in his expression. "Would you please explain why you're pounding on my front door at this hour of the morning?"

Blinking and forcing her thoughts back on track, she waved her hand, dismissing his concern. "I just got in and drove straight here. Are you Eli Pitts?"

Suddenly, he appeared suspicious. "Look, lady. It's four a.m. on a Wednesday morning. I suggest you go somewhere and sober up and leave me the hell alone." He made a move to close the door.

"Oh no, you don't." As she'd seen people do in the movies, she stuck out her foot, just in time to prevent him from closing her out. "This is too important."

He tugged once more, slamming into her foot and making her wince. "Come back later."

"Wait," she practically screeched. "Just tell me where my sister is. That's all I want to know. What have you done with Charla?"

Hearing the name, he froze. "Charla? My ex-wife, Charla?"

She managed to bite back a retort and nodded.

"Sister?" He peered at her. "So you're the evil older sister?"

"Ouch." Despite knowing Charla's antagonism against her, hearing him put it like that hurt. "I am," she replied.

"You'd better come inside," he decided, opening the door wide and motioning her to go past him. "Then you can tell me what she's done now and why you'd even think she'd be here."

Jackie followed him inside, waiting quietly in the foyer while he flicked on more of the lights.

"This way," he grumbled, leading the way in his flannel pajama bottoms and faded sleeveless T-shirt. His feet were bare, more proof that she'd indeed dragged him out of bed with her insistent bell ringing and door pounding. She knew she should feel bad about doing that, but her worry over her baby sister superseded anything else.

When they reached the kitchen, he pressed a button, preheating his coffee maker. "Coffee?" he asked, rubbing at his eyes, clearly trying to wake himself up.

Though she'd already had two cups on the flight and a huge to-go cup on the drive here in her rental car, she nodded. "Thanks."

"Great," he said without any real enthusiasm. "Have a seat. Let me get some caffeine in my system before you tell me what my ex-wife has gotten herself into this time."

She nodded and sat, managing to throttle her impatience. "Judging by the text she sent me, it's pretty darn urgent."

Instead of looking surprised, Eli appeared resigned. "Everything is urgent with that woman." Then his gaze sharpened. "Unless this is about my son. Please tell me Theo is all right."

"I don't know," she answered truthfully. "Take a look at this text and then we'll talk."

"'I urgently need your help,'" he read. "'My life is in danger. Please come home.'" After handing her back her phone, he poured two tall mugs of steaming coffee. "What does that mean?"

"I was hoping you could tell me." She accepted her coffee and took a sip. Strong and black, just the way she liked it. Eyeing him over the rim of her mug, she waited for him to ask if she needed cream or sugar.

"I don't have anything to put in it," he said, correctly interpreting her look. "Maybe milk from the fridge, but that's about it."

"This is fine." She took another drink. "Now, why don't you tell me what's going on with my sister?"

Instead of pulling out a chair and taking a seat near her, he continued to stand on the other side of the room, almost as if he didn't want to get too close. "I would if I could," he replied. "But Charla and I aren't exactly on friendly terms. Though she did call me a couple nights ago and asked me to pick her up at the Rattlesnake Pub. Apparently, the guy she's been seeing found out she was also dating someone else on the side and they got into a huge drunken fight." He gave her an apologetic smile. "She got thrown out of the bar and had no way to get home."

Drunken fight, multiple boyfriends. Filing this info away for later, she focused on one thing he'd said. "That means you might have been the last one to see her."

He shrugged. "I doubt it. That was Saturday night, so it's been a couple of days."

Not buying his story, she pressed for more info. "Have you heard from her since then?"

"No, but again, that's not unusual. Charla and I aren't…buddies. We co-parent our son. Usually, if we talk at all, it's about Theo. I have visitation with him every other weekend."

Theo. The nephew Jackie had never met. Just like this man. Charla had met him, married him, had his child and then divorced him, all while Jackie was in New York. She couldn't help but wonder what had happened to end their marriage so quickly.

Though her mother had filled her in while Jackie waited at the airport to board her flight, Jackie wanted to hear it from Eli. "What happened with you two? One minute I hear you and Charla were engaged, then happily married. She got pregnant almost immediately and the two of you had the perfect baby. Then *bam*. Separated and divorced."

His expression hardened. He took a long, deliberate drink of coffee. "That's right. Of course you didn't know. I forgot that you and Charla weren't even on speaking terms. Mind telling me why?"

"Didn't Charla tell you?" She couldn't resist. In fact, she really wanted to hear what kind of twisted reasoning Charla had come up with to explain cutting off her older sister.

"Look, Miss…"

"Jackie," she said, realizing she hadn't even introduced herself. "Jackie Burkholdt."

He dipped his chin in acknowledgment. "Look, Jackie. Charla is...dramatic. She loves to stir things up and thrives on drama. Even if you and she haven't talked for a long time, I doubt that much has changed."

"It hasn't." She held up her phone. "But for Charla to break her own decision to not speak to me after three entire years makes me think she's serious this time."

Expression unchanged, he regarded her. "Did you call her back?"

"Yes, I did." After draining the last of her mug, she set it on the table and pushed to her feet. "She didn't answer. I want to ask you one more time and please, think very carefully about your answer. Where is my sister?"

Narrow eyed, he glared at her. "I've already told you. I don't know. Now, I'm going to have to ask you to leave. This is a working ranch and I have to be out in the fields in a few hours."

Stonewalling. If he knew anything, he wasn't letting on. Which would make sense, if he'd done something to hurt Charla.

But the love in his voice when he'd asked about his son... She shook her head. One could exist exclusive of the other.

Eyeing him, she reminded herself she had no proof he'd harmed her sister. Just because it turned out to be the spouse or ex-spouse something like 90 percent of the time didn't mean this man had done anything wrong.

Back stiff, he escorted her to the front door, standing aside while she swept past him, closing and locking it behind her.

As she walked to her car, she turned and eyed the low-slung ranch-style house. It was homey, in a west Texas type way. No matter how hard she tried, she couldn't picture Charla ever living in a place like this. The remote location would make going into town more difficult, not to mention the rustic air of borderline neglect the place gave off. The white frame house could certainly use a coat of paint, and the untrimmed hedges and crazy rose brambles didn't help with the ranch's appearance.

Eli Pitts had come in from somewhere outside Getaway, bought the place and devoted himself to trying to turn around a farm many had considered long past its prime. Jackie's mother, Delia, had been positively effusive in her praise for him, especially once he and Charla had started dating. They'd been happy, according to Delia, and over the moon when Charla had gotten pregnant right away. Jackie had called, gotten voice mail and left a heartfelt congratulatory message for her sister. All the while aching with hope that this time, Charla would reach out and patch things up.

She didn't. Jackie continued to get updates from Delia, truly pleased that her sister had found such happiness.

Everything had seemed to be going along just fine, until it wasn't.

When Delia had told Jackie about the split-up, Jackie had once again tried to reach out to her baby sister. And yet again, Charla had refused to take her call. This despite the fact that Jackie's only "crime" had been taking a job out of state and moving.

Worse, no one took Charla's text seriously. Not their mother and certainly not Eli Pitts. Meanwhile, Jackie had taken a leave of absence from her publishing job in Manhattan, where luckily she had an amazing boss who'd been understanding when Jackie had walked into her office first thing Tuesday morning, asking to take vacation due to a family emergency. After that Jackie had purchased plane tickets at far too high a price, gone home and packed, made numerous phone calls and then traveled across the country on the basis that her baby sister truly needed her.

Exhausted and numb, Jackie climbed back into her rental car and headed toward town. She could either get a room at the Landshark Motel or stay at her mother's house, assuming Delia would let her.

She chose the motel.

This late at night, or early in the morning, depending on how you looked at it, downtown appeared completely deserted. Main Street stretched into the horizon, flat and empty. When she pulled up at the Landshark, a structure that had been old back when Jackie had gone to high school, a light shone from the office window. At least she didn't have to worry about the hotel not having any vacancies. Not many people stopped in this small ranching town in the middle of nowhere west Texas.

After checking in with a bored and disinterested front desk clerk, Jackie got her room key, located her room and got ready for bed, even though the sun would be coming up soon. She'd start looking for Charla after she got a few hours of sleep.

The shrill sound of her phone ringing woke her. Unsure of the time, Jackie fumbled in the dark room, located her cell and barely managed to hit the accept call button.

"Good morning," Delia chirped. "I heard you paid Eli a visit at four a.m."

"I did." Stifling a yawn, Jackie turned on the bedside lamp and sat up. "What time is it now?"

"Nearly nine."

That meant she'd gotten a few hours of sleep at least. Even though she felt as if she'd been run over by a truck. "Did he call you?"

"He did. Eli couldn't understand why you showed up there," Delia prodded. "I confess, I don't get it, either. You know the two of them split up. Their divorce was just finalized, uncontested by either of them. Why would you even think Charla would be there?"

Jackie sighed. "Every single news story when something happens to a young wife and mother, it's almost always the husband or boyfriend who's…" She stopped short, not wanting to alarm her mother without any proof.

"Charla's fine." Delia sounded certain. "She must have finally decided she wants to fix things between the two of you and figured a dramatic message was the best way to do it. You know how your sister is."

"I do." Again, correct. Charla never had been able to understand the concept behind the little boy who cried wolf. "But Eli might have been the last person to see her."

"Because he gave her a ride home from the bar Saturday night? I talked to her after that, you know. Your sister has always been a free spirit. She was really upset that Leo caused such a scene."

"Leo." Though still groggy, Jackie pounced on that. "What's Leo's last name?"

"How should I know?" Delia sounded slightly defensive. "And before you ask, no, I don't have any idea who all else Charla might have been seeing. While she and I are extremely close, she doesn't tell me everything. Just promise me you don't plan on storming into the Pub and demanding names."

Since that was exactly what Jackie planned to do, she tried to be noncommittal. "We'll see." Pushing out of the bed, she looked around the room, hoping to spy one of those small, in-room coffee makers. "If you hear from her, will you call me immediately?"

"Yes, I will. I'm sure she'll call me soon. We rarely go more than a few days without speaking to each other."

Jackie managed to swallow back a comment on that. Her mother rarely called her, except on holidays. And when Jackie phoned home, Delia often let the call go to voice mail and then never bothered to call back. She'd long ago managed to pretend that didn't hurt her.

Then Delia surprised her. "Since you're in town, will you stop by for dinner tonight? Around six?"

Dinner. At her mother's. Would wonders never cease?

"Sure." Keeping it casual. "I'll see you then." After hanging up, Jackie took a long hot shower, then headed out in search of coffee and food, in that order. Then she planned to stop by Charla's job, pay a visit to the day-care center that Theo attended, and if neither of those places turned up anything, Charla's apartment.

Later, fortified by a large coffee and a breakfast sandwich, Jackie drove to Levine's Jewelers. Charla had worked the counter since high school. She also took occasional part-time waitressing gigs at the Tumbleweed Café, mostly helping out friends who needed someone to cover their shifts. According to Delia, she'd also met her husband, Eli, there, too.

When she walked inside, Christopher Levine himself greeted her by name. Surprised that he remembered her, Jackie asked him when he'd last heard from her sister.

"I'm actually worried about her," Christopher said. "She called in sick four days ago, but I haven't heard from her since. I even took the liberty of going by her place to check on her, but she didn't answer the door. She's not picking up her phone, either, so I'm concerned she might be seriously ill."

Since Charla had worked for this man for years, Jackie showed him the text. "When I got that, I tried reached her, too. Since I couldn't, I took some vacation time at work and flew here. Now I'm trying to track her down."

Christopher shook his head and pushed his glasses up his narrow nose. "I don't know why she'd say she was in danger. I mean, we all know Charla could be a bit of a party girl, but she seemed to settle down now that she had a little one to look after." He sighed. "You might check at the Tumbleweed and see if any of her friends there know where to find her."

"Is she still picking up an occasional shift waitressing there?"

"Yes. She called it her fun money," he said. "I'm sorry I couldn't be of more help. But when you do get a hold of Charla, will you please ask her to call me? I need to know when she's planning on returning to work."

"I sure will." Feeling even more unsettled, Jackie got in her rental car and headed over to the Tumbleweed Café.

A wave of nostalgia swept over her as she stepped through the front door. With its same red vinyl booths and black-and-white linoleum floors, the place still looked exactly as it always had and probably always would.

"Jackie? Jackie Burkholdt?" an incredulous voice exclaimed. "It that really you?"

Looking up, Jackie spied Cassie Morgan, one of her best friends from her high school days. "Cassie!" They hugged, then pulled back to study each other. "You look great."

"So do you." Cassie cocked her head. She still wore her hair in long platinum waves, though she'd pulled that back into a ponytail for work. "What brings you to town?"

"I'm looking for Charla," Jackie said, keeping her tone light. No doubt all of Charla's friends knew that the two sisters no longer spoke. "Mr. Levine said she still picked up occasional shifts here."

"Oh. She does, but I don't know what's up with her," Cassie said. "She was supposed to cover for Julie the day before yesterday, but didn't show. And she'd agreed to open for Tabitha yesterday, but didn't." Cassie picked at her fingernail before looking up and meeting Jackie's gaze. "I'm a little worried. So are some of the others. We've tried calling and even going by her place. It's like she just up and disappeared."

Eli Pitts tried to go back to sleep after the visit from Charla's sister, but once up, he couldn't shut his mind down enough to doze. He managed to wait until a semi-decent hour before dialing his ex-wife, aware she occasionally worked the breakfast shift at the Tumbleweed. But as it usually did these days, his call went unanswered. Just in case, he left a voice mail, saying that he wanted to discuss Theo's visit this weekend. Their son seemed to be the only subject Charla was willing to discuss with him.

Which in the end was fine. Life went much easier without the amped-up level of drama that Charla preferred.

Eli hated that he'd made such a colossal mistake. His and Charla's relationship had been a whirlwind thing, and he'd been blindsided when he finally understood that the woman she'd pretended to be did not actually exist. By then they were married with a baby on the way. Charla couldn't seem to understand why she needed to stop partying. She'd sulked and pouted the entire nine months. As soon as Theo had been born, she'd insisted he be fed formula, so she could leave her newborn with Eli while she went out with her friends.

He'd taken it for a few weeks, hoping she'd get it out of her system and would come back and actually mother her infant. Instead, when he confronted her, she'd announced she'd met someone else and was leaving him.

Because he'd wanted full custody of Theo—after all, she obviously had no interest in her son—she refused to grant that. Instead, she'd gotten custody while Eli got visitation. He'd worried nonstop about his boy for weeks and months after that. Eventually, the smoke had cleared, the mayhem and destruction stirred up in Charla's wake had subsided and Eli had realized Charla managed to be a decent mother to their son.

He thought of the woman—Charla's older sister, Jackie—who'd shown up on his doorstep in the predawn hours. She'd been dark where Charla was fair, serious instead of frothy and apparently willing to allow herself to be dragged into whatever unique form of drama Charla had going now.

More power to her, he supposed. As for himself, he wanted no part of it. As long as Charla brought Theo over at the agreed-upon time, he was good.

Due to lack of sleep, he found himself dragging as he went about his normal routine on the farm. He hadn't yet reached a financial point where he could afford to hire full-time workers, so he made do with paying a couple of teenage boys to work part-time after school and on weekends. He sold high-quality alfalfa hay and always had a full slate of standing preorders, so he had high hopes that next year he might be able to expand and add a second crop. He'd been doing a lot of research and had his eye on grain sorghum.

Lunchtime rolled around and he decided to head into town and grab a bite at the Tumbleweed Café. Even though normally when he knew Charla might be working, he tended to avoid the place, the text she'd sent her older sister had him curious. Actually, more than curious. A bit worried, too, especially because if Charla truly had gotten into some kind of trouble, would Theo be safe?

He arrived at the popular lunch place shortly after twelve. As usual, he had to circle the lot three times before he found a space to park.

Inside, he bypassed the people waiting for a table and headed toward the lunch counter. One spot remained open, sandwiched in between two burly truckers. Eli slid onto the stool, nodded a casual hello and began scanning the restaurant for a sight of his ex.

He didn't see her.

"Hey, Eli." Sheryl Jones, one of Charla's friends, came over to take his order. "What can I get you?"

"Bacon burger," he replied. "Have you seen Charla?"

"No." She frowned. "I'm not sure what's going on with her. She hasn't shown up to work any of the shifts she agreed to cover in the last four days." Sheryl shook her head, sending her long earrings swinging. "It's not like her."

That was true. Charla acted flighty most of the time. The only exceptions were her jobs. She'd worked at Levine's Jewelers and the Tumbleweed Café since she'd been in high school.

"Have you tried to reach her?" he asked.

"Yep." Sheryl's brightly painted lips turned down. "Several times. I've left several voice mails. She hasn't returned a single call. A couple of the other girls even went by her apartment, but they didn't have any luck, either."

Eli pushed back a prickle of unease. "That's weird."

"I know. Even weirder, her older sister is in town, asking around for her."

He grimaced, deciding not to comment. "You know what? Would you make my burger to go please?"

"Sure thing." She bustled off.

While he waited, he thought about the text message Charla had sent her sister. My life is in danger. Drama, though not the kind Charla usually dealt in. But why would she feel jeopardized in any way? And if so, by whom? Finally, why would she reach out to her estranged sister instead of her ex-husband? At least Eli was local, which would increase his chances of being able to help her.

Of course, he would have been skeptical. Who wouldn't, after all the lies and fabricated stories she'd told him? Oddly enough, Charla never spoke about her older sister. When pressed, she'd clamped her mouth tight and said she couldn't discuss a betrayal of such magnitude.

"Here you go, hon." Sheryl returned, carrying a bag with his to-go box. He paid, already knowing the exact total including tip, and headed back out to his truck. He'd eat while he drove. Next stop, Charla's apartment. He'd call Levine's Jewelers on the way.

When one of Charla's coworkers at the jewelry store answered, Eli went ahead and asked about Charla, even though he could already guess the answer. Sarah said she, too, was worried about Charla and found her disappearance problematic. She asked Eli to call her if he learned anything new. Eli agreed, ending the call just as he reached Charla's apartment building.

When he pulled up and parked, he wasn't surprised to see Jackie Burkholdt walking across the parking lot. He hopped out of his truck and waved. "Any luck?"

"No." Changing direction, she hurried over toward him. "I stopped by the jewelry store first, and then the Tumbleweed. She hasn't been in to work in four days, either place."

With her sleek dark hair pulled back into an elegant bun, she appeared as different as the cool, quiet shallows were from her sister's blazing-hot sun. Something about her drew him, a thought that he immediately discounted as foolishness.

"So I heard." He grimaced. "I stopped by the Tumbleweed, too, and just got off the phone with Sarah, who works at Levine's. I guess we had the same thoughts."

Her cool caramel gaze searched his face. "Does that mean you're concerned, too?"

Ah, how to answer that? "I wouldn't say *concerned*," he replied cautiously. "Charla can be a force of nature. I know you and she haven't spoken in quite a while. But I'm guessing her personality hasn't changed much. I'm not sure why she might have felt compelled to text you what she did, but in my experience, she always has her reasons."

Jackie exhaled, a sharp little puff of sound. "I know what you mean, but I'm still worried. Until I moved away, Charla always knew she could depend on me for anything and everything. Despite her…anger at me, I have to believe she still knows that. If she is in trouble, I'm the one person she can trust to help her out."

He noted the way her voice trembled, despite her

obvious attempt to sound cool and collected. This actually made him like her just a little bit more.

"I know you're worried," he said. "But Charla and I have a son together. If something truly was wrong, I have to think she would have contacted me."

"To keep Theo safe?" she asked, frowning.

"Yes. Wouldn't that make sense? If Charla truly had some kind of trouble, why would she want to endanger her child?"

Her answer came slowly. "I guess." She looked around at the nondescript brick apartment building. "Then what now? I've checked her job and her home and came up with nothing."

"Let's check with the apartment manager. Bree knows me. I'm sure she'll let us take a peek inside Charla's apartment."

Though Jackie's frown deepened at this, she didn't protest.

A few minutes later, after explaining to Bree what was going on, they followed her back to unit 209. She unlocked the door and stepped inside. "Here we are," she said, glancing around. "Nothing seems out of place."

Eli stepped inside, thunderstruck. Theo's toys were strewn across the living room floor. Moving quickly, he hurried down the hall to his son's bedroom. That, too, appeared to be waiting for Theo and his mother to return home. If Charla had gone on the run, she hadn't packed anything.

This should have reassured him. Oddly enough, it didn't.

He turned to realize Jackie had followed him and

now stood in the doorway, gazing at the room's cheerful disorganization. When their gazes met, she swallowed. "What about day care?" she asked. "I'm assuming Charla took Theo to a day-care center."

"She did. It's right down the street from here." He took her arm. "We can take my truck."

Waiting while Bree locked everything up, he tried to get a grip on his emotions. Worry and fear could blind him if he let it.

Before they even went inside the day-care center, he suspected he already knew what they'd learn. "Theo hasn't been here in two days," the director told him. "We've reached out to his mother, but she hasn't returned our calls. Is everything all right?"

"I'm not sure." Eli scratched the back of his head. "Thank you. I'll be in touch if I find out anything."

Outside, he and Jackie trudged to his pickup and piled in.

"I'm getting worried," he admitted, starting up the engine. "I think it's time we talked to the sheriff."

The long, assessing glance she gave him made him wonder. "What?" he asked, slightly impatient. "I'm aware we don't know each other, but we both have the same concern."

"Do we?" Her cool gaze lingered. "Because from where I sit, you'd be the number-one suspect."

It actually took a minute for her insult to register. "Seriously? Please, enlighten me as to your reasoning."

"It's simple. Not only were you the last person to see her Saturday night, but if she went away for good, you would have the most to gain. My mom told me you tried to get full custody of Theo and lost. If Charla were out of the way, you could have your son with you a hundred percent of the time."

"That might be true," he replied, allowing some of his anger to show in his deep voice. "Except you're forgetting one very important thing. I would never hurt the mother of my child. And not only is Charla missing, if she truly is, then Theo is, too."

Staring out the window, she got quiet after that. He debated whether or not to simply drop her off at her car in Charla's apartment parking lot. Instead, he decided to bring her along with him to the sheriff's department. At least that way, maybe she could begin to understand that he wasn't the kind of person who would hurt any woman, for any reason.

Chapter 2

Remembering something about keeping your enemies close, Jackie forced herself to relax. She'd insulted Eli, she knew, but she couldn't bring herself to offer an apology. Not yet. She still wasn't sure about him. After all, abusers could be charming, too.

Even though she had no real reason not to trust him, she decided to keep herself aloof, at least until she knew more about what had happened to Charla and her son.

She knew her thoughts about him were irrational, to say the least. She didn't have one single valid reason to suspect him of causing harm to her sister. Everyone seemed to like and respect him, including her mother.

Now she'd see how the sheriff treated him.

While Jackie had never met Rayna Coombs personally, she'd heard a lot about her. Heck, Rayna had even made the national news, not once, but twice. Both times had involved serial killers. She appeared to be well respected by the townspeople and worked well with the federal law enforcement agencies. If anyone could help find Charla, Jackie suspected Rayna could.

After they parked, Jackie walked alongside Eli into the sheriff's department. She noticed the town had spruced up the exterior of the cinderblock building with a fresh coat of paint and a new sign.

Rayna Coombs herself stood in the reception area, sorting through a stack of papers on the desk. She looked up when they entered, her pretty face breaking into a huge smile. "Eli Pitts!" she said. "What brings you to visit me today?"

"This is Jackie Burkholdt," Eli said. "Jackie, meet Rayna Coombs, our sheriff."

They shook hands. Rayna studied Jackie, her expression quizzical. "You look familiar, somehow," she said. "Have we met before?"

"No." Jackie shook her head. "But you may have met my sister, Charla."

"Oh." If Rayna's smile faltered slightly, it didn't last long. She looked from Jackie to Eli and then back again. "What's Charla done now?"

Jackie tried to summon up enough outrage to protest the sheriff's assumption, but she couldn't. She hadn't been around the past three years and had no way of knowing what kind of trouble her sister might have gotten involved in.

"May we talk in private?" Jackie asked.

"Of course." Rayna led the way through a set of double doors, across a large common work area and into a small corner office. "Here we are. Take a seat." She closed the door and then went to her own chair back behind the large desk. "Now, why don't you tell me what's going on?"

Jackie showed her the text message, explained how she'd flown across the country to make sure her sister was okay. "But she hasn't shown up for work in two days, or taken Theo to day care. We went by her apartment, too. She's not answering her phone and some of her friends at the Tumbleweed are concerned."

"Even I'm a little bit freaked out," Eli agreed. "I know Charla does a lot of impulsive stuff, but she wouldn't involve Theo. Usually, she'd either drop him off at her mother's or leave him with me. This isn't like her."

"But she has done this before, right?" Rayna asked.

Eli nodded. "And I'm sure you've probably heard she and her latest man friend got into a drunken brawl at the Rattlesnake on Saturday night. Charla called me in tears and asked me to come get her, so I did. I dropped her off at her apartment. She said one of her friends was babysitting Theo."

"Which again, isn't unusual," Rayna pointed out.

"But she says her life is in danger," Jackie exclaimed. "I have to believe she's in very real trouble."

Listening, Rayna appeared to carefully consider her next words. "The problem we have here is that Charla is an adult. There's no evidence of foul play, so…"

"Does this mean you won't look for her until there is? Wouldn't that be far too late?" Jackie asked, keeping her tone calm and reasonable. "I want to find my sister now and protect her."

Eli and Rayna exchanged looks.

"What?" Jackie asked, pretty sure she already knew what the sheriff was about to say. "Look, even if Charla is a bit…dramatic, she and I haven't spoken to each other in three years. For her to actually text me, and with something like this, means I have to take it seriously. I'd appreciate if you would, too."

"I agree," Rayna replied, surprising her.

"Me, too," Eli seconded. "Charla's never involved Theo in any of her adventures before."

Which made Jackie wonder what kind of life her sister might have been leading. She decided she really didn't want to know. At least until her sister and nephew had turned up safe.

"What about your mother?" Rayna asked Jackie. "She and your sister appear to have a very close relationship. What are her thoughts on all of this?"

"She doesn't seem too concerned," Jackie admitted. "I'm going over there for dinner tonight and we'll talk more. But she's always been super indulgent of Charla's quirks, so it's hard to tell with her."

Eli shook his head, eyeing Jackie. "From my perspective, Delia acts more like Charla's friend than her mother sometimes. If Charla would have told anyone what's going on with her, she'd have told your mother."

"Good. Then maybe I'll find something out tonight." She considered, a thought occurring to her. "Why don't you come along? I'm sure you and Delia have a lot to catch up on."

Though his gaze narrowed, Eli didn't refuse. Instead, he muttered something noncommittal, which made Rayna grin.

"I'll start asking around," Rayna said. "And I'll let you know if I hear anything."

"Thank you." Jackie pushed to her feet. "And if I learn anything new at my mother's tonight, I'll give you a call."

"Perfect. Here's my card." Rayna stood, too. "We'll be in touch."

Eli opened the door and led the way. As they got back into his truck, he gave her a quizzical look. "Do you really think I should have dinner tonight with you and Delia? Don't you think she might find that a little weird?"

"Maybe." Jackie shrugged. "But what does it matter in the scheme of things? I'm hoping once she sees that you're also concerned, she might take this all a bit more seriously. Especially since her grandson is involved."

"I agree." He pushed the button to start the ignition. "But whatever else she might be, Charla loves Theo in her own way. I'm having trouble thinking she'd allow him to be in danger for even a second."

In her own way. Jackie filed that statement away for later. She had to admit, she found Eli Pitts attractive. But she couldn't let that blind her to the possibility that he might have somehow been involved in her sister's disappearance. He still might have been the last person to see Charla.

"Please come with me tonight," Jackie asked. "To be honest, having you there might make my mother open up more. She's always been defensive of Charla around me."

Though he shook his head, Eli didn't outright refuse. He drove her back to the apartment parking lot, pulling up right behind her rental car. "I'll go," he said quietly. "But only if we ride together."

"That sounds good," she replied, amazed at the way her stomach did a quick somersault.

"Are you staying at the Landshark?"

She nodded.

"I'll pick you up there. What time?" he asked.

"She wants to eat around six," Jackie replied. "So five thirty?"

"Perfect." He kept the truck running while she opened her door and climbed out. "I'll see you then."

Nodding, she watched him drive away. She told herself his words sounded more like a promise than a threat. While she honestly didn't think Eli Pitts was dangerous, she knew better than to let her guard down. Until her sister stood right in front of her and vouched for her ex-husband's character, she had no choice but to consider him a possible dangerous suspect.

Despite all of that, as she got ready for dinner, she found herself a bundle of nerves. Part of that would be because she hadn't seen her mother in three years. Delia had made it very clear on which side she stood when the rift had opened up between sisters. Despite Jackie's pleas for their mother to help mend things, Delia had steadfastly refused. Part of Jackie had trouble forgiving her for that. She probably always would. Parents weren't supposed to choose one child over another.

Once she set up her laptop and logged in to the motel's Wi-Fi, Jackie spent the next couple hours catching up on work. She could still do editing remotely, along with several other tasks that didn't require a physical presence in the office.

Finally, her stomach growled, reminding her she hadn't eaten anything since breakfast. Checking the time, she realized she'd have no choice but to wait until dinner now.

Dinner at her mother's. Which, if she was completely honest with herself, she dreaded. Part of the reason she'd asked Eli Pitts to accompany her was to act as a buffer between her and Delia.

After touching up her makeup, she brushed her hair and decided she was as ready as she was going to be.

She heard his truck pull up outside and swallowed back a sudden spate of nerves. This irritated her, because of all the reactions she might choose to have to her sister's ex-husband, sexual attraction wouldn't be one of them.

Instead of waiting for him to knock on her door, she let herself out, giving him a cheery wave as she walked to his truck. She'd decided on jeans and a T-shirt, with her feet in flip-flops.

When she climbed into Eli's truck, she noted he'd changed into a pair of well-worn khakis and a T-shirt that showed off his muscular chest and arms. He looked damn good. Eyeing him, she pretended her mouth hadn't gone dry and her heart hadn't skipped a beat.

"Hey there," he said, his warm smile friendly rather than flirtatious. Once she'd buckled herself in, he put the truck in Drive and pulled away. "Did you let Delia know I was coming?"

Crud. She grimaced. "I forgot. But honestly, she won't mind. She always speaks so highly of you."

He considered her words for a moment. "That's good to know. Hopefully, she'll have made enough food."

This had Jackie laughing. "I take it you and Charla didn't go over there for dinner very often?"

"No. We mostly met at restaurants or she came by the ranch." He gave her a curious glance. "Why?"

"Because Delia doesn't cook. She'll either have ordered to have something delivered or she'll have picked up tacos or fried chicken. And she always gets way too much. It'll be fine."

"I'll take your word for it."

He had his radio on low, tuned to the local country music station. A Garth Brooks song came on, one of her old favorites. She sang along under her breath. He glanced at her, noticing, and turned the volume up. Together, they sang along in a kind of clumsy camaraderie.

When the song finished, he turned the volume down and grinned at her. Flushed with pleasure, she grinned back.

"Here we are." He pulled over and parked at the curb in front of her mother's house.

Jackie stared at the small bungalow, still painted the same shade of pale yellow that she and her sister had hated. The manicured landscaping had grown out a bit, but overall it appeared time had stood still.

Slowly, she got out of the truck, stunned by the surprise rush of emotion closing her throat. Dimly aware of Eli moving to her side, she continued up the pathway to the front entrance. As she reached out to press the bell, the door flew open. Delia squealed, wrapping Jackie up in a tight, and unexpected, bear hug.

"I can't believe you're finally here," Delia said, acting as if Jackie had voluntarily stayed away. Then Delia's eyes widened as she spotted Eli standing on the front porch behind Jackie. "Eli? What are you doing here?"

"I'm sorry, Mom. I forgot to tell you I was bringing him," Jackie said. "He's been helping me try and figure out how to find Charla."

Delia frowned. "I told you to quit worrying. Your sister will turn up when she's ready to. I'm sure she's fine." She stepped back, motioning them to go past her into the house.

Jackie headed straight for the kitchen, unsurprised to see a huge bucket of fried chicken on the table. Eli followed a bit more slowly, clearly not sure how to respond to Delia's complete lack of concern for her missing daughter.

Once Delia reached the kitchen, she rounded on them. "Jackie, why are you so determined to make it seem as if something has happened to Charla?" she demanded. "Eli, you know her better than anyone besides me. It's not like Charla hasn't taken off before. She'll be back once she's had her fun."

Eli straightened and met her gaze directly. "While it's true Charla has done this before, this time she's involved Theo. She hasn't been in to work at either the jewelry store or the café, and Theo hasn't been to the day care in two days. She's not responded to anyone's phone calls or texts."

"That, combined with the text message she sent me saying she was in danger, seem to be a clear reason to be concerned," Jackie put in. She hated that her mother always seemed so blind to Charla's shortcomings, but right now Delia needed to open up her eyes.

Instead, Delia looked from Jackie to Eli with suspicion plain upon her face. "What are you two doing together anyway?" she asked. "Eli, I wouldn't have taken you for the sort of man who'd gang up on the mother of his child."

"Gang up?" Try as she might, Jackie couldn't keep her voice from rising. "Mom, I'm not the enemy here. Charla texted and asked for my help, remember? I took vacation time and flew the red eye across the country, for her. Because she needs me."

Uncertainty crossed Delia's face. Clearly, she didn't know how to deal with a reality where her two daughters weren't enemies. "Well," she said briskly. "How about we eat? Eli, I haven't seen you in a long time. I'm sure we have some catching up to do."

Eli wasn't sure what to make of the charged atmosphere between his former mother-in-law and her other daughter, but he suddenly understood why Jackie had asked him to come. During his brief marriage to Charla, he'd noticed how close she and her mother were, but he hadn't realized the full extent of Delia's willingness to turn a blind eye to her daughter's faults.

While clearly, Jackie could do nothing right in her mother's eyes. He didn't want any part of the strange dynamics and he resolved to try and make a graceful escape as soon as humanly possible. Somehow, he suspected Jackie wouldn't be averse to cutting short the visit.

Delia got out paper plates and napkins, along with plastic utensils. "I got extra crispy," she said. "And there's coleslaw, mashed potatoes and beans. Dig in."

Taking care to avoid making direct eye contact with Jackie, Eli sat. He hadn't had fried chicken in a while, and figured at least while everyone was eating, the thick tension might dissipate somewhat.

He dug in. Sitting across from him, Jackie did the same. Meanwhile, Delia nibbled on a drumstick, her gaze alternating between her daughter and Eli.

"How do you two know each other?" Delia asked suddenly. "Eli, were you acquainted before you met Charla?"

He hastily swallowed what he was chewing. "No. I first met Jackie yesterday, when she came pounding on my front door in the middle of the night."

"I heard," Delia drawled, glancing at her daughter. "What you didn't tell me is why would you do such a thing?"

Jackie sighed. "I was looking for Charla. I'm *still* looking for her. I know you don't think anything is wrong—and I really hope you're right. But until I actually see Charla and hear her tell me that she's okay, I'm not going to rest."

Delia shook her head. "Aren't you worried she's going to be upset to see you hanging around her ex?"

Outwardly, Jackie didn't react. Eli saw her hands tense on the table, but she picked at her piece of chicken with a single-minded intensity that matched her clenched jaw.

"Delia?" Eli cleared his throat. "I'm worried about my son. I know you and Charla are close. Do you have any idea where she might be?"

Delia considered him. Meanwhile, Jackie shot him a grateful look, abandoning any attempt to eat.

"Actually, I haven't heard from Charla in about a week," Delia admitted. "She's been busy, between trying to be a single mother and working two jobs." Somehow, despite the fact that Charla had been the one to end the marriage, Eli detected a note of accusation in her mother's voice.

He ignored this. Delia Burkholdt was no longer his problem. Finding his son was. "If you hear from her, will you let me know? She's supposed to bring Theo on Friday. It's my weekend to have him. I hope to hell she shows up."

Pushing to his feet, he found Jackie's gaze. "Are you ready to go?" he asked. If she wasn't, he figured he'd offer to return and pick her up.

But judging by the relief that flashed in her expressive eyes, and the way she jumped to her feet, she was just as ready to get out of there as he. "Yes," she said.

"But you've hardly eaten anything," Delia protested halfheartedly. Eli suspected she'd be glad to get them out of her house.

"I'm not very hungry," Eli lied.

"Me neither," Jackie seconded.

"Oh. Well, then…" Delia waved them away. "I'll let you two show yourselves out."

Marveling at the difference between this Delia and the one who'd been practically giddy with happiness hanging on his ex-wife, Eli strode for the front door. He opened it and stepped back so that Jackie could go ahead of him.

They rushed to his truck. Inside the cab he couldn't press the ignition button quickly enough.

"I'm not sure whether to laugh or cry," Jackie admitted, her mouth trembling and her eyes shiny, though she didn't shed a tear. "The bad thing is, I'm starving."

"Me, too." He made a snap decision. "How about we stop by the Rattlesnake for a burger and a beer."

"That would be awesome."

Her phone pinged. She glanced at it and shook her head. "She's still at it. Now you see why I was so eager to move to the other side of the country."

"I get that." He glanced at her, considering. "I've definitely seen a different side of her tonight. In fact, I'm still in shock."

With a weary sigh, she shrugged. "I wish I could say I was used to it, but I foolishly hoped after three years away, things might have changed. She's always doted on Charla and treated me like an afterthought."

"I'm sorry."

"Me, too. But in a way I guess it was a good thing. Gave me the drive to do something different with my life. I worked my way through college, graduated with honors and landed my dream job in publishing in New York." She smiled a little sadly. "Though Charla never forgave me for abandoning her, as she put it."

Incredulous, he stared. He'd known Charla was self-centered, but from the way she'd talked about her older sister's betrayal, he'd thought it had to have been something awful. "You're sure that's the entire reason?" he asked, letting his disbelief show.

"That's what she told me," she replied. "Though if she mentioned something else, I'd appreciate you letting me know."

"She was always deliberately vague," he said. "And now I understand why."

This made her laugh, a genuine sound of amusement that also succeeded in chasing the shadows from her eyes.

He pulled into the Rattlesnake Pub's half-full lot and scored a spot near the door. She jumped out and waited for him to join her. "It's been years since I had their Swiss-mushroom burger," she said. "I hope it still tastes as good as I remember."

Inside they were shown to a small booth near the back. When the waitress tried to bring menus, they both waved them away. "We already know what we want," Eli said, grinning. He ordered them both burgers. "What do you want to drink?" he asked Jackie.

"You mentioned beer," she said. "I'll have a Shiner please."

"Make that two." Since that happened to be his favorite beer. As the waitress moved away, he leaned back in the booth and studied the dark-haired woman sitting across from him. He refused to examine or even think about the strong attraction he felt toward her, which would be too weird since she was his ex's sister.

Thinking of Charla, he pulled out his phone and double-checked to make sure she hadn't texted or left a voice mail. Nothing. Looking up, he saw Jackie doing the same.

"You're really worried about her, aren't you?" he asked.

"Yes." She let out a puff of air in frustration. "I just don't understand why no one else is."

Their beers arrived and he took that moment as an opportunity to sip, and considered whether or not to say anything. Finally, he decided she deserved to know the truth about her sister. He'd try to be as tactful as possible.

"Maybe because Charla's done this before." He kept his tone mild, watching closely for her reaction.

"You and Rayna mentioned that before," she replied, a slight frown creasing her brows. "As did my mother. I was sort of afraid to ask. You mean she randomly disappears?"

"Yes. She takes off on a regular basis." He took another sip of his beer. "Though usually she doesn't take Theo with her. Saturday she claimed she'd left him with one of her friends. Usually, by now said friend would have shown up with Theo in tow. The fact that she hasn't is something that's got me concerned." He shrugged, refusing to give in to his early feelings of panic. "It's only Wednesday. I imagine Charla will pick him up and show up before Friday, since that's when she's supposed to drop Theo off at my house."

Though Jackie nodded, her expression remained troubled. "At the risk of sounding redundant, what about the text she sent me?"

"I don't know. Maybe that's her way of trying to reconcile with you."

Whatever response she'd been about to make, she didn't because their burgers arrived. Eli watched her as she accepted her plate from the waitress, enjoying the way she eyed her meal with a rapt, intent expression, as if she hadn't eaten for days.

He took another long pull on his beer before picking up his burger. Jackie had already taken a huge bite out of hers, no messing around and cutting it in half like some women did. He liked the way she went all in, then mentally chastised himself for even noticing.

They ate in a sort of companionable silence, she intent on devouring her meal, and he intent on trying not to watch her. He knew she didn't entirely trust him, and he supposed he couldn't blame her. She'd been away for three years and had missed out on a huge chunk of her sister's life.

Finally, she finished her burger and started on her fries. When she looked up and caught him watching her, she nodded. "Are you ever going to tell me what happened between you and Charla?" she asked.

The question was a reasonable one. Even if answering it truthfully—the only way he could—revealed him to be a complete and utter fool.

"Charla came into my life like a cyclone," he said, allowing himself to smile slightly at the memory. "You know how she is. So full of herself, brimming over with life. She waited on me at the Tumbleweed and when her shift was over, she drove herself out to my farm."

Jackie nodded, watching him closely. "I can see her doing that. Once Charla decided she wants something, she goes after it with everything she's got."

"Which is exactly what she did," he agreed. "It was crazy and beautiful and we were happy." He thought for a moment, and then amended that. "Or at least, I was. I didn't realize at the time that Charla lived her life kind of like a butterfly, flitting from one thing to another. I asked her to marry me. She asked to think about it. And then she discovered she was pregnant, so she said yes."

"That's the part of the story my mother left out," she

said quietly, pushing her nearly empty plate away. "I'd thought—I'd hoped—Charla might have grown out of that sort of behavior."

He shrugged. "It's okay. The person I thought I was marrying didn't exist. Part of the fault of that is on me." And part was on Charla, for pretending to be something she never could have been, though he didn't voice that. He was pretty sure Jackie understood.

"Charla seemed to enjoy being pregnant," he continued. "She thrived on all the attention, though she didn't like that she had to stop partying."

Jackie rubbed her temples, as if trying to ward off a headache. "But she did stop, right?"

"Yes. As far as I know."

She grimaced. "Tell me about when Theo was born. It's so hard to know I have a nephew and I've never even met him."

Impulsively, he reached across the table and lightly touched the back of her hand. "We'll make sure that changes."

"Thank you. I'd like that."

The waitress reappeared and collected their plates. He ordered another beer. Jackie declined, since hers was still half-full.

Once the waitress had gone, Jackie leaned forward. "I know all of this is incredibly personal, and I really appreciate you sharing it with me. Do you mind telling me what happened to end your marriage?"

Did he mind? Flashback of anger and tears, memories of him trying desperately to hold on to their little family, of Charla's scornful laughter and the way she'd called him a fool. Her partying, not coming home or spending time with her son for days. Eli had known the entire town saw and gossiped about it, especially since several people had taken it upon themselves to call him, informing him of his wife's every move. One older rancher had even gone so far as to advise Eli that he needed to get his wife in line. The man hadn't appreciated or understood Eli's laughter.

The end of Eli and Charla's marriage had been a time of great pain. Only Theo—and their love for him—had been a bright light shining in the murky darkness.

"It wasn't working out," he simply said. "Charla wasn't happy. She found someone else and asked for a divorce. I gave her one."

The waitress delivered his second beer, along with the check. "No hurry," she said. "Just let me know when you're ready."

He thanked her, returning his attention to Jackie. "She has custody of Theo, while I have visitation every other week. I also get him for two weeks every summer, and we alternate major holidays."

This schedule had been, to him, the worst of all of it. He loved his son and would have done anything for him. So did Charla, he knew, but as far as he could tell, Charla treated Theo more like an afterthought than the center of her existence.

Jackie watched him, the sympathetic expression in her dark eyes telling him she understood much of what went unsaid.

"Yet you still pick her up from a bar when she calls and asks?" she questioned, drumming her fingers on the table.

He winced, aware she had a point. "What else could I do? She and I might not have worked out as a couple, but she's still my son's mother."

"And you have no idea where she left Theo that night?"

"No. I'd made her a standing offer to babysit when Charla felt the need to go out, but she claimed she didn't like me being that deeply involved in her life, so she got various friends to do it."

Out of habit, he pulled out his phone and checked it. "She still hasn't responded tō my texts," he mused, scrolling over to various social media apps and checking the feed. "And she hasn't been active on Facebook, Twitter, Instagram or Snapchat. That's unusual for her."

Jackie leaned forward. "Does this mean you're starting to get worried?"

"Not yet," he answered truthfully. "But if she doesn't bring Theo on Friday, that will definitely change."

Reaching into his shirt pocket, Eli pulled out a business card and handed it to Jackie. "My number," he said. "Call me if you need anything."

"Thanks," she replied, accepting it. "I'll text you so you have mine."

"Sounds good. I'll let you know if I hear anything before Friday."

Promising to do the same, she got up and headed toward the door. He put enough cash on the table to cover both the meal and a nice tip, and followed her. Walking behind her, he couldn't help but admire the sway of her hips as she made her way through the room, or the way several other men eyed her. He had the strangest urge to catch up to her and put his arm around her shoulders, the classic gesture to show she was his.

Except she wasn't. Nor would she ever be. She was his ex-wife's sister, nothing more. Once Charla turned up, and he had no doubt she would as soon as she was good and ready, Jackie would head back to her life up north. Eli would continue to farm and raise his son, and Charla would continue sowing her wild oats.

On the surface it would appear that nothing had changed. Eli suspected that everything had.

Chapter 3

After leaving the Pub with Eli walking strong and silent behind her, Jackie once again climbed into the cab of his truck. She hadn't expected to like the man, but she did. She'd watched the hurt chase across his rugged face as he talked, saw him struggle not to say anything totally negative about Charla to her sister, and respected him for that.

He was easy on the eyes, too, she had to admit. However, she understood that the insistent tug of attraction she felt would be nothing but trouble for both of them were she to give in. So she wouldn't. After all, she was only in town to find her sister, make certain Charla was all right and meet her nephew. Bonus points for having time to catch up on everything she'd missed for the past three years. She might be worried, but she was glad Charla had finally reached out, whatever the reason. She could only hope her sister was, as everyone seemed to think, simply being dramatic.

One more day. Friday would roll around and Charla would either show up at Eli's farm with Theo, or she wouldn't. With all of her heart, Jackie hoped it was the former.

Eli dropped her off at Charla's apartments where she'd left her rental car. Thanking him, she got out of his truck and walked toward her vehicle, resisting the urge to glance back over her shoulder at him.

She unlocked the doors and got inside. Only then did Eli leave. After he'd driven off, Jackie got out and tried Charla's apartment one final time, unsurprised when she didn't get an answer. Wherever her sister might be, Jackie could only hope she was safe.

One more day, she reminded herself yet again. One. More. Day. Yet knowing that didn't help the roiling worry inside her. It made everything worse knowing she was alone in this. Even her own mother acted as if Jackie was a fool to worry about Charla.

Strange as it might be to understand, it seemed no one but she was truly afraid for her sister. Charla's friends had expressed concern, but mainly because she hadn't shown up at work to cover her shift. That seemed odd to her. Did Charla actually not have any real friends? As a child and a teenager, Charla had been popular. Everyone had wanted to hang out with her.

Clearly, not anymore. But then again, Jackie had been gone for three years. Everyone else had been here while Charla apparently burned a lot of bridges. To

Jackie, Charla would always be her baby sister. Spoiled, true. But deeply loved.

Driving back to the Landshark Motel, she made a detour for nostalgia's sake and drove past her old high school. The two-story tan brick structure looked exactly the same, just older. Getaway High, home of the Fighting Hornets. Jackie slowed, gazing at the imposing building, wishing she had better memories. She'd spent her entire time here studying hard, working toward her goal of coming out at the top of her class. She'd achieved this goal, despite her mother's baffling lack of support.

After graduating as class valedictorian, she'd been offered a scholarship to Texas Tech, enough to cover almost everything. Charla had been furious, accusing Jackie of leaving her to rot in a dying little town, as she'd put it. Only Jackie's promises to come home most weekends had mollified her.

Jackie had hoped her younger sister would study and work hard and follow in her footsteps. Instead, Charla had seemed determined to do the opposite. She'd partied hard and often, her grades falling so low that she almost didn't graduate.

So many memories here. Not all of them were good.

After leaving the high school, Jackie stopped by a small beer and wine store and picked up a bottle of Pinot Grigio and a few snacks. She had her e-reader loaded with manuscripts for work and planned to spend a quiet evening sipping wine and reading. It never hurt to get a jump ahead on the work that always seemed to pile up.

Back at the Landshark Motel, which took on a sad

appearance in the waning sunlight, she let herself into her room. Then she changed into her pajamas, poured a generous glass of wine, using one of the motel plastic water glasses, and climbed into the bed. Propping her back up with pillows, she got under the covers, took a sip of wine and began to read. These were from the slush pile, the unsolicited manuscripts aspiring authors sent in. There were always tons of them and Jackie enjoyed wading through them, aware that somewhere she might find a rare gem.

Of course, almost immediately her cell phone rang. Seeing her mother's name come up on the caller ID, Jackie was sorely tempted to let the call go to voice mail. Only the possibility that Delia might have finally heard from Charla forced Jackie to accept the call.

"Hey, Mom, what's up?" Jackie asked.

"I know you've been gone three years, but how could you have forgotten about the gossip in this town?" Delia demanded, her tone peeved. "I've already gotten three phone calls from people who saw you and Eli at the Pub."

"So?" Jackie asked, not bothering to conceal her impatience. "Are we not allowed to have a meal together?"

"People are saying you're poaching your sister's ex-husband."

"But I'm not," Jackie pointed out, rolling her eyes. "You know that, I know that and he knows that. What's the problem? Why are you even listening to gossip anyway?"

Delia sighed, a loud, dramatic sound that reminded Jackie of Charla. "Imagine what Charla is going to think once she gets home. She reached out to you in hopes of mending the rift between you and this is how you repay her?"

Jackie struggled to find the right words. Any words, actually, that wouldn't escalate the tension between her and her mother. Since the *rift*, as her mother put it, had been entirely Charla's doing, she wasn't sure what to say. In addition to that, while it was true Charla had reached out, she'd only done so because she needed help. Badly. No matter what anyone else thought, no matter how fickle her sister might be, in that moment when she'd sent Jackie the text, she'd honestly felt her life was in danger. Jackie believed that with every fiber of her being. It was why she'd put in an emergency request for vacation, bought an overpriced plane ticket, flown here and not only rented a car, but also paid for a hotel room. All of the money she'd saved for a trip to Key West with a couple of work friends would be depleted by the time she returned home.

Jackie had always been the one who saved her sister. Despite a three-year-long absence, she'd do whatever it took to save her now. Despite a lack of evidence, she would bring Charla home safely. If Charla's life truly was in danger, Jackie would stop the threat and protect her sister.

Meanwhile, Jackie could only cling to the hope that Charla had been wrong and that she wasn't too late.

On the phone Delia continued to worry about irrelevant nonsense. When she finally paused for air, Jackie jumped in. "Are you finished, Mom?" Jackie asked softly. "Because tomorrow is when we find out if Charla is actually missing. I'm trying to catch up on work and after that, I'd like to get some rest so I can be ready to see my sister again." As if there wasn't a doubt. Always the optimist, Jackie thought.

"There's more," Delia continued, her voice reluctant. "People apparently are taking bets on where Charla is and with whom."

This had Jackie sitting up straight. "People? What people?"

"I don't know." Delia sounded miserable. "She's not really well liked in town these days. Mostly because she can be a bit…careless. But Charla's a good person, a wonderful daughter and an amazing mother. I don't know why all these others can't see that. Instead, they chose to focus on her faults. Who cares if she likes to have a good time? She's young. She'll outgrow that eventually, like I did."

Jackie winced, glad her mother couldn't see her. When she and Charla had been younger, Delia had spent a lot of time hanging out in bars, too, leaving Jackie to watch over her baby sister. Delia had often come home drunk and passed out on the couch. Though Jackie had hated when that happened, it had been infinitely preferable to those nights when her mother hadn't come home at all.

Again, she wisely refrained from commenting. Delia had rewritten the past in her own mind and if her version of the truth bore no resemblance to reality, nothing Jackie could say would change that.

"I do have some better news, though," Delia said, her tone brightening. "I called a few of Charla's girlfriends and found out the names of Charla's latest two boyfriends."

"The ones who got into a fight at the Pub over her?"

"Yes. Wasn't that something?"

Unbelievably, Jackie heard an undercurrent of pride in her mother's voice. Grimacing, she poured herself a second glass of wine. "Yes, Mom, that was something. Did you pass that information along to the authorities?"

"Yes, I did." Delia's voice rang with triumph. "I called Rayna and passed both names along to her, just in case. She promised to talk to them. Which means if they know anything about where Charla might be, Rayna will get that information."

"Thanks," Jackie replied, impressed despite herself. "Does this mean that you're also beginning to worry about Charla?"

"A little," Delia admitted. "I'm worried about my grandson, as well. I usually see Theo several times a week, and it's not like Charla to keep him away from me for so long. But like you said, tomorrow is when she's supposed to bring Theo to Eli. If she doesn't show up, I know we'll all worry." She took a deep breath. "A lot. Is Eli going to let you know?"

"I hope so. Though what I'd really like is for Charla to call me first." She closed her eyes, allowing herself to picture it. Charla would be laughing, not even slightly apologetic for worrying anyone. They'd meet at Tres Corazons for dinner, have a margarita with their enchiladas and catch up on the past three years. Sisters once again.

"Well, call me the instant you hear anything," Delia ordered. "And if I hear from Charla first, I promise to do the same."

After ending the call with her mother, Jackie settled back against the pillows with her wine and her work, but she couldn't concentrate. She finally dug in her bag for a pad of paper and a pen and began making a list of what she knew about Charla and her disappearance.

She began with receiving the text. That had been late Monday night—actually, early Tuesday morning. Jackie hadn't seen the text until she'd gotten up around 8:00 a.m. Either way, the text had evidently been sent sometime after Eli had given Charla a ride home from the Pub.

Over to the side she listed the events that had occurred before Eli picked her sister up. A bar fight between two men.

She also listed how her sister hadn't shown up for work, four days at the jewelry store, which would have been Saturday, Monday, Tuesday and Wednesday, the day Jackie had arrived in town.

Two days. She'd only been back in Getaway for two days and it already felt like an eternity. She shook her head, half-relieved and half-worried that tomorrow they'd finally know something for sure.

And unless Charla called her, she still had to kill time Friday during the day. Eli had said Charla always brought Theo to the farm after five. After work. Where she hadn't been all week.

Pushing away the chill that ran down her spine, she decided to stop by the sheriff's office in the morning and chat with Rayna. Even though right now the general consensus seemed to be that Charla had taken off on some kind of lark and no one took her seriously. But if that actually was the case, what had she done with her toddler son? More than anything, Jackie hoped Charla showed up at Eli's farm tomorrow afternoon.

Somehow, Jackie didn't think she would.

Pulling out her phone, Jackie tried calling Charla again. The call once more went directly to voice mail. She also sent another text but got no response. Though almost everyone acted as if she was overreacting, she couldn't shake the feeling that this time something really was wrong.

If her sister showed up tomorrow—no, *when* her sister showed up tomorrow—Jackie vowed she'd suppress the urge to chew her out for all the worry she'd put her through. She'd hug her instead, she thought. They'd spend some time catching up, and then Jackie would bring up how worried she'd been. Since she'd taken a two-week impromptu vacation, she allowed herself to picture some of the things she and Charla might do. Girls' night out, maybe catch a movie or two. Heck, if Charla wanted, Jackie could even arrange for them both to fly back to New York, and she'd spend the rest of her time off showing her sister around the city.

Thinking such happy thoughts helped lighten the stressful uncertainty that had plagued her ever since arriving back home and not being able to locate her sister.

What if something really had happened to Charla and Theo, the nephew Jackie had never met? If so, Jackie knew she'd move heaven and earth to find them, as well as whoever meant to do her sister harm.

She thought about Eli, who should still be her number-one suspect if anything truly had happened to her sister, and wished she'd managed to put a bit more distance between them. Instead, after a mere two days, she felt as if he was her friend. She berated herself for being seduced by his earnest friendliness and handsome face. Still, all her life she'd been good at judging character, and she truly believed Eli was exactly as down-to-earth and real as he appeared to be. Someone like him would have been a steadying influence on her sister, though she could also see Charla deciding he was boring. Hopefully, Jackie would get a chance to hear everything directly from Charla's mouth tomorrow.

Hopefully. Definitely.

Friday morning. Finally. Eli opened his eyes, as usual well before his alarm clock went off, aware of a sense of both anticipation and of a niggling worry that he couldn't shake. Would Charla show? He had to believe she would. But then why hadn't she answered any of his texts or voice mails? They might not be able to talk about anything else, but they'd had an agreement to always stay in touch whenever it concerned their son.

Theo. Due to Charla's party-girl attitude, he'd asked for joint custody of their boy. Charla had laughed at him and the judge had apparently agreed with her that a child belongs with his mother. Instead of equal parenting rights, Eli received visitation, a standard schedule worked out by the judge that he'd apparently been using for over thirty years. Alternate weekends, two weeks every summer and switching holidays every year with Charla.

With no choice but to accept the ruling, Eli tried not to worry about his young son. At first, fears for his boy's safety had kept him up at night, but as time passed and Charla proved to be a fairly capable mother, some of his foreboding abated. At least when she went out partying, she always made sure Theo had a babysitter, sometimes her mother, sometimes Eli, mostly one or two of her friends.

Though missing Theo was a constant ache, Eli eventually got accustomed to his new reality. It wasn't what he wanted or hoped for, but it was what he got. He had no choice but to learn to live with it. He'd wanted to be present when Theo spoke his first words, began to crawl, took his first steps. Instead, he'd missed most of the major developments of his boy's life, though he made a big deal out of each new thing when he finally saw it.

His weekends with Theo were the best part of his life. Eli spent all the time in between them waiting for the next one to roll back around. So far Charla had never missed one or even been late. Eli always spent the entire day working to kill the hours until he got to see his son.

Today, though, with no response from Charla to his texts or phone calls, he wasn't entirely sure whether or not she would show. Even the thought had his stomach churning. He had no idea why she would do something like this, why now, unless she'd engineered all of this to make some sort of point to her older sister, Jackie.

He allowed himself to feel a flash of anger. Just a small one, quickly tamped down. He'd learned long ago not to allow himself to react emotionally to Charla and her drama. It wore him out. How like her this was. Charla had never cared about inconveniencing others; as long as she got what she wanted, the world was a bright and shiny place.

He knew Jackie was worried, but she hadn't been around her sister in a long time. She had no idea that acting like this—getting people riled up, disappearing for days without making contact—was normal behavior for Charla.

As far as Eli was concerned, Charla could live her pursuit of narcissistic bliss all she wanted, as long as Theo was safe. He had to be safe. The alternative simply wasn't acceptable.

Except he couldn't shake the unwelcome sense that something really had gone wrong.

Where was Theo? Why hadn't he been in day care? The only thing he could think of was that Charla must have gone on a trip and taken Theo with her. Even though to do such a thing was highly unlike her.

Worry over his son was the one aspect of all this that concerned him. To be fair, he knew Charla had a lot of close female friends, many of whom enjoyed looking after her toddler. This and only this knowledge is what staved off the pending frantic concern. He had to believe that whatever else Charla might have become, she would still make sure their son came to no harm.

But would she bring Theo tonight?

He worked hard all through the morning, throwing himself into the plowing, doing twice as many rows as he normally did. When he broke for lunch, he wolfed down a cold meatball sandwich, toyed with the idea of calling Jackie just to hear her voice and rejected the thought for the same reason.

Back at it, he worked right up until four thirty, then hurried back to the house to take a quick shower. Charla always dropped Theo off between five thirty and six, as stipulated in the custody agreement. He made a big pot of macaroni and cheese, Theo's favorite, and parked himself on a chair with a clear view of the road and driveway. Any minute now he hoped to see that telltale plume of dust kicked up by a car coming down the gravel road.

While waiting, he checked his phone, just in case she decided to text that she was on her way, as she sometimes did. Instead, there was nothing. A vague sense of unease settled around him, but he refused to give up hope. Theo would be here. He had to be.

Five thirty came with no sign of her and Theo. Pacing now, he fought the urge to check the clock every two minutes. But at 6:05 p.m. he'd begun to understand they weren't coming. Which meant Jackie might have been right all along. Charla could actually be in some sort of danger. If this was true, what about his son?

His phone rang, startling him. He snatched it up, his stomach twisting when he realized it wasn't Charla. Instead, Jackie was calling him, no doubt to confirm her sister's appearance. Or lack of.

He froze, not ready to actually say the words out loud. But realizing the ridiculousness of this reluctance, he answered the phone. "She didn't show," he said, his voice tight, just like the leash he had on his emotion. "Not yet, at least."

Silence, broken only by Jackie's harsh intake of breath. "No calls or texts, either?" Her voice shook, most likely because she already knew the answer.

"No." Finally, he allowed himself to say the unthinkable. "I'm worried about the safety of my son."

"And my sister," she added. "Both of them." She took a deep breath. "I think you need to call Rayna. Better yet, go see her in person. I can meet you there."

Feeling queasy, he agreed. "I want to wait just a few more minutes," he said. "Just in case they're running late."

Though she knew just as well as he that this was unlikely, she agreed. "Half an hour," she said, and ended the call.

While he waited, Eli paced. Front door hallway to back door. Around the living room coffee table, making periodic stops by the front window. Outside, nothing stirred up the dust on the gravel road. The late-afternoon sun continued to beat down, relentless in its brightness. Everything outside looked like a normal late-spring day. But it wasn't. Not even close. His son was truly missing.

He made it for twenty minutes before he snatched up his truck key fob and slammed from the house. He drove faster than usual but despite that, Jackie was already waiting for him in the sheriff's department parking lot. She took one look at his face and nodded, her expression grim. Side by side they walked in and asked to see Rayna.

The sheriff took one look at their unsmiling faces and motioned for them to follow her back to her office. Waving her hand at the guest chairs, she closed the door before turning to face them. "I'm guessing that Charla didn't show."

"No." This time Eli didn't even try to hide his worry. "What if something has happened to my son?"

"And what if something has not?" Rayna countered. "Let's think positive. While not showing up for the agreed-upon visitation isn't something Charla has ever done, that doesn't necessarily mean she and your boy have come to any harm."

While he appreciated her attempt to calm him down, Eli wasn't having it. "How about we find her?" he asked, a definite edge to his voice. "And my son."

Jackie squeezed his arm, which made him feel as if she offered her support.

"I know my mom gave you the name of Charla's two boyfriends," Jackie said.

"Yes, and we've already spoken to them," Rayna replied. "Neither of them claims to have heard from Charla since that night in the Pub."

"Other than Eli, I might be the only person who heard from her after that," Jackie interjected. "She sent her text to me early Tuesday morning."

Rayna nodded. "Then where has she been all this time?" Her steely gaze drifted over to meet Eli's. "It appears you might have been the last person to see her before she disappeared."

The words chilled him. Back to that again. "As if I would ever hurt her," he said, conscious of the way Jackie narrowed her eyes as she watched him. "Or my son. Come on, Rayna. You've got to do better than that."

Her curt nod didn't reassure him. "We're going to need to get the word out in town. I know people are already talking about this. Most of them assume it's simply Charla being Charla. I've spoken to Christopher Levine, too, and he said if Charla didn't turn up by tonight, he'd be willing to offer a thousand-dollar reward for information leading to her safe return."

"That's impressive," Jackie said. "When I talked with him, he seemed to think very highly of my sister."

Eli decided not to mention that Charla had claimed to have had an affair with her boss shortly after Theo had been born, confiding they'd also been together before she and Eli had met, though that had ended. The two of them had only picked up their relationship after she'd had her son. She'd then proudly shown Eli a large diamond ring the man had given her. Since Christopher already had a wife, it wasn't an engagement ring. Just a pretty and very expensive trinket, the kind a rich man might give his mistress.

If Rayna knew about the affair, she didn't say anything about it, either.

"What can we do?" Jackie asked, leaning forward. "Surely, there's some way we can help."

Rayna perched on the edge of her desk, her expression solemn. "I've already asked Delia for a list of Charla's friends—both male and female. Eli, if you can provide whatever information you might have, that would be helpful."

He nodded. Jackie, who now sat up straight at full attention, clearly waited for Rayna to say something to her.

"Jackie," Rayna finally said. "I know you've been away for a while and that you weren't involved in your sister's life recently. I'd ask you to help Eli here as much as you can. Also, I'm guessing your mother might need your support."

Eli could imagine how distraught Delia would be once she learned Charla truly was missing. She loved her younger daughter more than anything. In fact, he believed Charla had received her love of drama from her overly excitable mother.

"I will," Jackie agreed. "I'd like to ask you exactly what your plan is. Where do you go from here?"

Rayna nodded, her sharp gaze going from Jackie to Eli and back again. "Excellent question. I'm going to start with talking with all of her friends. I'd like to find out if she might have mentioned anything about taking a trip. We'll be checking the bus station and security logs out at the airport. I've put out an APB for her car, so if that shows up we might have a bit more info."

"I like that. Very thorough." Still, Jackie held up her phone. "And since she sent me the text message, can you ping her phone or check her GPS?"

"We already have." Rayna paused. "Her phone is not turned on."

This news hit Eli like a blow to the stomach. Charla and her phone were inseparable. She was always on the damn thing, either checking social media or one of her dating accounts.

"Dating accounts," he said out loud. "Charla had joined multiple dating websites. She claimed there weren't enough decent men in Getaway."

"We'll check those out, too," Rayna agreed. "Hopefully, Delia will have a bit more specific information for us about that." She cocked her head. "Unless you have more specifics."

"I'll make you a list of the ones I know she was on," he replied, and then took a deep breath. "What about an Amber alert for Theo? Can we do that? It might help him get spotted faster."

"I wish we could," Rayna replied. "Unfortunately,

since Charla is the custodial parent and has never been a danger to Theo, this doesn't meet the criteria of an Amber alert. I'm sorry."

For one second he allowed his desperation to show. "We've got to find them. We have to find my son."

"We will," Rayna soothed. "I'm putting all my best people on the case."

Chapter 4

Now that what Jackie had feared all along had come to pass, she refused to let go of that last shred of hope, despite the chill that had settled deep into her bones. Her sister and nephew would be all right. They had to be.

Meanwhile, Charla and Theo were officially missing.

Though she dreaded calling her mother, she figured it would be best to get it out of the way now. Excusing herself from Rayna's office, she crossed through the large work area, spied an empty conference room and slipped inside. Once she'd closed the door, she quickly pulled up her mother's contact info and took a deep breath before pressing Call Now.

Delia answered on the second ring. As soon as Jackie filled her in, her mother let out a bloodcurdling scream, so loud Jackie had to hold the phone away from her ear. She waited silently while her mother railed and cursed and sobbed, aware that there was nothing she could say to make things any better.

"I knew it," Delia declared after she'd finished her theatrics. "I just had this feeling something was wrong. All along, I knew."

Somehow, Jackie managed to refrain from reminding her mother that in fact, the opposite had been true. None of that mattered right now. "I'm at the sheriff's office now with Eli," she said. "Rayna is getting a plan put in motion. She's going to need a list of all Charla's close friends."

"Why would you think I'd have that?" Delia sounded both angry and frantic. "I'll do the best I can, but Charla didn't involve me in every aspect of her life."

Jackie blinked. Up until right this moment, her mother had talked as if she and Charla were super close, living practically in each other's back pocket. "Okay, Mom. I'm going to let you go now. I want to get back in there so I don't miss anything." She ended the call without giving Delia a chance to protest.

As expected, Delia immediately called back. Jackie declined to accept the call, sending it to voice mail, and left the conference room, heading back to Rayna's corner office. She opened the door quietly and slipped inside.

"There you are," Rayna exclaimed. "Why don't you and Eli keep each other company for a bit. I'm afraid I have to shoo you both off. I need to get to work." She glanced back at a stack of papers on her desk. "I promise I'll keep you informed."

Glancing at Eli, Jackie realized he was barely keeping it together. The thinly veiled, stark fear in his eyes had her taking his arm and leading him out of Rayna's office. "Let's go get a cup of coffee or something," she suggested. "I think it'll be better if we stay out of everyone's way and let them do their job."

He nodded and allowed her to steer him toward the exit. Once outside he glanced at her, his expression now carefully blank. "Where to?" he asked, the lack of inflection in his voice letting her know he definitely needed some time to process everything.

"How about we go for a drive?" Snap decision. Inside his truck he could rant and rave, if he wanted. Ask tough questions—and possibly answer them. Much better than in a crowded restaurant, where others would no doubt want to talk to him.

He shrugged, glancing at her. "I thought you wanted to get coffee."

"We can pick up some in a drive-through," she replied. "I think a ride might do us both some good."

Posture uncharacteristically stiff, he nodded and used his remote to unlock his truck. "If you say so. Let's go."

As she climbed into the passenger seat, her heart went out to him. She couldn't help it. Even though she knew she should consider him a suspect, especially since she didn't know him all that well. While his fear for Theo was palpable, he might be a damn good actor for all she knew. Without Charla there to tell her, she had no idea if she and Eli had been fighting. Maybe even over Theo.

Still, when someone needed comfort as badly as he

did, she had to offer it. Especially since she knew doing so would help her find a bit of solace as well. "They'll be found soon," she said, injecting a note of certainty into her voice. "I'm sure they're both fine."

"Are you?" A thread of bitterness seeped into his voice. "Because I'm beginning to wonder. What the hell did Charla get mixed up in this time? And how could she not take Theo's safety into consideration?"

Since she had no answer, she didn't reply. Instead, she looked out the window as he pulled onto Main Street.

"Where to?" he asked, barely glancing at her. "I'm assuming you have some destination in mind."

"You decide. Let's just drive around. Maybe out on the Farm to Market roads. If you want coffee, we can pick some up on the way."

"I think I'll pass on the coffee," he replied. "I'm already too agitated without adding caffeine. But we can pick some up for you if you want."

She shrugged. "That's okay. Let's go. Somewhere outside of town."

In response, he turned off Main Street and headed west. But instead of driving toward the highway, he stuck to the back roads, the ones that meandered through wheat fields and by cattle pastures, with numerous four-way stop signs.

Eyeing the passing scenery with interest, Jackie realized the last time she'd been this way had been as a young college student, home on break, with a group of friends looking for a pasture to have a bonfire and party.

Glancing at Eli, she wanted to ask him where he'd

grown up. Had it been in a small town like Getaway, or somewhere else? Was he even a native Texan?

But small talk not only seemed like too much effort, but also would have felt wrong. She'd suspected all along that Charla wasn't simply off on a lark. Eli, along with nearly everyone else, had just now come to the realization. He'd need time to grapple with the knowledge. While she needed to figure out what to do next.

The paved road gave way to gravel, and Eli slowed down some. On all sides of them the horizon seemed to stretch out forever. West Texas with its wide-open spaces and endless sky always made her feel a sense of peace. When she'd first arrived in New York, with skyscrapers blocking the sun and people hurrying everywhere, she'd battled claustrophobia. Eventually, she'd found her own pace and had managed to get used to the city. Having a place like Central Park to visit had helped a lot, too.

Eli slowed, swinging the truck to the left of the road to avoid a series of ruts. As he drove, some of the tension he carried seemed to dissipate. He sighed, fiddled with the radio and finally snapped it off.

"I just don't understand," he said, glancing sideways at her. "I get that Charla might have taken off. As you know, her doing so wouldn't actually be anything new. But Theo…my boy. She knows how much I love him. And he loves me, too. Why would she take my son away from me?"

The very real anguish in his voice made her eyes sting and her throat close. She hadn't expected to feel this sense of kinship with him, the man who still could be the one who'd actually threatened her sister.

"I don't know," she answered quietly. "Maybe she had no choice."

"There's always a choice. Always." He looked straight ahead, his rugged jaw tight. "I don't know what to think. The one thing Charla and I always agreed on was that our son would grow up with two parents who got along no matter what."

"I respect that," she said, meaning it. "But if someone was threatening Charla for whatever reason and she had to disappear fast, she'd have no choice but to take Theo with her. If that's the case, it won't be permanent. We just have to find out who's after her and why. Once she's safe, she'll be able to come back home."

"You really believe that?" he asked, his tone indicating he did not. "Since you've been back in town, you've learned a little bit about what kind of person your sister has become."

His cell phone chimed. Pushing a button on his dashboard, he had the vehicle read the text aloud. "Are we still on for tomorrow? Sasha Yacos."

Jackie glanced at him, her stomach in knots. "Girlfriend?" she asked.

"No." Turning left onto an even rougher road, he hardly glanced at her. "One of my students. I give group riding lessons to kids on Saturdays. I'm guessing news of Charla and Theo's disappearance is making the rounds. Sasha is wondering if we're still having the class. She'll probably be the first of many, now that word has gotten out."

More relieved than she should have been, she nodded. "How many groups do you have?"

"I usually have four," he answered, still seemingly

distracted. "I teach the youngest kids, the beginners, in the morning. After lunch I have two groups of older kids, one intermediate and the other advanced."

"Are you still going to have them?"

He thought for a moment. "I don't know. Actually, until that text, I'd completely forgotten about them." He turned again, this time onto a very narrow, very rugged road. Jackie realized he clearly had a destination in mind.

A shiver snaked up her spine. What if he was taking her to where he'd killed Charla and Theo, to show her the bodies before he murdered her, too?

Chiding herself for her foolishness, nevertheless, Jackie resolved not to let him catch her unawares. She might not be good at fighting, especially if he had a gun, but she'd recently taken up running. She was fast and she had endurance going for her.

"What do you think?" he asked, still talking about the riding classes. "Should I cancel them?"

"No." Despite her trepidation, she managed to speak calmly. "What purpose would doing that serve? In fact, if you don't mind, I'd like to come watch one or two of the classes. It might help take my mind off things."

"I don't know. I feel like I should be doing more. Out searching or something. Though I know Rayna's a professional, and a damned good one, it feels weird to do nothing when my son and his mother are missing."

Absurdly grateful that he'd included her sister, she nodded. "I know that feeling very well." They hit a deep rut, sending both of them bouncing. "By the way, where are we going?"

"There's an overlook," he said. "Notice how we're

going slightly uphill? When I first moved here, I discovered this place on one of my Sunday drives."

"What does it overlook?" she asked.

"You'll see," he replied.

At least he hadn't said something sinister, she thought. Still, she tried to remain alert, alternating between watching him and trying to notice landmarks in case she had to go on foot. Even though she knew her entire line of thought might be ridiculous, better safe than sorry.

"You still don't trust me, do you?" he asked, his voice casual.

Briefly, she debated how to respond, deciding to parry his question with one of her own. "Should I?"

"I didn't harm your sister," he replied. "Or my son."

An answer that really wasn't an answer.

One more turn, this time up a bit of an embankment, and he parked. Below them thousands of acres of farmland spread out. Along with a massive herd of longhorn cattle, roaming almost directly underneath.

Awestruck despite herself, she slowly got out of the truck and walked toward the highest point—a large, flat rock that made the perfect natural observation deck. He came up behind her and she tensed, remembering her earlier concerns.

"It's okay," he said quietly, a slight thread of humor in his voice. "I'm seriously not a murderer."

If her laugh sounded a bit nervous, he pretended not to notice.

He stood beside her, gazing at the majestic herd below. "If you're really that nervous, I can take you back to town."

With a sigh, she turned and looked at him. "I don't know what to think about you, Eli Pitts. Statistically, when women disappear, it's usually the husband or boyfriend who caused them harm."

"I'm neither of those things," he pointed out.

"That's splitting hairs. Ex-husbands, too, I think."

He considered her, his cowboy hat putting his face into shadow. "You're forgetting that Charla had several boyfriends. And while your theory makes sense, I also find it terrifying that you think Charla—and Theo— might have come to harm."

"I don't think that," she protested, swinging around to face him. "It's just one of many possibilities. More than anything, I hope Rayna locates them safe and sound."

He nodded, averting his face from hers. She watched him, aware he could see her intense scrutiny, her thoughts in turmoil. The slightest movement of his shoulders, the way he swallowed hard, not once, not twice, but three times, made her freeze.

Was he...crying?

Surely not. But then again...she knew enough to give him privacy, pretend not to see. But she couldn't seem to make herself move. Instead, she fought the strangest urge to wrap her arms around him and offer comfort the only way she could—through touch.

Would he rebuff her clumsy attempt if she did? Would it be better if she turned away and went back to the truck? While her internal debate raged, Eli continued to keep his profile averted, his entire body rigid, a testament to his attempt at maintaining self-control.

She had to see, to know the truth. Reaching out,

she touched his arm, making him instinctively turn to look at her.

Silent tears made silver paths down his rugged cheeks, spilling from his eyes, though he'd compressed his mouth in a tight line to keep from crying out in his pain.

"Eli…" She went to him, meaning only to hug him, but somehow his mouth, salty with tears, ended up pressed against hers. Need, raw and urgent, blossomed, and she kissed him instead. Part of her wished she had the power to kiss away his pain; the other, more primal part, only wanted to deepen the kiss, to turn it into more. This man, who'd once loved her sister and undoubtedly loved his son, had inadvertently borne his soul to hers.

Aching for them both, she could only offer this small touch, and hope they could somehow find a temporary respite.

Turning away, Eli blinked, trying to figure out what exactly had just happened.

Damn it all to hell. Not only had he cried, something he'd only done one other time, at his father's funeral, but gorgeous Jackie Burkholdt, his ex-sister-in-law, had kissed him out of pity, too. Pity. Even worse, at a time when physical attraction should have been the last thing on his mind, he'd found himself wanting to deepen the kiss, aching for *more*.

Clearly, Jackie hadn't felt the same. In fact, he couldn't actually blame her if she thought less of him.

"I'm…" He struggled to find the right words. An

apology might be in order, but damned if he wanted to apologize for something that had felt so right.

"It's okay," she murmured, her color still high. "I understand how easy it is to get carried away by a distraction like that."

A distraction. Odd choice of words, but maybe actually accurate. Because she'd wanted him, too, if only for that brief moment in time.

"Let's go back," he said. "It'll be dark soon and I'd like to be back in town." Instinctively, he checked his phone, just in case Rayna might have texted something. The screen remained blank.

Jackie nodded, her gaze still averted. "I agree." She checked her own phone, frowning. "Great. Just great. Delia has texted six times and left two messages. All the texts are her demanding to know what's going on, so I'm sure the voice mails will be the same."

He grimaced, climbing back into the driver's seat and waiting while she got in and buckled herself in. Several times on the way back he almost mentioned the kiss, but decided in the end it would be simpler to pretend it had never happened.

They made it to the outskirts of town before she spoke. "We have to believe that Charla and Theo are all right."

He nodded. "I agree. Because the alternative is unthinkable." And unbearable. He thought of his son, the bright spark of joy in Theo's clear blue eyes, his unruly shock of blond hair, his ready smile and infectious laughter. This time he managed to swallow past the huge lump in his throat. Damned if he'd cry again in front of Jackie. "I just want my boy back."

"I'm with you on that," she replied. "The sooner, the better."

After dropping her off, Eli made his way home. Knowing Theo was supposed to be here made his house feel emptier than usual. He turned on the TV, but couldn't settle on anything to watch so he turned it off. He went outside, making his usual rounds to check on the livestock, making sure the chickens were all penned up in the coop and closing all the barn doors. Because it was spring, darkness came later and later, but by the time he'd finished, the moon had risen in the starry sky.

Back inside he ended up going for a run on his treadmill, something he hadn't felt the need to do in a good while since the ranch kept him so busy. Forty-five minutes later, drenched in sweat, he stopped. A huge glass of water, a quick cold shower, and he felt as if he might be able to get some sleep after all.

Saturday morning Eli managed to get out of bed at his usual time, took a hot shower and made himself a large mug of strong coffee. The first group of kids and their parents would be there soon for the first riding class and he needed to be both awake and alert. Some of them trailered in their own horses, while others rode several of his.

After scarfing down a bowl of instant oatmeal, Eli made a second cup of coffee and headed outside. He raked the arena, using his tractor and a specific blade, before going over to the barn. He had four young riders who'd be needing horses, so he gathered up his calmest, most reliable ones—two mares and two geldings—and got them saddled and ready, tying them to the post just outside the riding arena. Staying busy was one way of keeping his mind off worrying about Charla and Theo. Since he hadn't heard from Rayna, he figured he'd call in between the first riding class and the second, just to see of there'd been any new developments.

He checked his watch. People should start arriving any moment. In fact, squinting into the sunlight, he swore he saw a plume of dust making its way up his road.

As the car drew closer, he realized that instead of one of his students, Jackie had arrived.

Despite everything, his heart stuttered in his chest at the sight of her long jeans-clad legs swinging out of her car. She wore Western boots, he noticed, and had tied her long, dark hair up into a jaunty ponytail.

Stunning and sexy, he mused, before shutting that train of thought down. "Good morning," he called out, using the same pleasant tone he used with his young students and their parents.

"Mornin'." She smiled and waved, looking around at his tied-up, well-fed horses and the freshly raked arena. "This is really interesting to me. I can't wait to watch the lessons."

"Thanks." He managed a hopefully impersonal smile. "Do you ride?"

"No. I never learned. I always wanted to as a kid, but Mom was a single parent and money was too tight."

On the verge of offering to teach her, he made himself close his mouth. Once Charla and Theo were found, Jackie would be going back to New York.

Luckily, more of his students began to arrive. At 8:55 a.m., his entire class of eight- and nine-year-olds had assembled, along with their parents. As usual, the adults all clustered together alongside the arena rail. He couldn't help but notice the way they all glanced at Jackie, who stood slightly apart.

Not his problem, he told himself, beginning the lesson by having everyone ride at a brisk walk around the arena. He made gentle corrections on body position, urging one boy to loosen his grip on the reins, another girl to sit up straight with her shoulders back and her heels pointed down.

From the walk to a jog, also known as a trot. Some kids had been born with a natural seat, able to adjust comfortably to the horse's pace. Others, too stiff or rigid, bounced, their elbows flailing. He corrected those, too, taking care to toss out an equal number of compliments.

Finally, the lope. A controlled canter. Their glee palpable, the kids grinned. Some outright laughed. They loved this.

Eli grinned back. The hour was nearly over. He clapped his hands, ordering them all back to a walk. "Line up," he said.

Once they'd all ridden into the center and formed a line, he gave them all a short pep talk, complimenting their skills, before urging them to take their horses for a walk to cool down.

After the students had ridden off, as usual all the parents surrounded him. Eli talked and joked around with them, ignoring one of the women's blatant flirtation attempts. All through this Jackie held herself apart, observing but not participating. More than one of the parents glanced her way, offering her a friendly smile, which she returned.

Eventually, the kids made their way back. Eli supervised the unsaddling of his horses and made sure the kids brushed out any sweat. Those who had brought their own mounts brushed out their horses, too. One thing Eli refused to allow was anyone who thought they could rush through taking care of the horses.

One of the women broke apart from the group and walked over to Jackie. Trying not to be too obvious, Eli kept an eye on them, just in case. The other woman hugged her and rejoined the group of other parents.

Right on time, everyone loaded up and left. He checked his watch, walking over to where Jackie still stood, her expression unreadable. "Well?" he asked. "What'd you think?"

"Pretty cool," she responded, raising her hand to smooth her hair. "Turns out one of the women I went to school with has a kid in your class." She grimaced. "That kind of makes me feel old."

This made him laugh. "Right."

She shook her head. "How long until your next class?"

"Just under an hour. I have to grab a couple of different horses for the kids who don't have their own. I don't like to use the same ones twice." He caught himself staring at her mouth, aching to kiss her again.

Talk about having absolutely no common sense. To cover, he checked his phone again. "Still no word from Rayna," he said.

Pressing her mouth into a straight line, she nodded. "I know. I can't seem to stop pulling out my phone.

This waiting is driving me crazy. Even though it's been more than a few days…" She let her words trail off.

He understood exactly what she meant. Before, the worry had been only speculation. Now it was something more.

"Would you like some coffee?" he asked. She accepted his offer. They walked back to the house together. He grabbed yet another cup before telling her he had to get the horses ready. "But you're welcome to hang out here in the house if you want."

"If you don't mind, I'd like to come with you to the barn," she said, surprising him. "I haven't really spent a lot of time around horses, but I'd like to. Plus, I've got to keep busy or I think I might lose my mind."

"That I get," he said. "Follow me."

To his surprise, she stayed for the entire next hour of lessons, as well, continuing to keep herself apart from the group of parents, but watching everything intently. He couldn't help but notice every time she pulled out her phone and actually took a weird kind of comfort in knowing she'd let him know if anything changed.

This time, one or two of the parents asked him directly about Charla, since word had already traveled around the town. He deflected, keeping his answers vague, relying on saying mostly he felt sure Rayna would find her.

All the while, he kept the terror at bay, well aware if he let it get past his shield, it would kill him. Every thought of his son, the bright and beautiful boy, brought a physical pain that he simply couldn't allow. He couldn't speculate, refused to think the worst and told himself he had no choice but to believe Theo would be found safe and whole.

When the second class was nearly over, Jackie turned and walked off, disappearing inside his house. Several of the parents watched her go, their expressions ranging from curious to speculative.

Again, after class he sent the kids down the road to cool the horses off, bracing himself for the chat with the parents.

This time several asked about Jackie, one in particular a single dad named Jared. "New girlfriend?" he drawled. "She's a looker, that's for sure."

"She is," Eli agreed. "She's also Charla's sister, Jackie. Jackie's in town to help look for Charla."

Jared winced. "Sorry, man," he mumbled. "I completely forgot." Expression sheepish, he moved away, ostensibly to check on his daughter.

Finally, all the students and their parents left and he made his way back to his house, his stomach churning, making him realize he needed to eat something. As he let himself into his house, he spied Jackie in his kitchen.

"I hope you don't mind, but I made us some lunch," she said, her smile not matching the grim look in her eyes. "Just sandwiches, but I'm thinking we need to keep our strength up. For when, you know, Rayna calls."

He nodded. "Thanks, I appreciate that." He dropped heavily into a chair at the table, eyeing the plate with a sandwich and chips that she slid in front of him.

Once she sat down across from him, they ate in a kind of bleak silence. He couldn't taste his food, but he managed to choke down the sandwich and most of the chips. "Thank you," he told her, noting she picked at her food. "I'm thinking about calling Rayna to check on things."

"I've been fighting the urge to do exactly that," she admitted. "But I've been…afraid."

He got that. "Because she said she'd call us and she hasn't. Which means she hasn't found out anything yet."

She nodded, her expression miserable. "It's Saturday. How much work does the sheriff do on the weekend?"

"You'd be surprised," he responded. "Especially in a situation like this with missing people. Rayna is really good at her job and takes everything very seriously. I imagine she and her people are out canvassing the town. Most people are home instead of at work, which makes it easier to ask questions."

"That makes sense," she admitted. "But even knowing this doesn't make my anxiety any less."

"Me neither," he admitted. He didn't tell her the various scenarios that had gone through his mind, each one worse than the next. All he could hope for was that none of them would turn out to be true. Charla had been known to be flighty. Maybe she'd taken Theo with her on some sort of vacation and had lost track of time.

Of course, that thought brought to mind images of Charla passed out drunk and some stranger taking off with his son. Better not to go that route at all. "I just hope they show up soon."

"Me, too," Jackie agreed. "Me, too."

Chapter 5

After watching Eli drive away, Jackie turned to go back to her motel room. But after a few steps, she stopped and reconsidered. She hadn't come all this way to sit around and do nothing. While she didn't want to interfere with Rayna's investigation, surely asking a few questions around town couldn't hurt.

With her decision made, she retraced her steps across the parking lot. Getaway had two main bars—the Rattlesnake Pub, where most of the older locals went, and The Bar, an ultra-modern drinking establishment specializing in craft beers and elaborate cocktails. While she figured her sister hung out mostly in the Pub, it wouldn't hurt to make a stop by The Bar and see if anyone there might know her.

Though she wasn't dressed stylishly enough, she figured her T-shirt, skinny jeans and boots would be okay enough to get her in the door at either place. Since so far all she'd heard about Charla's reputation had been worrisome, to say the least, she hoped she could find someone with a slightly different perspective.

Even though it was still relatively early, too early for the evening crowd, the parking lot at The Bar had very few empty spots. It must be happy hour. She found one and parked, taking a deep breath before getting out of her car. Since The Bar had opened after she'd moved away, she'd never been inside this place. She'd only learned about it because she kept up an online subscription to the Getaway newspaper.

Once inside, she stopped for a minute to let her eyes adjust to the dim lighting. The minimalistic decor managed to be both chic and inviting, not an easy task. Turning in a slow circle, she realized with a sense of surprise that she felt as if she'd stepped into one of the trendy bars back in Manhattan.

Though most of the tables and booths were occupied, there were still a few empty bar stools, so she made her way to the dark wood-and-granite bar and slid up on one. She didn't see anyone she recognized. Most of the patrons appeared to be barely over legal drinking age.

A smiling bartender with a man bun came to take her order. She asked for a draft wheat beer, whatever kind they kept on tap. When he requested her ID, she smiled and passed her still-valid Texas driver's license over. Since she didn't drive in New York, she'd kept it.

One brow rose as he studied it, but he handed it

back to her with a nod and went to get her beer. When he returned and slid a tall frosted glass across the bar to her, she showed him a screenshot she'd made from Charla's Instagram account. "Do you happen to know this woman?" she asked.

"Charla?" He grinned, which made him look even younger. "Sure. She's a regular, though she hasn't been around in a few weeks. She mostly liked to stop by after her shift at the jewelry store. She also works part-time at the Tumbleweed Café, so you might check there."

A few weeks. Disappointed, she took a sip of her beer. "I already tried that. I'm her sister and I'm just in town for a short time. I was hoping to see her while I'm here."

"Bummer." Looking past her, he scanned the room. "You might talk to that table over there, the six-top. Your sister hung out with them sometimes."

"Thank you." Grateful, she picked up her beer and headed over. The table of six had four men and two women. One of the men, a burly guy wearing a knit beanie and sporting a nose ring, watched her approach.

"Hi," she said, refusing to allow herself to feel awkward. "I'm looking for my sister, Charla, and the bartender mentioned y'all were her friends."

One of the women snorted. "I wouldn't say *friends*, exactly," she said. "Maybe more like frenemies."

"Speak for yourself," a man wearing round, wire-rimmed eyeglasses and a cotton shirt buttoned all the way to his collar reprimanded. "Charla is good people." He eyed Jackie, appearing to consider his next words. "But as I'm sure you know, Charla is missing. Everyone in town is talking about it. And Rayna—that's our sheriff—has already been by here asking if anyone knew anything."

"She has?" Impressed that Rayna clearly was on top of things, Jackie thanked them and turned to head back to the bar.

"Wait." The other woman, a slender waif with short, wavy blond hair, stopped her. "Have you talked to Serenity? It might sound weird, but she knows things other people don't."

"I haven't, but that's a great idea." Serenity Rune, a self-styled psychic, ran a combination floral/metaphysical shop downtown. Jackie would try to swing by there soon, since she knew Serenity wasn't open on Sunday.

Back at the bar, Jackie asked for her tab. Once she'd settled that, leaving a few dollars for the bartender, she took one final sip of her beer and left.

Next stop, the Rattlesnake Pub. From experience, the Pub would be much louder, more raucous and likely full of people Jackie and Charla both had gone to school with.

There, with the lot already full, she had to park down the street. Getting out of the car, the loud thump of music escaped the building, making her realize it must be late enough that the live band the Pub always hired on Friday or Saturday night had already started.

Pushing through the door, she stepped inside. Just inside the door, a bouncer wearing a black cowboy hat, leather vest and boots stopped her, asking for her ID and a three-dollar cover charge.

"It's not even seven," she protested. "I'd think charging cover would start around nine. When did y'all start charging a cover charge, anyway?"

"We only do on Friday, Saturday and lately Sunday nights. That's when we have live music," he responded.

"That's new," she said, handing both over.

"Not really." He passed back her license and studied her face. "Your name sounds vaguely familiar, but I don't recognize your face."

"I've been away from town for a while," she admitted. "I'm Charla Burkholdt's older sister, Jackie."

He did a double take at that. "Wow. You two look nothing alike."

Jackie had heard this her entire life. Not only was Charla blonde and Jackie brunette, but Jackie was tall and lean while Charla short and curvy. "True. Anyway, I'm trying to find my sister. I was hoping maybe some of her friends here might have an idea where she might have gone."

He shook his head. "Everyone in town is wondering where she up and disappeared to. Rumors are flying like crazy. Anyway, the sheriff was here earlier asking around. You might talk to her and save yourself some time."

Wow. Rayna continued to impress her. Jackie nodded. "Thanks. That makes a lot of sense. Since I'm already here, I might as well have a drink and look around."

"Knock yourself out." A group of people came through the door and he turned his attention on them, leaving Jackie to make her way inside.

Inside, everything looked just the way she remembered it. In keeping with its name, the Rattlesnake Pub had been decorated in a Western theme. Old black-and-white photos of popular country music artists adorned the walls. It had occupied this building for as long as Jackie could remember.

The main part of the Pub had zero empty tables and a lot of people milling around with drinks in their hands. Jackie headed straight for the long bar on the right side, even though she could see there were no bar stools available and people stood three deep in line waiting to order drinks. If it got this crowded so early on a Sunday night, Jackie didn't like to think about what it must be like on Friday or Saturday.

Then she caught sight of a poster advertising the musical act tonight and understood. A very famous and very popular country music singer would be performing tonight. Often some of the greats liked to make pit stops in small Texas towns, and Getaway often made that list. In view of this, three dollars as a cover charge wasn't nearly enough. This crowd must have come from Abilene and all the small towns in between.

Well, Jackie thought, maybe someone in this crowd might have more insight as to where Charla could be.

Deciding to circulate instead of getting a drink, Jackie wove her way through throngs of people, searching for a familiar face. If she was completely honest with herself, she inexplicably hoped to find Charla here, beer in hand, laughing with her friends over some stupid joke. Which made no sense, but she couldn't shake the feeling.

Though she had to have grown up with at least some

of these people, Jackie didn't see anyone she recognized. Then a woman at one of the tables glanced up and did a double take while Jackie tried to place her. The woman pushed to her feet and hurried over, walking confidently despite wearing what had to be at least four-inch heels. "Jackie Burkholdt? Wow! Long time, no see."

Staring, Jackie scrambled to remember the woman's name. Finally, it came to her. "Pam Milan?" Jackie had been off-and-on friends with her in high school. They embraced, Pam's strong perfume almost making Jackie sneeze.

"I heard you were in town," Pam exclaimed, tugging at her arm. "Come sit with us. Have you had any luck locating your sister?"

"Not yet." Having to lean close to be heard over the noise, Jackie's nose twitched at the strong perfume.

"Come on, come on," Pam insisted. Jackie followed the other woman over to the already crowded table. Someone grabbed a spare chair and pulled it up. "Sit, sit."

"Thanks." Now Jackie recognized a couple of the others, one or two of them former classmates. If she remembered right, the stocky man with the receding hairline had also gone to Tech, where he'd played football. She didn't remember much about him other than that. And the woman with the super-short chic hairstyle had been on the drill team.

Pam performed introductions. A few of the others were several years younger, which explained why Jackie hadn't recognized them. Two people were from the next town over. When Jackie asked, she learned none of them had even talked to Charla lately and most of them didn't even know her. Most of the conversation centered on the country music star performing tonight.

After a couple of minutes, Jackie pushed to her feet and excused herself, saying she really needed to ask around about her sister. Pam waved goodbye, hollering at her to stay in touch. Jackie responded with a vague wave of her hand, moving back into the even more crowded room.

This time, instead of waiting in line at the bar for a drink that she didn't really want, Jackie decided to make her way through the room and look for people she might recognize as friends of her sister's. At first, she didn't see anyone, but then as she neared the dance floor area, she spotted Bobbi Jo Fleming, who'd once been one of Charla's closest friends. Bobbi Jo kept her straight, shoulder-length hair platinum and favored large, gaudy jewelry and short, tight skirts.

Laughing with a drink in one hand, Bobbi Jo's expression changed when Jackie made eye contact with her. She blinked her obviously false eyelashes and set her drink down on the table as she stood. "Jackie? Is that really you?"

"Yes, it is. It's great to see you." Jackie moved closer and they made small talk as best as they could over the noise. Unfortunately, that meant they had to stand uncomfortably close, and like Pam, Bobbi Jo also applied her perfume liberally. Though Jackie tried not to inhale, her eyes began to water. Quickly, she asked about her sister.

"I heard you were here looking for Charla," Bobbi Jo drawled. "I'll tell you up front I don't have any idea where that girl got off to. She seemed to have finally gotten her act together, being a mom and all. Until last Saturday night, when both her boyfriends showed up here at the same time and got into a huge fight." She rolled her heavily made-up eyes. "It got so bad they were all kicked out. Charla took that hard. This is her bar, you know. She loves this place, calls it her home away from home. Her ex had to come pick her up. After that, no one has seen or heard from her."

Her ex. Eli. Once again, he appeared to have been the last person to see her sister.

Jackie chatted with Bobbi Jo a few more minutes before excusing herself and moving on. After three complete circles around the room, weaving in between groups of people, she decided to leave the Pub and go back to her motel room to get some sleep. She planned to be up bright and early in the morning to keep trying to locate her sister, though she hadn't been able to make an actual plan. In a town as small at Getaway, there were only a few options. Once those had been exhausted, she wasn't sure where else she could look or what else she could do. She tried to take some comfort from the fact that Rayna appeared to be on top of things.

Her thoughts kept returning to Eli. On the way back to the motel, she stopped and got a salad at the burger place, since she couldn't remember when she'd last eaten. It tasted surprisingly good, and she devoured it, along with another cup of her wine. She wondered how Eli was coping and reached for her phone half a dozen times to call him. In the end, she decided not to disturb him, just in case he'd actually managed to get some rest.

That night, she slept poorly, her sleep interrupted

by horrible dreams featuring her sister and the nephew she hadn't even met yet.

Finally, sometime after midnight and two hours of tossing and turning, she fell into a deeper sleep. When she opened her eyes again, sunlight beamed through the space in between the curtains, and a quick glance at her phone revealed it was nearly seven. She rushed through her shower, applying minimal makeup and putting her hair in a ponytail before dressing in a comfy pair of jeans and a T-shirt. She slipped on her favorite running shoes, since she figured she'd spend most of the day on her feet.

Her phone chirped just as she'd grabbed her car keys to head out. A text from Eli.

I'm headed to the sheriff's office, it said. In case you want to meet me there.

Yes, she sent back. On my way.

She arrived at the sheriff's office just before he did. She'd gotten out of her car when she saw his truck pull into the lot. Waiting while he parked, she felt her heart jolt a little at the sight of him striding toward her, well-worn jeans slung low on his narrow hips, a gray cowboy hat on top of his head.

"Mornin'," he greeted her, his gaze weary. "I hope you slept better than I did."

"Probably not. I'm really worried," she confessed. "As I'm sure you must be. I stopped by both The Bar and the Rattlesnake Pub last night and asked around about Charla. Rayna had already been there, so she's definitely doing due diligence."

After removing his hat, he used his fingers to comb

out his hair. "That's good. Let's see if she has time to talk to us and tell us what she's learned, if anything."

Inside, they once again found Rayna digging through paperwork on the front desk. She looked up when they entered, smoothing away her frown when she saw them. "Hey, you two," she said. "Come on back to my office."

As they followed her through the main area, Jackie couldn't help but hope this meant she had something substantive to tell them. A quick glance at Eli revealed a similar hopeful expression.

Once they were all in, she closed the door and walked around behind her desk. "Take a seat," she said, though she remained standing behind her desk. "I'm afraid I have some bad news."

Jackie gasped. Eli gave her a stricken look, before swallowing hard. "What is it?" he asked. "Did you find Charla?"

"No." Rayna looked from one to the other, wincing. "I'm sorry. I should have been more careful with my choice of words. I've gotten some more information that might explain why Charla took off."

"Do you really think that's what she's done?" Jackie asked, still trying to regain her equilibrium. "Taken off?"

"It's possible. Christopher Levine was already in to see me," Rayna said, the downward turn of her mouth letting them know it hadn't been pleasant. "He says his books are off. Way, way off. As you may know, Charla acted as his bookkeeper."

To Jackie's shock, Eli rolled his eyes and made a dismissive sound. "The two of them were also having an affair. If his books are off, I guarantee he had something to do with it."

"An affair?" Jackie couldn't believe it. "Charla has known Christopher Levine since she was a senior in high school. Not only is he a lot older than her, but he's married." Even as she spoke, she remembered her sister showing off diamond earrings and necklaces, jewelry she'd supposedly purchased using her employee discount. Now she had to wonder if they'd been gifts from the jewelry store owner.

Rayna said nothing, her gaze alternating between Eli and Jackie, clearly waiting to hear them out.

"Yes, an affair." Eli shrugged. "Apparently, it was going on before she met me, though Charla claimed it was over a few months before we started dating. Strictly platonic, she said. Until it wasn't. She said they resumed the relationship sometime shortly after our son was born." He glanced at Jackie. "I didn't find out until after she asked for a divorce, just in case you're wondering."

Swallowing, Jackie nodded. She felt numb. If this was true, then she had to wonder if Charla had really been embezzling from Levine's. She had to wonder why. What the heck was wrong with her sister?

"Do you have proof?" Rayna finally asked. "I'm talking about your theory on the books. Because if you do, I need it quickly. Christopher wants to press charges."

"Against Charla?" Still reeling from the accusations of Charla having a long affair with a much older man, Jackie struggled to keep up. "I don't understand."

"Embezzling." Rayna's crisp reply. "According to

Mr. Levine, your sister may have made off with a large sum of money over time. Not to mention various items out of his storeroom stock."

"In other words, stealing money and jewelry," Eli said, his expression impassive.

"Why? Why would Charla do something like that?" Jackie asked, feeling sick. "She's worked at Levine's since high school. She was very proud of that. She also worked at the café, and took care of her son. Why on earth would she jeopardize her entire life like that?"

"Maybe she felt like Christopher Levine owed her for something?" The ache in Eli's tired voice made Jackie want to slip her hand into his. "Anyway, isn't the burden of proof on him?"

"It is," Rayna agreed. "Though honestly, from the way he was talking, he's got quite a bit of evidence proving his claim. He's getting all of that together and bringing it by in about an hour."

"Meanwhile," Jackie said, "Charla's still missing."

"And Theo," Eli added.

Rayna nodded, tapping her pencil on a manila folder. "I think at this point we have to consider the possibility that she might have left of her own accord."

Not again. Despite beginning to feel as if she might never have known her sister, Jackie felt obligated to mention the text. "Remember, she said she felt as if her life was in danger. Maybe that had something to do with this." She took a deep breath. "I have to think only pure desperation would make her steal from Levine's."

Eli gave her a skeptical look, but didn't comment.

Rayna considered her words for a moment. "Whatever her motive might have been, that wouldn't make this any less of a crime. If Mr. Levine's claims turn out to be true, once we find Charla, we'll have no choice but to arrest her."

Though Jackie nodded, hearing this hit her hard. "I'll have to tell my mother," she said, wincing as she imagined Delia's reaction.

"I'm sorry." Rayna reached across her desk and touched Jackie's arm. "I wish Charla would come back and help clear all this up. But she won't—or can't—so there's that."

"Can you search her apartment?" Jackie asked. "Maybe if she left a laptop behind, or has a computer, you could find some hint on it."

"We can't do anything without a warrant," Rayna replied. "Once Mr. Levine presses charges, we shouldn't have any difficulty obtaining one."

"A warrant," Jackie echoed, hardly able to believe what she was hearing.

Shaking his head, Eli looked from one woman to the other. "If Charla did take off on her own accord, and I agree that now it's entirely possible she did, she would never be that careless. But most importantly, what about my son? I'm still worried about him, and I consider him to be in danger, no matter what the reason for their disappearance."

"I understand." Rayna stood. "And I promise to keep you both posted if anything new develops. Now, if you'll excuse me, I have to get ready to meet with Christopher Levine."

Jackie pushed to her feet. Next to her, Eli did the same. "Thank you," she said. "Please continue to keep me informed."

"Us," Eli corrected. He took Jackie's arm and rather than make a scene, she let him. At least until they cleared the doorway, when she gently tugged herself free, walking ahead of him all the way outside. He walked her to her car, waiting to speak until she'd pressed the key fob to unlock the doors.

"What, are we enemies now?" he asked.

Coolly, she turned. "I'm not sure what you mean. We barely know each other." Truth, even though when they were together she honestly felt as if she'd known him forever.

Evidently, he shared that sentiment. "Come on, Jackie. It's just me. What's going on?"

Fine. "You appeared awfully ready to believe that Charla could be a criminal."

"You don't?"

Staring at him, she struggled to find the right way to respond. In the end, she settled on truth. "I don't know. But ever since I've been back in town, I've learned one bad thing after another about Charla. I mean, I always knew Mom spoiled her—I did, too—but she wasn't an awful person."

"I know," he agreed. "We're all complicated."

Was that a warning? She narrowed her eyes, unsure how to respond.

Before she could, he leaned in and kissed her. A hard press of his mouth against hers, sending liquid fire right through her veins. Her gasp had her opening her mouth to him, and she mentally said the hell with it and kissed him back, right there in the sheriff's department parking lot, for all the world to see.

* * *

Eli wasn't sure why—maybe it was the vulnerability in Jackie's amber eyes—but he leaned in for what he intended to be a quick kiss. Just a press of his lips on hers, maybe for reassurance or some other reason he didn't want to think too deeply about.

However, the instant their mouths touched, all self-control went up in a blaze of heat. To his stunned shock, she yanked him closer, until he pinned her with her back pressed up against her car, and kissed him as if she wanted much, much more.

Only the sound of a car honking its horn in the street made him come to his senses and break away.

They stared at each other for a moment, both breathing heavily, her mouth slightly puffy, making him ache to kiss her again.

He started to apologize but realized he would never be sorry for a kiss like that, so he settled for quick nod and turned away. So aroused he could barely walk, he felt her gaze on him the entire time he made his way back to his truck.

Damn.

Only once he'd driven off did he allow himself to think about what had just happened. If he knew this town—and he did—news of his and Jackie's kiss would be all over Getaway by dinnertime. For himself, he didn't worry too much, but he could imagine Delia's reaction to learning her daughter had been kissing her favorite other daughter's ex. It wouldn't be good. In fact, he imagined it would be spectacularly awful.

For him, that kiss had been worth it. For her... He wondered what Jackie thought. Even though they barely knew each other, he wanted her. From her sensual reaction, he believed she felt the same way. However, even he understood what a huge mistake giving in to that desire would be in the middle of all this. Now was definitely not the time to be worrying about his libido. His focus needed to be on finding his son and bringing him home safe. End of subject. Since the monumental mistake he'd made with Charla, he'd prided himself on his self-control. He needed to call upon every ounce of it now.

Thus fortified, he drove home. Rayna had seemed quite certain that Christopher Levine had a good case that Charla had not only embezzled from his store, but had stolen precious gems, too. Shockingly, the idea that Charla could have stolen from her employer barely surprised him. He'd realized some time ago that he'd never really known her. The things she'd done since the moment he'd met her, and her complete and utter lack of remorse, meant anything was possible.

In fact, if she'd gotten away with a significant amount of money, he'd bet she'd taken Theo and escaped to some tropical beach. She'd always talked about living in the Caribbean. If he had even the slightest idea what island she'd gone to, he'd hop a plane himself and hunt her down.

The only thing that gave him pause was the weird text she'd sent Jackie. She hadn't contacted him or Delia, but her estranged sister. He didn't understand the logic behind that, but since Charla never did anything without a reason, he knew there had to be one. He just had to figure out what it might be.

Now once again his thoughts had circled right back

around to Jackie. She truly worried over her sister and appeared to be having a difficult time adapting to hearing the truth about her. Had Charla really changed that much in three short years? Somehow, he doubted that.

Since he had plenty of work to do on the farm, he drove back there. Recently, he'd taken in two young geldings to train, one as a cutting horse, the other for the client's daughter to show in stock seat equitation. He knew if he could train even one successful cutting horse, his reputation would be made and he'd have a waiting list of people wanting to bring their horses to him. His current financial woes would be over.

Working with the first horse, a flashy sorrel quarter horse called Ro, he let himself get lost in the movements. Focusing on the animal drove everything else out of his mind. When he made the connection with a horse, magic happened. This, a gift he'd recognized ever since he'd been a young boy, had made him realize what direction his life had to take. Other people found magic in numbers and became accountants; those with a gift of words, authors. He'd been born to train horses and had worked his fingers to the bone in his corporate job in Houston to save enough money to buy the small ranch here in rural west Texas, where property sold for much less than it did in areas near big cities.

As soon as Theo was old enough, he planned to teach his son to ride. He wanted to see if his boy had inherited his gift with horses.

Theo. Mingled anger, worry and sorrow filled him, which he quickly pushed away. Still, the horse underneath him faltered in his stride, clearly sensing some of his rider's unrest.

Eli got his mind back on track and finished the training session. As he unsaddled the gelding, he put him on the hot walker to cool him down while he went to get the other horse.

By the time he finished with both horses, after brushing them out and returning them to their stalls, he realized he'd managed to skip lunch. He returned to the house, made himself a quick sandwich and checked his phone. A text from Rayna confirmed what he'd already guessed to be true. Charla was a thief and had most likely gone on the run.

With his son.

He supposed he should be glad that would mean Theo wasn't in any danger, but Charla had single-handedly wrecked his entire world in one fell swoop. The worst of it was that he still didn't entirely understand why she would do such a thing. They hadn't been good married, but he believed they got along just fine as coparents.

He saw a notification for a missed call. Jackie's number. She'd also left him a voice mail. After hesitating, he finally played it back. She'd simply asked him to call her. No doubt because she'd received the same text from Rayna.

Leaving his phone in the kitchen, he walked down the hallway to Theo's room, with its race-car bed and football-shaped toy box full of toys. The room sat untouched between visits, though Eli kept fresh sheets on the bed.

Eli stood in the doorway, finally allowing anger to fill him. Only once before in his life had he felt this furious sort of helplessness—when he'd lost his bid for joint custody of his son. This situation, while in its own way worse, brought about the same urge to do something, *anything*, but he was unsure of what. He needed to find his son. But he had no idea where to start looking.

Chapter 6

Jackie read the message again and again. Rayna's text had been short and to the point.

After reviewing the evidence provided by Mr. Levine, we have issued a warrant for Charla's arrest.

She'd sent it to both Jackie and to Eli.

Which meant Charla was a thief. Jackie sat for a moment, staring at her phone with a lump in her throat and a knot in her chest. She couldn't help but wonder how Eli had reacted when he'd received it. Because this new information made it likely that Charla had taken off on her own with Theo.

The only anomaly had been the text Charla had sent Jackie. Why claim to be in danger? And why involve

Jackie at all? Though bringing it up so often made
Jackie feel as if she was beating an already dead horse,
she couldn't let go of the very real fear she'd sensed in
her sister's message.

Had Christopher Levine found out about her embezzling and gone after her? Or had she been using
someone—one of her other boyfriends perhaps—to
fence the stolen jewelry and things had gone sideways?

Jackie sighed. Either way, now Charla had a warrant for her arrest. Time to call her mother. She'd put
it off as long as she could. While she knew news like
this should probably be delivered in person, she felt
safer talking to Delia on the phone. She had an idea
her mother's reaction wouldn't be pretty.

Taking a deep breath, she figured she might as well
get it over with. Otherwise, if Delia heard from the Getaway grapevine before Jackie got a chance to tell her,
there'd be even more hell to pay.

Delia answered on the second ring. "Do you have
news of your sister?" she demanded, forgoing any type
of greeting or pleasantries at all.

"Sort of." Speaking quickly, she filled her mother
in on everything Rayna had said, including her re-
cent text.

When she'd finished, Delia's unusual silence felt
unnerving.

"Oh, no," Delia finally said, her voice quivering.
"That would certainly explain how she could afford
all the extravagant jewelry gifts she gave me over the
years. She told me she had a huge employee discount."

Stunned, Jackie wasn't sure how to respond.

"I wonder if I take everything and return it to

Levine's, if Christopher will drop the charges," Delia continued. "It's worth a shot."

"Mom, I think there was a lot more involved than just a few pieces of jewelry," Jackie said, still cautious. "While Rayna didn't give an amount, it appears Charla has been embezzling money from the store for years."

Again, Delia went quiet. When she finally spoke, her response lacked conviction. "She wouldn't do that. Would she?"

Jackie didn't have an answer for that. But she did have a few questions. "Mom, if Charla were to escape somewhere, to some tropical island or something, where do you think she'd go?"

"How would I know?" Now Delia let her frustration show. "She was always talking about taking a beach vacation. Maybe the Bahamas or Jamaica. But I refuse to believe she'd run away without at least saying goodbye to me."

Before Jackie could say anything else, Delia said a quick goodbye and ended the call. At least her mother hadn't yet heard any gossip about Eli and Jackie kissing. When that happened, and it would, Jackie figured there'd be hell to pay.

Before she could think too much about it, Jackie called Eli. The call went to voice mail, making her wonder if he'd be avoiding her now. Ignoring the pang in her heart at the thought, she left a brief message, asking him to call her. She couldn't stop thinking about him, not only about that kiss, but about the raw vulnerability he'd allowed her to see.

Restless, tired of being confined to a small hotel room, Jackie decided to go out instead of turning in for the night. While mostly to keep from letting boredom drive her up a wall, she also figured she could see if there were any other people there who might know Charla.

Decision made, she quickly applied her makeup and then grabbed her favorite pair of trendy torn jeans, high-heeled shoes and a low-cut blouse. Since this outfit was one of her standard choices, she'd brought the jewelry she always wore with it—black dangly earrings shaped to look like feathers, a silver necklace that nestled perfectly in her cleavage and several bracelets on one arm. Satisfied after checking her appearance in the mirror, she got into her car and drove to the Rattlesnake.

As she pulled into the packed parking lot, she could hear the steady thump of the band's bass. At nearly ten, the Pub's crowd appeared to be partying in full swing and she only found a spot because someone else happened to back out.

She paid her cover charge and allowed them to stamp the back of her hand. Once inside she could barely squeeze past a large group of people who had apparently been unable to find seats, so had decided to stand close to the exit.

Immediately, Jackie headed for the bar and got in line. When her turn finally came to order, instead of her usual beer or wine, she asked for a large margarita. If she remembered right, they were good here.

Then, drink in hand, she began to circulate the room.

A woman eyed her as she walked past. "Wait," she said, touching Jackie's arm. "Aren't you Charla's older sister?"

Wondering if she'd ever get used to the efficiency of the gossip in Getaway, Jackie nodded. "I am."

"I'm Marissa, one of Charla's friends," Marissa explained. She wore her jet-black hair in a short, trendy cut and used heavy black eyeliner to outline her eyes. "I heard you were in town looking for her."

"I don't suppose you've talked to her or seen her lately?"

"No." Marissa took a long drink of her wine. "Rayna has already been around, asking questions. Maybe you should talk to her."

"I have. I just feel like there's no harm in talking to people myself. Plus, I needed to get out of that hotel room," Jackie admitted.

"The Landshark?" Horror echoed in the other woman's voice.

"Yep."

"I feel ya. Anyway, check out that guy over there playing pool." Marissa jerked her head to indicate. "He was one of the guys Charla dated."

Eyeing the burly man wearing biker's leathers, Jackie's eyes widened. "Was he one of the guys who got into a fight over her?"

"I think so." Marissa went back to sipping her drink. "Though if he was, they kicked him out. I'm not sure how he managed to get back in."

"Different bouncer, no doubt," Jackie said absently. "I'm going to go talk to him."

"Are you sure that's wise?" Though a stranger, concern echoed in Marissa's voice. One of her friends, who'd been silently observing the conversation, voiced her agreement.

"Normally, I'd be a bit apprehensive," Jackie admitted. "But this is a crowded bar. I should be safe here."

Marissa shrugged and turned away.

Jackie took a deep sip of her margarita and strode over to the pool table. She watched while the man took his shot. When he'd finished, she summoned up a smile and asked him if she could talk to him a minute.

"Honey, I can do more than that." He moved closer, too close. When Jackie took a step back to get away from him, she bumped into another man. Apologizing, she managed to maneuver herself into what looked like a safe spot.

Unfortunately, the band chose that moment to launch into a loud, raunchy song that had most of the bar singing along. Aware there was no way this man would be able to hear her from any sort of distance, Jackie moved a tiny bit closer than she felt was wise. "I'm Charla's sister," she said, looking up to find him staring down her shirt.

He smirked as he let his gaze travel slowly back up to her face. "You don't look like her."

"I know. I get that a lot." Hoping the band would soon settle down, she indicated the pool table. "I think it's your turn."

To her relief, he took his cue and went back to studying the table. He made several shots in rapid succession, clearing all of the solids from the table. "Pay up, Joe," he ordered, holding out his hand. His opponent, the hapless Joe, who looked as if he was three sheets to the wind, dug out a twenty from his pocket and handed it over.

"Now, where were we?" big biker dude asked her.

As he leaned in close, she got a whiff of strong whiskey and cigarettes. "I'm Scott, by the way. Oh, I know. You were about to show me if you can kiss as good as your sister."

"No, no, I wasn't," Jackie replied emphatically. "I just wanted to ask you if you happened to have any idea where Charla might be."

Ignoring both her refusal and her question, Scott lunged for her, hauling her up against him and pressing the full length of his large body against her. Furious and scared, she tossed the contents of her glass on him, coating the front of him with margarita.

Instead of deterring him, if anything, this appeared to spur him on. "Oh, so you like it rough, do you?" He pushed her hard, slamming her back into the wall.

Disbelieving, she looked around for help. To her shock, no one seemed to be paying them the slightest attention.

"Get. Away. From. Me," she ordered, teeth clenched. "I mean it. Don't touch me!" This last, she shouted. But with the band playing the raucous chorus, they drowned her out.

Except he heard. He had to. Because the glint in his bloodshot eyes turned mean. He used his big hands to pin her shoulders against the wall.

Desperate, she brought her knee up, hard. But somehow, he managed to block her. He swooped in, about to plant his wet lips on hers, when suddenly someone jerked him off her.

"Leave her alone."

Eli. Grateful, Jackie moved away from Scott, who turned unsteadily to face Eli.

"Mind your own damn business," Scott snarled, bringing up his fists.

Eli stood his ground. "Jackie," he said without taking his eyes off the larger man. "Go ahead and move away. There are bouncers near the door. Go get one of them and send him over here."

Heart pounding, Jackie hurried away to do as he'd requested. She spotted a man who looked as if he might be a bouncer and tugged on his arm. He bent down so he could hear her. Quickly, she told him what was going on. "Over by the pool tables."

With him leading the way, they pushed through the crowd, arriving just in time to see Eli sidestep as Scott swung at him, before landing his own punch on Scott's chin.

Though Scott staggered, he didn't go down. Instead, he hauled off and managed to get a blow in on Eli's eye. Eli staggered backward, but launched himself at Scott again, shoving the larger man backward into the pool table, sending balls flying.

By now, people had begun to notice and a crowd had formed.

"Break it up," the bouncer ordered, pushing his way through and grabbing a hold of Scott. Unwisely, Scott swung at him, and the bouncer clocked him hard, knocking him down. But not out. He lurched back up to his feet.

The band, apparently catching wind of all this, stopped playing. By now, the entire bar seemed to be craning their necks to see what was going on.

Meanwhile, Scott continued to curse and swing

wildly, his eyes bulging, looking for all the world like an enraged grizzly bear.

A second bouncer joined the first and together, they managed to subdue Scott, who continued cursing at them. Jackie rushed over to Eli. His eye had already started swelling. With a muscle working in his jaw, he seemed furious.

"The police are on their way," someone said. "And probably an ambulance."

"He started it," Scott shouted, struggling to break free of the two bouncers. "I want to press charges for assault."

Jackie spun around. "You tried to feel me up and kiss me, despite me telling you no. He *defended* me from you. And if anyone is going to press charges, it will be me."

"Come on," one of the bouncers said, herding Scott away. "You can tell it all to the police."

The second bouncer stayed with Jackie and Eli. "Don't worry," he said. "That guy Scott is a known troublemaker. Plus, we have cameras on the pool area, so I'm sure we have everything on film."

Jackie nodded. "Can I get some ice for his eye?" she asked. One of the waitresses, hearing her request, went to the bartender and returned with some wrapped up in a dish towel.

When Jackie pressed it to his eye, Eli winced. "I've seen that guy before," he said. "I think he might have dated Charla."

"He did, or so I was told," Jackie replied. "That's why I tried to talk to him in the first place."

The band started up again and everyone returned to what they'd been doing.

"Come on back with me," the bouncer ordered. "The police will come and talk to you there. It's much quieter."

A few minutes later two police officers entered the back room with an EMT in tow. "Go ahead and check him out," one of the officers gestured to the EMT before turning to Jackie. "We'll go ahead and take your statement, ma'am."

Jackie told them exactly what had happened and why. When she'd finished, he nodded.

The EMT finished taking Eli's blood pressure.

"And you, sir?" the officer asked Eli. "Do you concur with her version of events?"

"Yes." Eli met Jackie's gaze. "I'm not a violent man," he muttered. "But I will fight to defend someone I—" he glanced at Jackie and swallowed "—care about."

Jackie's heart stuttered. Had he been about to say *loved*?

Meanwhile, the EMT nodded, using a penlight to check Eli's pupils. "I get it." He wrote something down and then stood. "Looks like you're okay to go. Put some ice on that eye and take ibuprofen every six hours."

Eli nodded, wincing slightly at the movement.

"I'll take care of him," Jackie volunteered. Eli shot her a grateful look.

"Good. You do that," the EMT said and walked off.

"We'll be in touch." The police officer nodded to his partner. "You are free to go."

"Let's get you home." Jackie took his arm. "We can pick up your truck tomorrow."

He let her lead him to her car and help him into the passenger seat. "You know, I can probably drive my truck."

"Maybe." She gave him a soft smile. "But let's not take any chances. I'm sure your truck will be fine until the morning. I'll drive you back over to pick it up."

Finally, he gave a weary nod. "Okay."

"What were you doing in the Rattlesnake anyway?" she asked, pulling out onto Main Street.

"Probably the same thing as you," he replied, eyes closed. "I couldn't sleep and thought it might be nice to get out and have a drink. I got your message and thought I'd call you back in the morning. If I'd known you were awake, I would have asked you to join me. Next time, I'll ask."

Next time. The simple statement gave her a visceral thrill. Foolish, she told herself. But still, she couldn't keep from smiling. "I assume you got Rayna's text," she began, but a quick glance over at Eli revealed he'd fallen asleep. Or was, like her mother used to say, just resting his eyes. She couldn't tell very well in the dim light, but she'd bet he'd have a hell of a shiner in the morning.

As she pulled up in front of his ranch, he woke, his hand instinctively going to touch his eye. "Ouch," he said.

"We'll put some ice on it as soon as we get inside." After turning off the engine, she got out and went around to his side, intending to open the door for him. But by the time she got there, he was already out.

"Thanks, but I'm okay," he said when she held out her arm just in case he needed the support. Figuring his male pride might be stung, she nodded and simply fell into step beside him.

As he unlocked the front door, she wondered if he would ask her in or send her away.

Eli hurt far more than he wanted Jackie to know. Not just his eye, but his pride. When he'd seen that drunk jerk pin her up against the wall, he'd seen red. He'd rushed over, his only thought the need to get that guy off her. The fact that the other man outweighed him by at least seventy-five pounds hadn't mattered.

Instead, it had taken two bouncers to bring the guy down. No shame in that, he told himself. Yet, he still felt as if he'd somehow failed her. And the way she hovered over him, as if she thought he'd collapse at any moment, didn't make him feel any better.

Five steps inside his house and he turned to face her. Silhouetted by the front porch light, she appeared achingly beautiful and fragile. "I'm sorry," he said. "I should have been able to protect you."

"That's what you're worried about?" she asked, slipping inside and bumping the front door closed. She wrapped her arms around him, holding on tight. "If you only knew how it felt, having you rush to my aid. No one has ever done that for me."

No one. Not just no man, but no one. This made him wonder what her childhood must have been like, living with two narcissists like Delia and Charla.

Unable to resist the soft shape of her body pressed against him, he held her, breathing in the sweet scent of her hair. He ached to tell her how he'd begun to feel about her, but he knew the timing wasn't right. He didn't know if it ever would be.

Finally, she released him. "Let's get some ice on that eye," she said, her voice brisk.

In the kitchen, she pulled a bag of peas from the freezer and handed it to him.

Accepting it, he sank into one of the kitchen chairs and pressed it to his eye. "You don't have to stay if you don't want to," he said.

Hands on hips, she regarded him, her dark eyes shadowed. "Are you asking me to leave?"

He decided to be honest. "No. I'm only giving you your options. Don't feel you have to watch over me out of pity."

"Pity? Is that truly what you think I feel?"

Now he felt like a jerk. "I'm not sure of anything at this point," he said softly. "Everything is off kilter. Just pretend I didn't say that, okay?"

Instead of responding, she crossed the room and gently took the frozen peas away from his face, placing them on the table. Then, straddling him, she leaned in close. "Let me show you exactly how I feel."

Then she kissed him. It wasn't a gentle press of her mouth on his, but instead, a fierce, raw claim of possession. His body instantly responded as they opened their mouths to each other. She laughed when she felt the strength of his arousal pressing against her. Then, gaze locked on his, she began to move against him, still fully clothed. The friction, unbelievably sensuous, nearly had him losing all control.

"We can't," he gasped, though damned if he could

think of a good reason why. Then he remembered. "No condoms. I, er, haven't exactly had a reason to buy any."

"That's okay," she breathed. "We can still have fun with our clothes on." And she proceeded to show him exactly how.

After, with her body still trembling, she stayed where she was, just hanging on to him. He couldn't believe it—he hadn't done anything like this since he'd been a teenager—and even then the release hadn't been nearly as powerful.

This woman. He smoothed her hair away from her face, placing a soft kiss on her temple, which made her smile. "Come on," he finally said. "Let's get cleaned up and get some rest. We can talk about Rayna's text in the morning."

"I should go." Moving awkwardly, she climbed off him and disappeared into the bathroom.

While she was gone, he grabbed the frozen peas and put them back on his eye. Damn, she confused and delighted him. He'd never met a woman like her and doubted he would again.

A moment later she returned. She'd smoothed down her formerly disheveled hair, though her swollen lips revealed her to be someone who'd just been thoroughly kissed. "We'll talk tomorrow. I'll come by and take you to get your truck. How about nine?"

Distracted, he managed to nod.

"I'll let myself out," she told him, and left as quickly as if she thought he might chase after her and beg her to stay.

Bemused, he locked up and jumped into the shower to clean up.

The next morning he woke up and winced when he touched his eye. A quick glance in the mirror proved Jackie's prediction had come true. He looked like he'd gone ten rounds with an enraged grizzly and lost.

Jackie pulled up at five minutes until nine. She sent him a text, letting him know she was out front.

Just the thought of seeing her again sent his pulse racing. He felt like a besotted kid, aching for her when she wasn't around. Slugging down the last of his coffee, he went outside to meet her.

"Good morning," she said as he got into her car. "That eye looks like it must hurt. Did you manage to get any sleep?"

Back to impersonal yet friendly.

"I did. How about you?" he asked politely, taking his cues from her. With her aviator sunglasses on, he couldn't see her eyes.

"As best as could be expected after learning my sister now has a warrant out for her arrest."

Aware they might be treading on dangerous ground, he nodded. "It's surreal. But then again, this entire situation with Charla and Theo defies belief."

She drove, quietly competent, clearly lost in her own thoughts. As they pulled up to the Rattlesnake Pub where his truck sat alone in the empty lot, she sighed. "I'm sorry about last night."

"Don't be." He waited until she'd parked to plant a quick kiss on her cheek. "I'm not."

Leaving that there, he smiled and got out of her car. "Talk to you later, I hope."

Absently, she nodded, her color high. "I'm sure we will."

He stood next to his truck and watched as she drove off. Damn, he had it bad. He didn't know what he was going to do when she took off back for the east coast.

Hopefully, the rest of the world would have settled down by then. Somehow, with Charla wanted for theft and embezzlement, he knew things would change. But at least he'd have Theo back, and the constant worry that lurked in the back of his mind would be gone.

Chapter 7

Her phone rang, the caller ID displaying a number she didn't recognize. Though Jackie usually let calls like that go to voice mail, Charla's having gone missing changed everything. She answered it, hoping against hope it would be her sister. Maybe Charla had to use another phone.

"Is this Charla's sister?" a feminine voice asked. Once Jackie answered in the affirmative, the woman identified herself as Melanie. "I think my boyfriend might have spotted Charla. I called you instead of the sheriff," she said, "because Charla is my friend and I don't want her to get in any more trouble. I heard about the jewelry store thing."

Already? Shaking her head at how fast gossip traveled in this town, Jackie thanked her before she asked where.

"Big Bend National Park. He and a friend went camping there. He swears he saw someone who looked just like her ahead of him on one of the hiking trails. He says he called out to her, but she kept going. He tried to catch up with her, but says she was gone."

As far as Jackie knew, Charla had never gone hiking. She was more of a Zumba or yoga in the gym–type person as far as exercise. "How sure is he?" she asked. "As far as I know, Charla doesn't hike."

"Zach got her into it," Melanie replied. "He was one of her boyfriends. He's a personal trainer at the gym. You might check with him and see if he's been hiking with her lately."

"Thank you," Jackie replied. She ended the call.

More than anything, she needed to talk to Eli. Even though she'd just dropped him off and calling him again sort of felt like stalking. Still, this was too important to simply let slide. She punched in his number again.

He answered immediately. "Missing me already?" he teased.

Despite herself, she blushed. "I am, but that's not the only reason I wanted to talk to you." She filled him in on what Melanie had said.

"I know Zach," he replied. "I know he and Charla went out a few times, but they both liked to play the field. From what I know of Charla, she's not much into outdoor activities."

"I think we need to go talk to him," she said. "Just in case that really was Charla up in Big Bend." Then, realizing she'd said *we*, she walked back her words a little. "Or I can go talk to him, if you're busy. I'll report back to you what he says."

"How about you pass the info along to Rayna and let her investigate?" he suggested.

Exhaling, she struggled to find the right words to convey her feelings. "I'd like to check this out myself," she finally said. "I don't expect you to understand, but I'd really like to talk to Charla before she gets arrested."

He sighed. "I know what you mean. She's your sister. I get that. But if she really did embezzle and steal, she needs to pay for her crimes."

"I agree. But I still can't get past her text to me. She said she was in danger. What if she still is?"

"I'll go with you," he finally said. "We'll talk to Zach and then decide if we want to drive out to Big Bend. I'll have to get one of my part-time workers to come stay at my ranch and take care of the livestock since it will be an overnight trip. You know how long that drive is."

"I do." It had always been one of her favorite road trips. "My friends and I used to go out there on spring break and hike when I was in college." She wished she'd kept her old hiking boots. "If we end up going, we'll need to stop somewhere and pick up supplies. Have you ever been hiking?"

He laughed, the low, husky sound giving her goose bumps on her skin. "Only on horseback, and I have a feeling that doesn't count."

"Are you up for it?" she asked, ready to go alone if he wasn't.

"Sure. But I'll need to stop by my place to arrange the care of the ranch and to pack a few things. So let's talk to Zach and then we can make our decision."

Though she already knew she'd be going no matter what Zach had to say, she agreed.

"I'll pick you up in fifteen minutes," Eli continued. "I need to make a quick stop at the drugstore first. The gym is right off Main Street, so not too far."

"Sounds good. Since the weather is nice, I'm just going to wait for you outside. I'll sit by the pool."

As usual, when she caught sight of Eli's pickup, her heart did a funny little skip. Shaking her head at herself for acting like a teenager with a crush, she hurried over and climbed inside.

"Hey there." His slow smile had her inwardly melting. "Let's see what Zach has to say."

Though the gym seemed on the smaller side, there were quite a few people working out, several on the line of treadmills or elliptical machines. Eli waved at the receptionist as they walked past, heading toward the free weight area.

"There he is." Eli pointed to an extremely muscular man helping a woman do push-ups.

When Zach turned, his piercing blue eyes meeting hers, Jackie caught her breath. She hadn't expected such patrician features along with the superhero build. But—she looked again—there was a certain kind of self-assured smugness in his expression. As if he knew exactly how she or any other woman would react at the first sight of him.

Apparently hearing her reaction to Zach, Eli glanced at her and rolled his eyes. "Charla's type," he said. "Poor Christopher Levine didn't stand a chance."

The comment made her grin because he was right. In high school, Charla had valued appearance over everything else. Despite that, as far as Jackie was concerned, Zach couldn't hold a candle to Eli's easy confidence.

"Eli, man." Zach clapped Eli on the back. "Long time, no see." He squinted, taking in Eli's black eye. "Wow. I heard about the bar fight, but that looks bad. I'm just about finished up with Madeline here, so I can talk to you then."

Eli nodded.

Jackie struggled to keep her expression neutral. Once again, the speed at which gossip traveled in this town surprised her. Zach sauntered away. Slowly, Jackie let her gaze follow him. "How long did Charla and Zach date?" she asked.

"Not too long." Eli shrugged. "Zach is Charla's twin, personality wise. And as you can imagine, he's really popular with the ladies."

"I can see that," she said. "He seems awfully sure of himself."

"I can't blame him. He's really a nice guy, despite the fact that every single woman falls all over herself the first time she sees him." He eyed her. "Speaking of that, are you feeling okay? Or do you need to sit down?"

She laughed. "I'm fine. Zach is rather startling, but he's definitely not my type."

"Really?" He sounded skeptical. "What is your type, then?"

Heart pounding, she locked gazes with him. If she told him the truth, that he was her type, it would sound as if she was flirting or trying to get a reaction. She swallowed hard and managed a shrug. "I don't really know." That part was definitely true. She'd simply left out the part about the zing of physical attraction she felt just being in the same proximity as Eli.

With a slow nod, Eli appeared to accept her answer. "Here he comes," he said.

"Eli, what can I do for you today?" Zach asked, his gaze sliding past to Jackie. "And who's your friend?"

Jackie held out her hand, introducing herself before Eli could. "I'm Jackie Burkholdt. Charla's sister."

He shook her hand, a slight frown creasing his brow. Though his smile remained in place, something flickered in his eyes.

"I heard about Charla taking off," he said. "I'm guessing that's why you're in town?"

"It is," Jackie replied. "But Eli and I wanted to come see you to ask about hiking."

"Hiking?" Voice puzzled, Zach looked from her to Eli.

"Someone reported that they thought they saw Charla hiking out in Big Bend," Eli interjected. "Since we heard you got Charla into it, we thought we'd ask if you might have known anything about this."

"Once," Zach said. "I took Charla hiking one time. We went to Palo Duro and took easy trails. She hated it. Complained the entire time. I seriously doubt she would have gone hiking anywhere, never mind Big Bend."

"That's kind of what I thought." Eli stuck out his hand. "Thanks, man."

"No problem." Someone called Zach's name. "Gotta go. My next client is here."

A petite blonde woman waved at him, eyeing him as if she'd like to eat him up.

"Come on." Eli took Jackie's arm. "I think we've found out what we came for."

Following him outside, she waited until they were in the truck before telling him. "I'm going out there anyway. You don't have to go with me, though you're certainly welcome to if you want."

About to start the engine, he turned and looked at her. "You realize there's, like, a ninety-nine percent chance she won't be there, right?"

"I do." She lifted her chin. "But because there's even a one percent possibility that she will, I have to go. I can't let the chance that I might find her slip out of my hands."

For one heart-stopping moment, she thought he might kiss her again. Instead, he shook his head and pressed the button to turn the motor on. "I get that. And because I do, I'm going with you. Though honestly, I'd feel better if someone had mentioned seeing a toddler, too."

He dropped her off at the motel to pack, telling her he'd text when he was on his way back. "It'll be at least an hour," he said. "I've done my horse training for the day, but I've still got to line up someone to come stay at the ranch. Plus, I need to dig out my old camping gear and see if I can drum up a pair of hiking boots."

"I'm going to have to stop and buy some," she said. "And unless you have an extra sleeping bag, I'll have to purchase one of those, too."

"I'll let you know."

Nodding, she slipped out of his truck, telling herself she was imagining the way she felt his gaze on her back as she walked away.

* * *

After waiting to make sure Jackie got into her motel room safely, Eli exhaled before putting the truck in Drive and pulling out into the street.

While he seriously doubted they'd find Charla anywhere near a hiking trail, there wasn't any way he could bring himself to stay here while Jackie took off on her own. Though she hadn't asked, he wanted to protect her. There were too many potential mishaps that could happen to a woman alone in the wilderness. At least if he went with her, she'd have backup.

Now he only had to figure out a way to protect her from himself.

Back at the ranch he called Jimmy Stephens, one of the teenagers who worked for him part-time. Jimmy seemed thrilled to come stay at the ranch and earn extra cash, so Eli asked him to come by now.

With that taken care of, Eli went out into his garage to locate his camping gear. When he'd lived in Houston, he'd frequently taken solo camping trips on the weekends, though he'd packed everything away when he'd purchased the ranch.

He located the tent without too much trouble, and a sleeping bag. He knew he had another one somewhere, because at one point he'd talked the woman who'd been his girlfriend at the time into going camping. She hadn't even lasted the entire night, asking him to take her home when she'd learned she'd have to walk to the public restroom.

In addition to the tent, he loaded up all his other supplies. The portable stove, the lantern, a coffeepot and some cooking pots and eating utensils and plates. Everything he'd once enjoyed using. He even managed to locate his battered old hiking boots, a little stiff from disuse, but he figured they'd loosen with use.

He threw a few clothing items into a small duffel bag, including a coat since he knew the nights might get chilly.

While he knew they'd only be gone one night at the most, he couldn't help but wonder how Jackie would take to the primitive conditions. She'd said she'd done hiking trips in the past, but hadn't mentioned anything about staying in the wilderness. He guessed he'd be finding out soon.

Once he'd stowed all the gear in his truck, he grabbed his ice chest and set about loading it up with provisions. He also packed dry goods, figuring the more he brought, the less they'd have to buy when they got to the national park.

Right before he left, he sent Jackie a text to let her know he was on his way. When he pulled up to the Landshark, he spotted her sitting in one of the chairs near the pool. She stood and grabbed her bag, a carry-on size, and hurried over to his truck.

As she climbed into the passenger seat, her silky long brown hair swirling around her, he was struck by a mental image of that hair spread underneath her on a pillow, her body naked and welcoming his.

Damn. Instant arousal. He shifted in his seat to hide it and managed a hopefully banal smile. "We can stop at the sporting goods store on the way out of town."

"Perfect." Her warm smile stirred his body again. What the hell?

Looking away, he shifted into Drive and pulled out into the street.

After stopping at Ramos's Sporting Goods, where Jackie purchased a pair of hiking boots, they hit the road in earnest.

She'd been happy to hear he'd brought an extra sleeping bag and camping gear.

"What if she crossed the border into Mexico?" she asked. "I mean, if she really did embezzle from Levine's, maybe she's going to try and hide out there. I can see her in one of the resort towns, hanging out in a bar on the beach."

Suppressing a twinge of panic at the idea of Charla spiriting his young son across the border, Eli sighed. "Maybe, but I still think she would have flown, maybe under an assumed identity. Charla wouldn't do it the difficult way, which is why I truly don't think we're going to find her hiking in the Guadalupe Mountains. Are you sure you want to make that drive?"

She studied him for a moment before replying, her expression thoughtful. "Seriously, you don't have to go with me. I know this trip probably won't turn up anything, but while Rayna is doing everything she can to find Charla and Theo around here, what can it hurt? Maybe there will be some clues."

"Maybe." But he wasn't hopeful. "I left a message for Rayna, letting her know where we're going and why."

Glancing at him sideways, one corner of her lush mouth kicked up. "Me, too," she said. "Though I didn't mention it to my mother. It's already bad enough that she's accused me of trying to *poach* my sister's ex, as she put it. Even though I explained to her that we are both just trying to find Charla and Theo, I could tell she didn't believe me."

This so boggled his mind, he could only shake his head in disbelief.

According to his phone, the drive would take a little over six to seven hours. When he passed this information on to Jackie, she grinned. "That's about right," she said. "Depending which route you chose. I'm assuming you're taking I20 west to 385 south?"

"I am." He paused. "Unless you prefer another way."

"I'll leave that up to you since you're driving." She stretched, the seat belt tugging at her shirt and drawing his gaze to her torso. Instantly, he forced his attention back to the road.

"And though some people might find the scenery boring," she continued, apparently oblivious to the direction his thoughts had taken, "I think it's beautiful."

"Me, too," he admitted. "I grew up in Houston. The first time I made a trip to west Texas, I knew that's where I belonged. Something about the wide-open spaces and the unbelievable skies got to me. Plus," he added drily, "I really enjoy the noticeable difference in humidity."

This earned a laugh. "I've been through parts of Houston when I went to Galveston," she said. "I agree with you there. What did you do in Houston before you came to Getaway and became a ranch owner?"

"I worked as a financial analyst for a huge corporation," he answered, somewhat reluctantly. "Though I hated every minute of it, I knew what I wanted to do. I saved as much as possible so I could buy my place." He'd also made several lucrative investments that continued to pay small dividends.

"But the horse training, the riding lessons. How did you learn those skills?"

He shrugged. "My uncle is a big-time cutting horse trainer. He owns his own place up near Conroe. From the time I was eight years old, I spent every summer up there. Plus a lot of weekends during the school year. He taught me everything I know. And he gave me my lifelong love of horses."

"Wow. I'm impressed."

"What about you?" he asked. "I know you work in New York City, but what do you do? And how did you choose your career?"

"I've always loved to read," she said. "Neither my mother nor my sister could understand why, but I did. I discovered romance novels in high school. I studied hard so I could graduate at the top of my class and get financial assistance to college. I went to Tech." Her voice rang with pride. "I majored in English. As soon as I had my degree, I began applying for my dream job, working for the largest publisher of romance in the world."

"And is that where you work now?"

She beamed. "It is. I love my job and my life. Life in New York City took a little getting used to and I was lonely at first, but now that I've been there three years, I love it."

Though he nodded, his heart sank just a little. Honestly, he knew he should be glad to hear her say that. Maybe now he could stop himself from occasionally imagining a future together with her.

About halfway through the drive, they stopped and grabbed some tacos at a little hole-in-the-wall place.

They made it to the Rio Grande Village Campground before nightfall. Since they'd planned to go hiking first thing in the morning, this meant he'd have plenty of time to set up camp, build a fire and make them a hot meal.

The tent seemed a lot smaller than he remembered, but he managed to fit both sleeping bags in, side to side. There wasn't a whole lot of wiggle room. And yet he wouldn't have been able to account for his body's reaction if he and Jackie had been forced to share one bag. In fact, just thinking about what such a thing would be like had him semi-aroused.

"Should we make a campfire?" she asked, rubbing her hands together against the chilly night air. The mountainous desert could be hot as Hades during the day, but as soon as the sun went down, a chill crept over the landscape, deepening with the darkness.

"Sure," he said, noticing she'd already assembled a nice stack of twigs and sticks, using crumpled newspaper as a base. He rummaged in his supply box and located the long-handled lighter and used it to catch part of the newspaper on fire. It wasn't long before they had a decent-size fire going.

"I can heat us up some canned meat and beans, if you're hungry."

At that, she made a face. "No, thanks. Though I do wish we had some marshmallows," she said, grinning at him. The flickering fire made copper highlights dance in her dark hair, making he appear earthy and mysterious and sexy as hell.

Abruptly, he pushed to his feet. "I'll be back in a few," he rasped, heading toward the campground restrooms, when in fact, he needed to go for a walk in the darkness and get his head back on straight.

Right now, with everything going on in his life, he had no reason or right to crave a woman this much. But he did. And he wasn't entirely sure how to turn that need off. All he could hope for was to try and resist it.

He made one complete circle, almost back at their spot before turning around and going back the way he'd come. As he approached, he saw Jackie still seated by the fire, gazing pensively off into the darkness.

His reappearance seemed to briefly startle her.

"Nice night," he said, dropping to a seat on the wooden picnic table bench. "And yeah, marshmallows or s'mores would really taste good right now."

This made her laugh. "You definitely took the snack craving up a notch."

"I have a box of protein bars if you want one," he told her. "Assorted flavors, so there might be something you like."

"No, thanks." Turning her attention back to the fire, she lapsed into quiet, once again giving him the opportunity to study her.

Instead, he tore his gaze away, trying to stare at the flames, as she did. The silence should have felt companionable, but this kind of silence led to self-examination, and right now that was the last thing he wanted. Better to get up and find busywork instead.

Since he'd already set up the tent and the sleeping bags, he began going through the supplies he'd packed, sorting them. He knew better than to let them remain outside while they slept, but he could at least see what they had by meal.

"I thought we could set out on our hike right after sunrise," she said softly. "It'll still be relatively cool. We can ask about Charla when we meet up with other hikers. I'd also like to try and find some park rangers. What do you think?"

As a plan, it lacked structure, but since he still believed this entire trip would turn out to be pointless, he agreed. "We might also show her picture to the other campers."

She nodded. "I'm thinking I'll turn in early."

His heart skipped a beat. Maybe that would be the best way to deal with their enforced closeness. If Jackie went into the tent first and fell soundly asleep, he might have a lot less trouble sliding into a sleeping bag next to her and nodding off.

"Worth a shot," he said out loud, earning a quizzical look from her. "I mean, you go ahead. I'm going to finish going through our provisions and get them stored in the truck cab for the night. No sense in attracting any hungry wildlife."

Her eyes widened at that comment, but she only nodded, stifling a yawn. Her sinuous stretch drew his gaze to her slender body, sending such a strong bolt of desire through him that he shuddered. How the hell was he going to be able to sleep inches away from her for an entire night?

Clearly, she had no such worries. "Good night, then," she murmured, climbing to her feet and disappearing into the dark tent. A moment later she used her flashlight to see, illuminating her silhouette. He stared at her across the flickering firelight, hoping against hope that she wouldn't undress, though honestly, he prayed she would.

But of course, like him, she'd be sleeping in her clothes. She simply used the flashlight to adjust her sleeping bag and climb into it. Then the light went out, leaving him alone with the campfire and his aching body.

Again, he decided it might be best to find busywork, as if by doing that he might wear himself down enough to be able to find sleep. He stowed their provisions, dumped dirt on the campfire to extinguish it and stood facing the tent. He could do this. By now, Jackie should be deeply asleep. He just needed to slip inside, get into his sleeping bag and close his eyes.

Like Jackie, he carried a small flashlight, which he used to find his way to his side of the tent. Standing quietly for a moment, listening to the deep, even sound of her breathing, he pushed away the ever-present ache of wanting her. Moving slowly and deliberately, he took care not to shine the light on her, not wanting to risk causing her to wake.

After removing his shoes, he went to crawl over Jackie to get to his sleeping bag, hoping he could do so without disturbing her. Halfway there, he honestly believed he was going to make it when she sat up abruptly, her forehead colliding with his midsection.

"Eli?" The husky note in her voice made him swallow hard.

Before he could reply, she reached for him and pulled him over to her. "Come here," she said. "It's too cold not to share."

Chapter 8

Jackie had been trying to stay awake until Eli joined her, though he took so long she found herself dozing, despite the occasional bouts of shivering. She swore cold seeped in from the hard ground underneath the tent and her sleeping bag. Though she'd kept her jeans and sweatshirt on, she'd begun to rethink shucking her jacket. When she woke up with her teeth chattering, she crawled out from her sleeping bag and retrieved it. The jacket helped somewhat, though her legs and feet were still cold.

If only Eli would turn in for the night, she suspected the two of them could generate enough heat to banish this awful chill. Because despite the fact that he'd laid out two separate sleeping bags, she fully intended that they share one.

Just the thought brought a surge of warmth. She was

going to do this; she'd known that ever since they'd started discussing this trip. She craved him with a fierceness that consumed her. She knew he wanted her, too—heat blazed from his gaze every time he looked at her. He might be her sister's ex, he might be someone she'd never see again once she got on that plane to fly back to New York, but damned if she was going to let this opportunity to experience making love with him slip past. Somewhere deep inside she suspected she'd never meet another man like him. A man's man, rugged and tough and independent, yet also generous and kind and giving. And sexy, too. Sexy as hell. And apparently avoiding her.

Finally, the flickering glow from the campfire went out. Which meant Eli was about to come inside the tent. While she'd been waiting, she'd run through several different scenarios to tempt him, most of them involving her being totally naked, and discarding them all due to the cold. They'd undress each other, she thought, and make their own warmth, skin to skin.

The tent flap opened. Though he kept his flashlight pointed away from her, it provided enough light for her to view his outline. She tried to keep her breathing slow and steady, mimicking sleep, though she wasn't sure why.

As Eli began to clumsily attempt to crawl over her without touching her, she sat upright, hoping he'd think he'd awakened her. Acting on instinct, she reached out and tugged him close to her, letting him know she was cold.

She wanted to say she needed his warmth, but what came out was a simple declaration. "I need you," she said, seconds before his mouth covered hers in a fierce, intense kiss.

He kissed her as though he'd been starving for this, and the way she returned the kiss had to let him know she felt the same. Somehow, he managed to fit inside her sleeping bag, zipping it up to create a tight cocoon of warmth.

His hands slid over her body in ways she'd only dreamed of until now, her clothing an unwanted barrier. She touched him, too, sliding her hand up under his shirt, feeling his muscular stomach contract at her touch.

She needed more. All of him, nothing between their bodies.

Unfortunately, there was no way they could manage to remove their clothes in the narrow confinement of her sleeping bag.

Eli must have realized this about the same time she did. He broke away, his breathing jagged. "Before we go any further," he rasped. "Are you sure you want—?"

"Yes." Interrupting him, she pulled him in for one more long, deep kiss. By the time he lifted his head, she figured he had no doubt what she wanted. "Now, let's unzip this thing so we can undress."

They made quick work of shedding their clothes, urged on by both desire and the chilly night air on their bare skin.

"Go," he ordered. Laughing, she dove back for the still-warm sleeping bag. He didn't move. "I've got a condom," he said. "I bought some. I just need to get it out of my wallet."

Eyeing his muscular body silhouetted in the darkness, she managed a nod.

He made a sound in between a grunt and a groan and moved over to the clothes he'd just shed. A moment later he clicked on his flashlight and located his jeans, pulling out his wallet and the condom he now apparently kept stashed there.

Breathless, she watched as he opened the wrapper and tugged it over his huge, swollen arousal. He looked up, flashed a grin and then turned the flashlight on her. "I want to see you," he rasped. "You're even more beautiful than I imagined."

In response, she moved aside the sleeping bag and opened her arms. "Get over here, you."

A moment later he covered her body with his, the proof of his desire pressing hard against her belly. Moving against him, this time she opened her legs, arching her back in a silent plea.

"Not yet," he rasped, but she already knew he was lost. She shimmied, he groaned and then he buried himself deep inside her.

"Oh," she managed, loving the way he completely filled her. And then he began to move.

Deep and hard and fast, then slowing, until she thought she might lose her mind. She begged, she pleaded, she tried to urge him on with her body, but he kissed her instead.

Finally, just when she thought she might shatter into jagged little pieces, he groaned and finally released his iron control. *This* was what she wanted, needed, and she felt her body start to dissolve as she found her release.

At the moment her body clenched around him, he

shuddered with his own release. They clutched each other tight, riding the waves together.

Finally, she stopped shuddering, depleted and fulfilled and in a dazed sort of awe at what had just happened. He continued to hold her, still buried inside her.

"That was…" he began. She silenced him with a quick press of her finger against his lips. Right now, in the aftermath of what had been the most intense lovemaking she'd ever experienced, she didn't want to talk or analyze; she simply wanted to be still and let the moment wash over her.

As if he understood, he didn't speak again, though he finally rolled away from her and rummaged in his pack for something to use to clean himself up.

"Do you want your clothes?" he asked. "It's getting colder."

She opened one eye, looking up at him illuminated by his flashlight. "No. I'm betting between you and me, we can manage to keep each other warm."

This made him chuckle, even as he made his way back to her. Once he'd crawled in beside her, he zipped the bag closed and then gathered her in his arms.

She let herself drift off with her face against his broad chest. Pure happiness, she thought, the last thing that went through her mind before she gave in to sleep.

When he woke her the next morning, she could tell by the absence of darkness inside the tent that the sky had begun to lighten, even though the sun had barely skimmed the edge of the horizon.

"Mornin'," he murmured, nuzzling her neck before his mouth found hers. Already wearing protection, he nudged her with his aroused body, making her laugh and pull him close. They made love again, less frantically this time, slow and unhurried, though he soon had her arching her back and urging him to go deeper, faster.

Again, they climaxed together, and he held her until her body stopped shaking. She could get used to this, she thought.

"Great way to start a morning," he muttered, stroking her shoulder.

"It is," she agreed, unable to keep from smiling. "So how many condoms do you keep in your wallet?" she asked, only half teasing.

"I had three," he replied. "That means we have one more left in case we want to do this again."

This had her smiling, even though she ached inside. This man, this amazing, sexy, rugged man, was something she'd never thought she'd find. Not here, not in New York, not ever. The fact that he'd once been married to her sister mattered less than knowing she would soon have to leave him forever. He didn't belong in New York any more than she belonged in Getaway. Heart both full and heavy, she got dressed, grabbed her bag with its change of clothes and toiletries and accompanied him to the campground showers.

The morning air still carried a chill leftover from the darkness, though she could tell the day would heat up with the sun. At the facility she and Eli went their separate ways. While she dreaded the icy shower, she figured if she rushed it might not be too bad.

She was wrong.

Teeth chattering, she got herself clean in record time. Glad Eli'd had the foresight to bring towels, she dried herself off and pulled on clean clothes, dressing in layers. Her hair was another story. Since there was only so much drying she could do with a towel, she had no choice but to let it mostly air dry before putting it into a braid.

Walking outside, she saw Eli waiting. The sight of him, so tall and muscular and handsome, brought on another rush of longing. To cover, she made a show of studying her new hiking boots. "They're not broken in," she told him, lifting one foot so he could see. "Here's hoping I don't have blisters a couple of hours in."

He shook his head but didn't comment. Once she reached him, he walked with her all the way back to their tent.

"Canned meat and beans or protein bars?" he asked, his eyes crinkling at the corners. "Sorry, but I didn't bring anything perishable like eggs or bacon."

"Protein bar, please," she said instantly. "The idea of eating canned meat makes me feel nauseated. I tried it once in college. While I'm not sure if it was that or the peppermint schnapps, I've never been so sick in my life."

Still smiling, he made a face. "Sounds like it might have been both. That's a bad combo right there." Handing her a box of protein bars, he shrugged. "Help yourself. They're assorted."

She chose a blueberry and almond bar plus an apple cinnamon nut combo and passed the box back to him. "I grabbed an extra for my backpack," she said.

"Good idea." He did the same. "Let me make a small campfire and brew us some coffee."

Grateful, she nodded. "That would be heavenly."

She sat on the wooden picnic table bench and watched while he brought a small fire to life, expertly handling a battered metal coffeepot. He'd brought stainless steel mugs and once the brew had finished, filled two and handed one to her.

After taking a cautious sip, she made a sound of approval low in her throat. "This is really good."

Her comment made him grin. "Not what you were expecting, I take it?"

Instead of answering, she drank again.

They allowed themselves a few minutes to drink their coffee before disassembling the tent and stowing all their gear back in the pickup. When they'd finished, he turned to her. "As I'm sure you know, there are a lot of trails out here. Do you want to try beginner hikes or something more challenging?"

She considered. "What do you think Charla would be most likely to do?"

"None of this," he responded. When she made a face at him, he sighed. "I don't know." He pointed to a sign. "Since we're already in the Rio Grande Village Campground, let's take this nature trail. It's only three quarters of a mile and since it's relatively easy, probably something Charla might have done."

"Then after this, I'd like to see if we can try the Santa Elena Canyon Trail," she said. "Though I'm not sure how far it is from here."

"We can ask."

Side by side, they set off on the trail. This early in the morning, they only encountered two other hikers. Jackie showed them a photo of her sister, but neither had seen her.

The short hike didn't take long, but by the time they'd returned to the trailhead entrance, she could feel soreness at the back of her heels.

"Are you okay?" He must have noticed her limping.

"New boots." Grimacing, she waited while he unlocked the truck. "I'll survive."

"I thought we'd stop at the visitor center next. Show Charla's picture around and see if they've seen her. Usually, you can find a park ranger there, too."

She nodded and buckled her seat belt. "Two for one. I like it."

Unfortunately, Charla hadn't been by the visitor center, and the park ranger they talked to hadn't seen her, either. Jackie's spirits sank. With Charla's blond prettiness and vivacious personality, people tended to remember her.

"Maybe you're right," Jackie admitted as they climbed back into the truck. "This trip might have been a complete waste of time."

"Maybe," he allowed, starting the engine and backing from their spot. "At least as far as finding Charla and Theo are concerned." He met her gaze, his own intense. "But I want you to know that I wouldn't trade last night or this morning for anything."

Blushing, she looked away, making a show out of watching the scenery go past.

"Do you still want to go on that other hike?" he asked. "We can if you want. Your choice."

She thought for a moment and sighed. "The likelihood of us finding anyone who's seen Charla is slim to nothing. I guess we might as well head back home."

Home. The instant she finished speaking, she regretted her word choice. Getaway wasn't her home, not anymore. She could only hope Eli hadn't noticed and drawn the wrong conclusion.

Home. Eli wondered if Jackie realized what she'd said. If she meant what she'd said. Probably not, he decided. After all, lots of people referred to the place they'd grown up as home, even if they resided elsewhere. That was most likely all she'd meant. Not a reason for his heart to skip a beat and hope to make his chest tight.

"I'm sorry," he said. "I wish we could have had better luck."

"Me, too."

They stopped for more coffee at a gas station. After the restless night he'd had, Eli knew he'd need the caffeine for the long drive home. He knew he needed to address the elephant in the room, but wasn't sure of the best way how.

"I'm thinking we need to talk," he finally began as they drove down a two-lane highway in what seemed to be the middle of nowhere.

Though she'd been dozing, his statement had her blinking and sitting up straight. "About last night?" she asked, her tone cautious.

"Yes." He glanced her way, trying to read her expression but couldn't. "That was—"

"A mistake?" she interrupted. "Because so help me, if that's what you're going to call it, you'd better think carefully. We still have several hours remaining on this drive."

Not quite sure how to take that, he considered.

"What would you call it, then?" he asked. "And for the record, I was going to say it was amazing."

She flashed him a quick smile. "Good save. And yes, it was amazing. But that's all it can be. No strings, no emotions. Just a onetime thing. You're my sister's ex-husband after all."

"Two-time thing," he corrected, watching her smile broaden.

"And yes, I know you're going to be returning to New York," he finished. "I get it. But I wanted to make sure what happened doesn't make things weird between us for however long you're here."

Her brows rose. "Definitely not. We're both adults, Eli. It doesn't have to mean anything."

But what if he wanted it to mean something? Wisely, he bit back those words. He realized he had begun to fall for Jackie, though clearly, she didn't feel the same way.

Of course she didn't. It seemed he was eternally doomed to be a fool for love.

"Good," he managed. "You're in agreement, then? What happened changes nothing between us."

"Maybe one thing," she drawled, reaching over and placing her hand on his arm. "Sex is a great defuser of tension. So I recommend whenever things get too intense, we help each other out."

With her touch burning his skin, her sultry tone had his body stirring. He swallowed hard, working on concentrating on the road. "Sounds good," he managed to say, pleased that his voice sounded relatively normal. "Anytime."

She laughed. "I like you, Eli Pitts," she said. "A

lot. If you ever find yourself in New York, please look me up."

"I will." He knew she had no idea how sad that made him. He'd never go to New York and felt pretty sure she knew that. "Just curious. How long are you here for?" he asked.

"I took a two-week vacation," she replied. "Though I'll ask to extend that unpaid if I have to. I can't leave until we find Charla."

Playing devil's advocate, he had to ask, "What if your boss says no? What will you do if he tells you either come back or lose your job?"

"She," Jackie corrected. "My boss is a woman. And honestly, I can't see her doing that. She knows what's going on and how important it is for me to find my sister."

"But what if she has to?" he pressed. "If work is piling up and they really need your warm body there to help out."

She glanced sideways at him, a slight frown creasing her brow. "Are you asking me if I'll stay here if they fire me?"

Put that way… "Sorry," he said, feeling sheepish. "I guess I was. I have no idea how it works in your line of work. I know when I worked for a large corporation, if I asked for too much time off, they would have fired me."

"Well, I'm hoping that's not the case with my employer. I love my job and I'm damn good at what I do. I've been doing some editing remotely and I can always pick up more. If that's not enough, I'll deal with that bridge when we cross it."

Now he felt like a jerk for even bringing it up. "Look,

I shouldn't have said anything. I guess I was just wondering if there was any scenario that would have you staying in Getaway indefinitely."

"Eli…"

He gave her a rueful smile. "I know, I know. Still, you can't blame a guy for trying." He'd already revealed far more than he knew he should about his growing feelings for her. The last thing he wanted to do was to scare her away. "The lovemaking was really awesome," he added, hoping she'd think sex was all he cared about.

"Ahhh, now I get it." Her brow cleared. "You know, since you feel that way, I'm sure we can get together again at some point."

Glancing at her, he grinned, relieved to see the matching sparkle in her eyes. "I'd like that," he said. "A lot, actually."

The sound of her laughter made everything right with the world. Or at least as right as it could be with his son and her sister still missing.

The thought sobered him. He'd always considered himself an optimistic person, but Charla and Theo's prolonged absence had made even him begin to imagine worst-case scenarios.

"They'll be all right, you know," he said, aware she'd know exactly what he meant. "They have to be, because nothing else is acceptable."

"I know." Her quiet reply matched her determined expression. "I won't have it any other way."

Spoken as two people who believed they had total control of not only their own destiny, but that of others. He could only hope they were right.

His cell phone rang.

"It's Rayna," he said, his heart skipping a beat. After a quick deep breath, he answered.

"Are you sitting down?" Rayna asked. "Is Jackie with you?"

Not sure how to take this, he answered in the affirmative.

"Put me on speaker," Rayna demanded. "I want Jackie to hear this, too."

Quickly, he did as she requested, filling Jackie in.

"Can you both hear me?" Rayna asked. She continued without waiting for an answer. "We have Theo." Her triumphant tone made her sound fierce. "Safe and unharmed."

Stunned, it took him a second to find his voice. He glanced at Jackie, who had her hand over her mouth and tears in her eyes. "How? Where?"

"One of Charla's friends brought him in. It seems Charla left him with her last Saturday before she went out and never returned to pick him up." Rayna paused, and then continued. "Apparently, this is not unusual and this friend has watched Theo for several days before. Charla pays her well, she said."

"What friend?" he asked. "Do I know her?"

"I don't think so. She lives in Abilene. Her name is Natalie. When Charla didn't pick up her phone or return her text messages, Natalie drove here with Theo to find her. When she couldn't do that, she contacted us."

"Where is Theo now?" Eli asked.

"Here at the police station," Rayna replied. "Though Delia is on the way to pick him up."

Heart pounding, he swallowed. "Tell Delia I'll be there as soon as I can."

"Will do, but I'm going to need you to stop by and talk to me first." Rayna's tone had gone grave. "Because Natalie had quite a bit to say about why Charla left. Apparently, she felt threatened by you. She told Natalie that she believed you wanted to kill her, so you could have sole custody of Theo."

He opened his mouth, but no words came out. "That's ridiculous," he finally managed, horribly aware that Jackie had gone stiff and still in the seat next to him. "You know that, Rayna. Don't you?"

"I know you're a good man," Rayna replied. "I know how much you love your son. But we still don't have any idea where Charla is. And now I can't discount the possibility of foul play. While we don't have any evidence, I'm thinking we might need to turn this search in a new direction."

"What's that mean?" Jackie asked, the sound of her broken voice shredding his insides. "Do you mean you're now considering this a homicide investigation?"

"Not yet," Rayna hastened to reassure her, her tone soothing. "We have nothing to base that on."

"Like a body?" Jackie finished flatly.

Rayna paused. "Yes. We have no reason yet to believe Charla met with serious harm."

"Yet. Except for the text she sent me, saying she was in danger. And now her friend says she felt threatened by her ex-husband, the man I'm currently alone with in the middle of nowhere."

"What do you mean?" Rayna asked. "Where are you two?"

"Driving back from Big Bend," Eli answered. "We

followed up on a lead. Someone said they thought they saw Charla hiking a trail up there."

"Charla hiking?" Rayna made a dismissive sound. "I can't see that happening."

"Me neither." Eli glanced at Jackie. She stared straight ahead, refusing to look at him. Her entire posture radiated anger and something else.

"We're on our way back," Eli said. "I'll text you when we're getting close."

"Sounds good."

Eli pressed the button to end the call. He glanced at Jackie, but before he could speak, her phone rang.

"Hello?" she answered. "Hi, Mom." Then, raising a brow at Eli, she pressed the button to put the phone on speaker.

"That man killed your sister," Delia said, her voice full of venom. "I hope you understand now why I didn't like you hanging around him."

Eli started to speak, but Jackie held up her hand to silence him. "We don't know that Charla is dead," she said, her voice full of pain. "And until we know that for certain, I refuse to hear anyone say such a thing."

Delia went silent. "I agree," she finally said, much more subdued. "I have Theo with me."

"That's what Rayna said," Jackie began.

Eli couldn't take any more. "I want to talk to my son," he said. "Please put Theo on the phone."

"You're with *him*?" Delia screeched. "How could you?"

The rueful look Jackie shot him told him he should have kept his mouth shut. He acknowledged she might be right. With emotions running so high, no way in hell would Delia allow him to talk to his son right now.

Why would Charla say such a thing? He'd never threatened her, and the last time he'd seen her, things had been cordial. At least as cordial as it could be with her inebriated and upset about her two boyfriends coming to blows. He hadn't engaged with her, simply listened as he drove her back to her apartment. She'd made sure to tell him Theo was with a sitter she trusted and while he'd wanted to ask her why she hadn't asked him to keep their son, he knew drunk Charla might be apt to take the question the wrong way, so he hadn't.

He listened as Jackie attempted to calm her mother down. But Delia wasn't having it. She began to swear, calling both Eli and Jackie several colorful terms, until Eli decided he'd had enough.

"Delia," he said as loudly and firmly as he could. "Not. In. Front. Of. My. Son."

In response, she ended the call.

"Jackie," Eli said, reaching out to touch her with one hand, meaning only to console her.

"Don't touch me," she said, jerking away. The look in her eyes as she pressed herself into the passenger door shattered his heart. "Not right now."

Chapter 9

When Eli reached for her, Jackie gasped out loud, in-stinctively shrinking away from the man she'd just made love with. All along, her gut had told her one thing and common sense another. Maybe because she trusted her instincts, she'd managed not to listen to common sense. Now she was trapped in a moving vehicle with the man who might have harmed her sister. *Might have* being the operative words. She took several deep breaths in an at-tempt to calm herself down. Just because her mother had gone off the deep end didn't mean she had to.

At her instinctive reaction, Eli's tortured expression made her feel a twinge of remorse, which she quickly squashed. She needed to keep her head clear and try to look at this objectively.

"Sorry," she muttered. "I just don't know what to think."

"What Charla's friend said, you know that's not true, right?" he asked, his husky voice breaking. "I would never hurt the mother of my child. I'm not sure why Charla would even say such a thing, or if she even did, but I've never done anything to threaten her. Not once, not even when I learned she'd cheated on me multiple times."

Keeping her own face neutral, Jackie nodded. Truthfully, right now with her head spinning and her stomach churning, she wasn't sure how to react or what to think. "I understand," she said, trying not to reveal her inner trepidation. Had this man, this man she'd begun to fall in love with, done something to harm her sister? Was that why he'd been so certain they wouldn't find Charla in Big Bend? She wanted to ask him, but then again, she didn't. Because of course he would say no and if she couldn't convince him she believed him, would he hurt her, too?

"Do you?" A hint of bitterness crept into his voice. "Because I'm getting a totally different vibe from you. Come on, Jackie. You've gotten to know me pretty well. Do you really think I'd hurt Charla?"

She sighed. His pointed question put everything in focus. "I'd like to think no, but if there's ever been anyone who had a better reason, I don't know of them. She was awful to you, you had to constantly worry about your son and from all accounts, you were the last person to see her when you picked her up at the Pub on Saturday night. Plus, according to all the true-crime dramas and books I've read, if the wife goes missing or has been harmed, the husband or the boyfriend or ex usually did it."

"For real? And do you actually believe that? About me?"

"I did at first," she admitted. "Now I'm not so sure." Possibly foolish, but as she'd gotten to know Eli—and who was she kidding? The spark between them had become an inferno—she'd found herself believing there was no way he could ever do such a thing. Maybe her attraction to him blinded her; perhaps she'd one day come to regret her naivete, but for now she'd go with that. Innocent until proven guilty. The Eli she'd gotten to know, the ruggedly tender man in whose arms she'd just spent the night, would never have hurt her sister or any woman. She couldn't be wrong. Dear heaven, don't let her be wrong. Because if she was, more than just her heart could be at stake.

"I believe you," she said softly. "Unless you give me a reason not to."

Keeping his gaze on the road, he nodded. "Thanks. I won't."

They both lapsed into silence, broken only by the monotonous sound of the tires on the pavement. She wondered what he might be thinking. She could only imagine the relief he felt knowing that his son was okay.

If only she could say the same about her sister.

Half turning in her seat, she studied Eli's rugged profile. While she couldn't help but wonder if she was letting her attraction to him blind her, she also trusted her gut. And right now, every instinct told her this man hadn't harmed her sister. Then why did she have to keep convincing herself of that?

She took a deep breath, aching to be back on comfortable ground. Her conciliatory nature had been one of the things her mother and sister considered a flaw, though Jackie disagreed.

"I'm sorry for doubting you. You must be overjoyed knowing Theo is safe," she said, offering a verbal olive branch. "I'm really looking forward to finally meeting him."

"I am," he replied, shooting her a quick glance. "And relieved. More than anything, I want to gather him up and hug him. Only then will I know it's actually true."

Touched, she swallowed past the sudden lump in her throat. "I can imagine. I only wish Charla would be there, too."

"She'll turn up," he said. "She always does."

More silence. A quick glance his way revealed he stared straight ahead as he drove, noticeably lost in his own thoughts.

"Do you know this Natalie person?" she finally asked. "Did she often babysit Theo?"

"No." Expression remote, he barely took his gaze off the road. "I've never met her. Hell, Charla never once mentioned her name. I'm glad she took care of Theo, but I have no idea why Charla would make such a claim. Assuming she did."

"Assuming she did." She mulled that over for a moment. "What reason would Natalie have to lie?"

"I don't know." A hint of anguish had crept back into his voice, and the tight set of his jaw revealed his inner turmoil.

"I'm sure Rayna will figure it all out," Jackie said. "She seems good at what she does." Despite everything, or maybe because of what they'd shared, she had to push down a strong urge to comfort him. Finally, she decided the hell with it, and squeezed his shoulder. He reached up and covered her hand with his. They rode several miles that way, each lost in their own thoughts.

"I'm glad you're still on my side," he finally said, removing his hand, which made her feel oddly bereft, so she moved hers, too.

"Does my opinion matter that much to you?" she asked, genuinely curious.

He grimaced. "I like you, Jackie. More than like you. I get that you'll be returning to your job and the east coast once all this is over, but this thing between us—whatever you want to call it—is unreal."

"It is." Still, that skeptical part inside her wondered if he was deliberately highlighting their mutual sexual attraction to ensure she stayed on his side. After all, she'd all but admitted she felt the same way. But now she'd be a fool not to have some doubts. She couldn't help it—she'd only known this man a short period of time. He was her sister's ex, after all. Now someone had actually said Charla felt threatened by him. Was that what she'd meant when she'd texted Jackie that her life was in danger?

And how awful was it that even now, when Jackie looked at him, she still wanted to kiss him?

Concentrating on the road, Eli drove fast, his quiet competence and concentration reassuring. Theo had been found. But where was her sister? Would Charla really willingly leave her son for so long?

Jackie knew Charla had grown up spoiled. As the older sister, both she and their mother had doted on her. From the moment Charla could walk and talk, Delia had made it clear that Charla's wants and needs had precedence over anyone else's. Wanting to be a good big sister, Jackie had willingly gone along with this plan. With Charla merely two years behind her in school, Jackie had gladly done without so that Delia could afford to buy Charla the latest fashions, the expensive makeup and designer purses. In truth, Jackie hadn't cared about any of that stuff anyway.

Looking back now, she could see that she'd allowed herself to enable Charla's bad behavior. Jackie had done late homework for her and had even written more than a few of Charla's term papers. A doting—and blind—Delia had refused to give her darling younger daughter anything resembling a curfew, so Charla had taken to partying and even experimenting with drugs.

That was where Jackie had put her foot down. To her surprise, Charla had gone along with Jackie's demands to not partake of the drugs, though she'd balked at the request to make new friends.

Which was why, when Jackie had graduated at the top of her class and had made plans to go to Tech, she'd been dumbfounded at Charla's demand that she remain here in town instead.

When Jackie had attempted to explain, Charla had refused to hear a word she said. Instead, all Charla could think about was herself. "You *owe* it to me to stay until I finish high school," Charla insisted. "You can always go to college later."

After Jackie had left for school and her dorm room, both Charla and Delia refused to speak to her for months. Instead of being proud of her elder daughter, Delia believed Jackie was being selfish.

When Jackie came home for Thanksgiving break,

the ice had barely thawed. While away, she experienced the normal freshman homesickness, but when she was back home she'd begun rather quickly to plan her escape.

Things had improved slightly when she returned for winter break. She'd taken Charla shopping, purchased her lots of small gifts that she could barely afford, and as long as she did whatever her younger sister wanted, things were fine.

Looking back, Jackie could see the pattern. Charla took; Jackie gave.

Which was why Charla hadn't bothered to attend Jackie's college graduation. Delia had shown up begrudgingly, explaining away Charla's absence with shrugs and a vague explanation. Because she knew her sister's nature and loved her anyway, Jackie had pushed away her own hurt feelings. When she'd returned home after graduating, Charla hadn't even congratulated her. Jackie had known she should have confronted her, but she'd once again let it slide. After all, she was busy, applying for jobs at various publishers, hoping to put her degree to good use.

It wasn't until Jackie had accepted her editorial assistant job in New York that she'd actually come to understand how self-centered her baby sister had become. Excited to share her good news, Jackie had informed her mother and Charla at the same time. Delia had simply stared, before mumbling a congratulatory phrase and turning away. Charla had turned almost purple with rage. She'd thrown a fit.

Jackie had stood in stunned disbelief as her sister stomped around their small kitchen, yelling out curse words, calling Jackie names, accusing her of being too big for her britches. Charla sneered as she broke a few plates by hurling them at the wall. Instead of reprimanding her, Delia had simply left the room. Frozen, Jackie wasn't sure what to do. She hadn't expected this reaction at all. She foolishly believed her own sister would be happy for her.

Finally, Charla had given Jackie an ultimatum. Stay in Getaway or consider all ties severed between them. "Stay and do what?" Jackie had asked. Charla didn't have an answer so Jackie had simply shaken her head and continued making her plans to move to the east coast.

Though Jackie had assumed Charla would get over her pique with time, she hadn't. In fact, the first Christmas when Jackie had called her mother to see about making plans to come home, Delia had told her not to bother. It would be too upsetting to her sister, Delia had said.

This had hurt, naturally, but really shouldn't have come as a surprise. Jackie had gone on with making herself a new life in New York, trying not to feel like an orphan.

Looking back, Jackie realized both she and her mother had become Charla's enablers, always making excuses for Charla's bad behavior and questionable choices. Since she never had to face any consequences, Charla had never had the opportunity to learn from her mistakes.

She must have been shocked when Eli actually gave her some pushback. Evidently, becoming a mother had done nothing to curb Charla's narcissistic tendencies.

And still, despite her sister's refusing to have anything to do with her for three years, Jackie had dropped
everything and rushed home when she'd received Charla's text message. Only to learn that instead of finally
growing up, Charla had clearly gotten worse.

What a mess. Jackie couldn't believe she'd actually
thought she'd be able to fly out here and do what she'd
used to do—fix her sister's problems. Instead, she'd
managed to create a few of her own.

When she'd stormed out to Eli's ranch, she hadn't
expected the flare of instant attraction. He was her sister's *ex-husband*, for Pete's sake. She also knew if she
were a disinterested third party on the outside looking
in, she might be tempted to think she was a fool, easily swayed by a handsome, sexy man.

Maybe she was. She wasn't sure of anything anymore. Her head began to ache as she continued to gaze
out the window at the rugged landscape. Part of her
wished she could hightail it back to New York and lose
herself in her work and her social life. Once Charla was
found, of course.

The other part of her, a part she hadn't even known
existed, ached to remain here and explore her devel-
oping relationship with Eli. Even allowing herself to
think this blew her mind. Talk about complications,
not to mention high drama, especially once Charla returned. And Delia...

No. This line of thought had to stop right now. She'd
returned to town for one reason and one reason only—
to help her sister. If she couldn't manage to enjoy the
company of a handsome cowboy without getting her

emotions all tangled up, then she'd need to establish a safe but friendly distance.

Decision made, she relaxed as they drove past the starkly beautiful landscape and wide-open sky. West Texas wasn't for everyone, but anyone who'd grown up here knew they'd always belong.

Overwhelmed with joy at the knowledge that he would soon see his son again, Eli tried to process the rest of what Rayna had said. It made absolutely no sense. This woman Natalie's claiming that Charla had been afraid of him, worried that he would hurt her, might as well have been another language, with something vital lost in translation.

He wasn't a violent man. Never had been. Even in the darkest part of his marriage. When it seemed he couldn't even look at Charla without provoking an argument, he'd hung on tight to his temper. He'd rarely raised his voice, never mind his hands, no matter how much she'd provoked him. And as addicted to drama as Charla was, she'd deliberately provoked him a lot.

He'd actually been relieved when she'd declared she wanted to move out. But only if she'd left their son. Seeing how much that meant to him, she'd refused. She'd actually laughed when he told her he'd intended to fight her for custody.

When he'd lost, she'd laughed again. His steadfast refusal to visibly show his frustration had made her lose interest in tormenting him further, and they'd settled down to work out the details of his visitation dates with their son.

Oddly enough, while his and Charla's marriage

hadn't worked out, they'd actually gotten along better as coparents. She'd been free to live her life unfettered by a husband. He'd never once passed judgment on her lifestyle, other than the times he'd expressed concern about their son. She'd always insisted Theo was being well taken care of, knowing Eli had no choice but to believe her.

So why would Charla—or this Natalie person— make such a bogus claim? He supposed he would be finding out shortly. At least he had the small comfort of knowing how good Rayna was at her job.

The most important thing was that Theo was safe. Delia might try to give Eli a hard time when he went to pick him up, but in the end, she'd have no choice but to release the boy into his father's custody.

The closer Eli got to home, the more his impatience had him rattled. The drive felt as if it took far too long, and he caught himself pushing ninety miles per hour more than once, though he immediately adjusted his speed as soon as he realized. Though Jackie never commented, she seemed a bit fidgety, too.

Her first reaction to hearing this Natalie person's lies had cut him to the core. He understood, and actually couldn't blame her. At least once she'd thought things over, she was willing to give him the benefit of the doubt.

While Eli had his son back, Jackie's sister was still missing. He could imagine how disappointed she must be that Charla hadn't turned up with Theo.

Again, he wondered where Charla had gone. If she'd really stolen from her employer, did she truly value money more than her son? Clearly, since she'd left him with a friend and never gone back to pick him up.

Unless...what if she truly considered her life in danger? After all, she had sent a text to Jackie stating that. Maybe Christopher Levine had gone after her, once he'd learned of her embezzlement. And then there were her warring boyfriends, one of whom might have decided to make her pay for cheating on him.

To be honest, while Charla had a lot of friends, she'd also made quite a few enemies. Christopher Levine's wife, for one. Eli couldn't imagine she'd been happy to learn about her husband's mistress. The fact of that same mistress stealing from them might have been the last straw. No doubt Rayna had already made a similar list, just in case.

They arrived in town just before dinnertime. He drove straight to the sheriff's department as Rayna had requested, though he really wanted to go directly to Delia's and hug his boy close.

"Let's do this," he told Jackie, swinging into a parking spot. "The quicker I can get this over with, the sooner I can see Theo."

Rayna waited for them in the reception area. The rest of the sheriff's office had emptied out, leaving only the much smaller night crew on duty.

Unsmiling, Rayna nodded at them as they walked through the door. She wore her fiery red hair in a neat bun, and her flinty gaze meant she was in professional law enforcement mode. "Come back with me to my office," she ordered. "I have a few questions to ask you."

Eli nodded, resisting the urge to check his watch because he knew Rayna wouldn't appreciate it. With

Jackie right beside him, he followed Rayna back to her office.

Back behind her desk, Rayna waited until they were both seated before dropping into her own chair. Again, she outlined what she'd already told them on the phone. When she'd finished, she sat back in her chair and stared hard at him across her desk. "Eli, do you have any idea why Charla would say such a thing?"

"No." He inhaled. "In fact, I'm not entirely sure she did. What do you know about this Natalie person who Charla entrusted with our son?"

"We checked her out. She has a clean record, no prior arrests. Works a steady job and appears to be an upstanding citizen. She's older than Charla, and says she picks up extra money by taking babysitting jobs." Rayna tilted her head. "Are you sure you've never met her? Tall, leggy brunette with bright blue eyes?"

Why did he feel like that last question might be a trap?

"I don't recognize the name or the description," he said cautiously. "Why do you ask?"

"Because this woman had quite a bit to say about you," Rayna responded. "None of it positive. She talked as if she knew you well, not just on hearsay from Charla. And she seemed very adamant in her statement that you were a danger to her friend."

Not sure how to respond to that, Eli settled on a careful shrug. "I honestly have no idea who she is or why she would feel that way. Let me set the record straight. I never threatened Charla or gave her the slightest indication that I'd ever hurt her. She and I had a friendly divorce and despite the disagreement over who should have custody of Theo, once the decision was made, I accepted it."

"But you didn't like it," Rayna pressed.

Aware of Jackie quietly watching, Eli nodded. "No. I did not. Theo comes first with me. I didn't—don't—believe that Charla feels the same."

"Which might imply motive," Rayna drawled. "However, right now all we have is hearsay. I know you, Eli, and I'd like to think this woman is wrong. We will continue looking for Charla. As long as we find her alive and well, you have absolutely nothing to worry about."

Beside him, Jackie stiffened. Since he knew her absolute worst fear was that something awful had happened to her sister, he decided not to protest. He nodded instead. "Thank you. If we're finished here, I'd like to go see my son. I've been worried sick. I need to see for myself that he's all right."

"Go ahead." Rayna stood, smoothing down the front of her uniform. "Do you want me to go with you? Delia is aware of the accusations Natalic made. I'm thinking she might refuse to let you have your boy."

"I don't think that will be necessary," he began. Jackie placed her hand on his arm.

"Rayna needs to come," she said, her eyes full of concern. "You've seen a brief glimpse into how dramatic—and crazed—my mother can be. You heard her on the phone earlier. If she truly believes you've touched one hair on my sister's head, she'll be out for your blood. Seriously."

Realizing she might have a valid point, he agreed.

"I'll drive right behind you," Rayna said. "When we get there, I'll hang back, unless there's trouble."

Trouble. He thought of how Delia had screamed curse words over the phone. His gut clenched. Around his innocent little boy. Theo had to already be confused and afraid with all the changes and not seeing his mother for so long.

By the time they pulled up to Delia's small house, his insides were churning. All the lights were on and the front porch was well lit. Eli and Jackie got out and waited for Rayna to catch up. Then, all three of them walked up the sidewalk and climbed the three steps up to the front door, though Rayna hung back, waiting on the edge of the front porch, as she'd promised.

Taking a deep breath, Eli pressed the doorbell, listening as the chimes sounded inside. They waited a moment, and then two. No one came to the door. He glanced at Jackie, letting her see his frustration and the worry he tried to suppress. What if Delia refused to come out? Was it possible she wouldn't let him see his own son?

"Let me call her," Jackie said, her voice soothing, apparently noticing his rising panic. "Clearly, she's home."

She pressed the button to dial her mother, putting the call on speaker. Three rings in and Eli began to worry Delia wasn't going to answer. But midway through the fourth ring, Delia picked up.

"What do you want?" She sounded tired. In the background, Eli could hear his son chattering in toddler-speak.

"We're outside, Mom," Jackie said. "Me and Eli and Rayna. Could you please answer the door?"

"I'm not giving my grandson to the man who might have harmed my daughter," Delia declared. "And you can't make me."

Rayna spoke up. "Actually, Delia, we can. Eli is Theo's father. Eli has not been charged with any crime and he has every right to have custody of his son. You need to turn the boy over or I will have to arrest you."

In response, Delia snarled several harsh curse words. But a moment later she yanked open the front door.

"Wait out here," she demanded, the tight line of her mouth and her furious gaze matching her angry voice. "I'll bring Theo and his bag out to you. I don't want any of you people setting foot in my house."

Jackie started a little at that. *You people* apparently included her own daughter.

"Mom," Jackie began, but then shook her head when Delia wheeled around and glared at her. "There's no reason for you to act like this."

Delia's lip curled as she faced Jackie. "How dare you," she snarled. "You'd better be careful, girly, or Eli will do to you whatever he did to Charla. Though you'll actually deserve it for being stupid enough to trust him."

Narrow eyed, she swung her gaze to Eli. "And when they arrest you and throw you in jail, I'll be raising your son anyway. I'll make sure and tell him all about what kind of person his father turned out to be."

With that, she stomped back inside her house, slamming the door behind her.

Eli briefly closed his eyes, trying and failing to let

her vindictive fury wash over him and away. He needed his mind clear of turmoil for his son.

"Don't take her too seriously," Rayna said softly from behind him. "She's just worried and hurting right now. She'll come around eventually."

Jackie didn't say anything. Judging from her strained and hurt expression, her mother's words had cut her deeply. Though Eli knew she, too, worried about her sister, at least she didn't truly believe he'd done something to hurt Charla. He was thankful for that at least.

A moment later the door opened. Delia stood framed in the doorway, still scowling, holding Theo's small hand in hers. At the first sight of his son peering around at them in confusion, Eli thought his heart would explode. "Theo," he said, holding out his arms. "I'm here. Daddy's here."

The instant he caught sight of his father, Theo froze. "Daddy?" he asked, the uncertainty in his small, wavering voice tearing at Eli's heart.

Immediately, Eli crouched down, putting himself at the same level as his son. "It's me, bud," he said. "I don't know where you've been, but I've sure missed you." He continued to hold out his arms, willing to wait until his boy came to him.

Theo jerked his hand free from Delia's and launched himself at his father. Easily, Eli caught him, swinging his boy up and out and around, making Eli squeal with joy. Then, after making two full turns, Eli gathered the toddler close and hugged him tight. Tears pricked at his eyes. His son. Alive and safe.

At that, Delia shoved a small suitcase and a car seat out onto the front porch and closed the door just short of a slam. A moment later they all heard the sound of the dead bolt clicking into place.

Little Theo flinched. "Gamma?" he asked, his plaintive tone tearing at Eli's heart. Judging from his scrunched-up face, Theo was trying to decide whether or not to cry.

"She's okay," Eli soothed. "I promise. Your gamma is fine."

"Come on," Rayna said, putting a hand on his shoulder. "Take your son home. Get him settled. If you need anything, you know how to reach me." Turning, she headed back to her patrol car. "As for me, I've got to get back to work."

Jackie picked up the suitcase and the car seat and took them over to Eli's truck. "You'll have to put this in there," she said, holding up the car seat. "I'm afraid I don't have the slightest idea how."

Though Theo clung tightly to him, Eli managed to untangle himself and handed his son over to Jackie. "Hang on, Theo," he said. "Let me get your car seat ready, okay?"

Thumb in mouth, the toddler nodded. Shifting him to one hip, Jackie rocked him side to side while Eli made short work of installing the child safety seat. He gently took Theo back from Jackie and got him buckled in. "Ready to go to Daddy's house?" he asked, ruffling his son's hair.

Eyes wide, Theo nodded. "See Mama?" he asked.

Feeling as if he'd just been sucker punched, Eli swallowed hard. "Not just yet, little guy. Just me and you and your aunt Jackie here." He glanced at Jackie. "Do you mind coming back to the ranch with me?" he asked, keeping his tone casual. "Or if you'd rather, I can drop you off at the Landshark."

She glanced from him to Theo, who appeared to be on the verge of falling asleep. "I'd like to come with you," she answered softly. "It's about time I get to know my nephew."

Eli tore his gaze away from his son long enough to smile at her. "Great," he said, his heart full. "I'll introduce you. Let's go."

Chapter 10

Jackie's stomach did a dip the instant his eyes connected with hers. Warmth bloomed inside her, the same aching sense of need she always felt around him. Damn. What was it about this man?

During the drive out to his ranch, she noticed the way Eli constantly watched his son in the rearview mirror. The absolute love and tenderness in his expression told her more about what kind of man Eli Pitts truly was than anything else.

When they finally made the turn onto the rough gravel road that led to his place, she couldn't suppress the feeling she was going home.

Home. That word again. Growing up, Getaway had been the home she couldn't wait to get away from. Often, she'd believed that was why the dusty little west

Texas town had been given such a moniker; because people couldn't wait to leave it behind. Despite the town's official story that the name had been chosen by early settlers to keep people out, she'd always believed this.

The past three years she'd slowly made New York City her home. When she'd first moved there into her small apartment with a roommate she hadn't known, she'd found the crowded chaos both terrifying and lonely. It had taken her a while to make friends, to develop a social life, but she'd finally found her groove. She loved her job, loved the hustle and bustle of the city, and even if she was still single, she'd learned being alone didn't always equal loneliness. She'd dated a few times, nothing serious, but she hadn't actually been looking for that anyway. She wanted to focus on her career.

Now back in the place she hadn't been able to wait to leave, she found herself finally able to see the charm of small-town life. Though honestly, she knew Eli Pitts had a lot to do with that. She shook her head, mentally chastising herself. She'd never been the type of woman who'd let a man derail her from her chosen path.

Jackie had been surprised when Eli asked if she wanted to come back to the ranch with him. She'd actually expected him to drop her off at the motel so he could spend some quality time with his son. The fact that he'd allow her in his special family moment made her feel all squishy inside.

Theo was absolutely adorable. He'd certainly received the best attributes of each parent—Charla's thick platinum-blond hair and long-lashed baby blue eyes along with Eli's features. This child would be a heartbreaker someday, making her wonder what Eli had looked like as a toddler.

Eli. Everything always came back to Eli. Clearly, she had it bad. When she wasn't worrying about her missing sister, she couldn't stop thinking about him. Or aching for the slightest contact of her skin to his, even if it was just a bump of their arms. She'd actually caught herself imagining a life on the ranch with him, even though staying in Getaway had never been something she'd ever even remotely considered.

Charla would be found, she knew. She had to be since the alternative simply wasn't acceptable. And when she returned, she'd be facing charges of theft and embezzlement. Would she have to go away to prison if convicted? Jackie might not know much about her sister anymore, but she did believe someone like Charla would wilt away if confined to a prison cell.

Glancing at the child now soundly asleep in the back seat, she turned to Eli. "Do you think Charla might have gone on the run because she knew Christopher Levine was about to find out what she'd done?"

Keeping his voice pitched as low as hers, Eli answered, "I'm pretty sure that's the situation. I'd guess Rayna's working with that scenario in the back of her mind."

Once he'd pulled up in front of his garage and parked, Eli turned and watched his sleeping son. His unguarded expression, so full of wonder and love, stirred an ache low inside her.

"I wonder if we can get him out of that car seat and into the house without waking him," Jackie said.

"I've done it before." His quiet confidence was even more endearing.

She got out, closing her door quietly, and stood back, watching while Eli carefully unbuckled his son and lifted him from the car seat. Holding him close to his chest, he handed Jackie the keys so she could unlock the front door.

Once inside, Eli carried Theo down the hall into his bedroom. Gently, he cradled his son in one arm while pulling back the covers. To Jackie's amazement, the little boy continued to remain deeply asleep, even when Eli removed his shoes and covered him with the sheet and blanket. Meeting her gaze, Eli motioned at her to follow him. On the way out, he turned off the light.

Instead of immediately leaving, Eli stood in the doorway of his room for a few minutes, just watching him sleep. Jackie stood next to him, memorizing the tender look on his face as he gazed at his son. Finally, Eli put his arm around her waist and tugged her with him. "Come on," he murmured.

Though she'd half expected they'd go to his bedroom, he led her down the hall toward the living room instead. But they'd only taken a few steps when he pressed her against the wall and covered her mouth with his.

As always, passion flared at the first touch of his lips to hers. She got a sense of celebration in his touch; joy, too. His boy was safe. Now, if she could just say the same about her sister.

The thought acted like ice water on flames. She wiggled out from under him, marching down the rest of the hallway and into the kitchen. He followed, equally out of breath, his arousal straining the front of his jeans.

Though her entire body ached for him, she managed to avert her eyes. "I'm starving," she declared, a little more breathless than she would have liked. "Could we make a couple of sandwiches, maybe open a can of soup?"

His bemused expression almost made her crack a smile.

"Sure," he replied. "Go sit and I'll make us something. Would you like a beer?"

Almost tempted to offer to do it herself, she nodded instead. "Sure. Thanks."

He handed her two and then began rummaging in the cupboards.

Carrying them with her, she took a seat at the kitchen table and popped the top on hers, taking a long drink. She was all too aware she'd end up staring at him too closely, so she pulled out her phone and checked social media. She needed something to distract her from her craving for him. Even so, she couldn't resist looking up frequently, watching him as he moved around the kitchen, preparing their meal. Despite her every intention, being here with him in his kitchen felt incredibly intimate. All she needed was for him to put on some soft music and they'd be dancing around the room.

The random thought made her smile and she glanced back at her phone, scrolling past the constant parade of pets and scenery and memes.

"Here you go," Eli said, sliding a plate with a sandwich in front of her and another opposite her seat. "Soup coming right up."

His warm gaze heated her blood. She put down her phone, debated jumping to her feet to see if she could help and decided to remain seated. Watching him, his quiet competence sexy as hell, desire thrummed through her blood. She drank another sip of beer to cover it.

After carrying two bowls of soup over, he sat. "I thought you were hungry."

"Oh, I am." She picked up her sandwich, ham and Swiss with mustard on wheat bread, and took a bite. Looking up, she found him watching her, his own meal uneaten in front of him. The heat in his gaze made a shiver snake up her spine.

Unbelievably, she blushed.

"Do you mind sleeping in the guest room tonight?" he asked. "Because the only way I can take you back to the motel is after Theo wakes up, which probably won't be until morning. Are you okay with that?"

Images of him sprawled in his bed, with her tucked in beside him, flashed through her mind. "The guest bedroom will be fine," she said, refocusing her attention on her food.

After they ate, she offered to do the dishes, but he insisted. Once again, pleasantly full this time, she sat and watched him, admiring the way his jeans rode on his narrow hips, and the shape of his butt.

He checked on Theo again before asking Jackie if she wanted to watch TV. She agreed, feeling both relaxed and oddly on edge. She kind of liked feeling so cozily domesticated here in his home with him, but knew she shouldn't.

When she took a seat on the couch, he joined her,

though he sat at the opposite end. Though he'd picked up the remote, he made no move to turn the television on.

"Where do you think Charla is?" she asked. "I don't get why she'd leave her son."

Eli opened his mouth and then closed it. "I'm not sure," he finally answered. "From the way she's been acting lately, I think she might have decided she couldn't live her best life and take care of a toddler, too."

"Her best life?" she echoed. "What do you mean?"

Again, he considered her, appearing to weigh his words. "If Charla did steal from Levine's, and say the amount was…substantial, she might have decided to take the opportunity with the stolen money to reinvent herself somewhere else. She always seemed to be struggling with what kind of person she wanted to be."

"True. I get that. But what would make her decide to become a thief? I know my sister likes to party and could be superficial and shallow, but to steal from her employer?" And abandon her child, she added mentally. Not to mention dump a man who, from all appearances, had made a pretty fantastic husband and father.

Or, she reminded herself, it could all be an act.

"Earth to Jackie," Eli said softly. "I don't know where you went, but as far as your question about what Charla was thinking, we won't know until we can ask her." With that, he turned on the TV.

"Anything in particular you want to watch?" he asked, scrolling through the offerings on Netflix.

"I've just finished a couple of shows," she replied,

deciding not to tell him she'd binge-watched them. "How about a movie?"

They settled on a light romantic comedy that had good reviews. As the movie began, she found herself wishing he'd slide over from his end of the couch and sit closer to her, but figured in the end it might be best if he didn't.

Evidently, he felt the same way, because he kept a good bit of distance between them the entire movie. As the ending credits rolled, she got to her feet and quietly asked him if he'd mind showing her where she'd be staying.

"Sure," he said. "There are already clean sheets on the bed. I keep it made up just in case."

The small room had been simply decorated. A double bed, a single nightstand with a plain lamp, and a dresser were the only furniture. A few generic framed prints hung on the walls, and three colorful throw pillows brought a touch of color to the room. Eyeing them, Jackie realized she could see her sister choosing them. At least at one point, Charla must have tried to decorate the house.

"I'll leave you fresh towels in the bathroom," Eli said, his tone formal. "Is there anything else you need?"

Without turning to look at him, she slowly shook her head. "I'm good, thank you."

He turned and left without another word. Aching, she closed her door and turned down the covers.

When she woke the next morning, she sat up in bed blinking, looking around the unfamiliar room, disoriented. Eli's guest room. And judging from the absolute silence in the rest of the house, everyone else must still be asleep.

Needing coffee, she tiptoed toward the kitchen, stopping short when she caught sight of Eli rocking Theo in a chair she hadn't noticed in one corner of the den. Eli crooned wordlessly to the dozing toddler.

Heart struck, she froze, unable to speak past the lump in her throat.

As he glanced up, a slow smile spread across his face. "Hey," he said softly. "Good morning. He woke up hungry at five, so I changed him and made him breakfast. He'll sleep for an hour or two and then I can take you back to the motel."

She nodded and cleared her throat. "Sounds perfect." Not trusting herself to speak again, she turned and made her way to the kitchen.

Though it felt like she was hiding, she sat at the table and drank her coffee. Her equilibrium couldn't take seeing Eli and his son right now. Emotion washed over her as she thought of her sister and the bad choices Charla had made.

Once she'd finished her coffee, she went back to ask Eli if he wanted her to make something for breakfast. She couldn't make herself just rummage in his fridge. But when she got to the den, he and Theo were gone. Listening, she thought she heard them down the hall in Theo's room. A rush of overwhelming longing hit her, so hard she momentarily couldn't catch her breath.

Suddenly, she wanted to get out of there. As soon as possible. She'd shower once she got to her motel room.

Heart pounding, she forced herself to walk down the

hallway toward Theo's room. Eli had gotten the boy dressed and right now had knelt down to tie his shoes.

"Hey," she said, standing in the doorway. "Would you mind running me back to the motel?"

Looking up, Eli studied her. "You sure you don't want to shower and have breakfast first? Theo's already had his bath and I showered earlier."

"No, thank you." She kept her tone polite. "I've got a few things I need to do today, so I'd really like to get back."

"No problem," he replied. "Let me grab the keys and we'll head out."

When he dropped her off at the Landshark, Theo giggled and blew her a kiss from his car seat. Touched, she blew him one right back. Eli smiled. "I'll touch base with you later, okay?"

"Sure."

Back inside her room, she rushed through her shower, planning to go out and grab a meal somewhere. After blow-drying her hair, she got dressed. She felt oddly lethargic, as if she'd spent the entire night making mad, passionate love with Eli. As if.

Her cell rang. Rayna. Jackie answered on the second ring.

"Hi, Rayna. What's up?"

"Can you come downtown?" Rayna asked. "I have something here that you need to see."

"Of course," Jackie answered. "Should I tell Eli?"

"Not this time," Rayna replied, surprising her. "I'd like to talk to you alone."

Jackie promised to be there in fifteen minutes. She finished applying her makeup, slipped on a pair of flats and grabbed her keys. She made it to the sheriff's department in ten.

The receptionist smiled at her as she walked through the door. "Go on back," she said. "Rayna is expecting you."

As usual, Jackie found the door to Rayna's office open. The sheriff sat behind her desk and looked up at Jackie, unsmiling.

"What is it?" Jackie asked, dread coiling low in her belly. "Is something wrong?"

"This came." Rayna held out an envelope. Jackie recognized Charla's distinctive, almost childish, handwriting on the outside.

"Go ahead," Rayna urged. "It's addressed to me, but I think she meant part of this for you."

As Jackie accepted it, her heart pounding, Rayna touched her arm. "A word of caution before you read it," Rayna said. "I'm not sure I believe what she wrote at all. Keep that in mind, okay? There's no reason to freak out. Especially if you notice the postmark date."

Slowly, Jackie opened the envelope and pulled out a single sheet of paper. Definitely her sister's handwriting, though clearly Charla had made an effort to tone down her usually exuberant scrawl.

If you're reading this, most likely I'm dead. Jackie gasped aloud, raising her gaze from the paper to meet Rayna's.

"Keep going," Rayna urged, the set of her mouth grim. "Like I said. Take it with a grain of salt."

Heart pounding, Jackie nodded. *I had an arrangement with a friend to mail this if they didn't hear from me by Wednesday. I think my ex-husband is working with Christopher Levine to have me killed.*

Now Jackie understood Rayna's comment. Her skepticism made sense. Only someone as self-involved as Charla would try to make anyone believe those particular two men would work together for anything, never mind murdering her.

She continued reading. *My son is with a friend of mine named Natalie Beaumont. My mother will need to raise him. I know she'll make sure he remembers me. And if my sister showed up after I sent that text—which I doubt—tell her too little, too late.*

But I want Eli and Mr. Levine punished for taking my life.

Promise me you'll do this, or I swear I'll haunt you.

After dropping Jackie off, Eli took his son to the Tumbleweed Café for breakfast. He knew just about everyone in town had been worried about Theo and it would do them all good to see him in person.

From the back seat, Theo chortled. He'd brought along one of his favorite toys, a stuffed alligator with whom he liked to converse in his own mostly unintelligible language.

After parking, Eli unstrapped Theo and carried him inside. As usual, the café was packed. Several people looked up when he entered, and then did a double take when they saw his son.

On his way to the table, he stopped and talked to several people. Once he and Theo were seated, he requested a booster seat and ordered breakfast. Theo wanted pancakes, so he got those, plus a fried egg platter for himself.

He'd just pushed his plate away when his cell rang. His heart skipped a beat when he saw the caller was Rayna.

"Any news?" he asked, hoping she'd gotten a lead as to Charla's whereabouts.

"Sort of," Rayna replied. "But not what I think you're hoping for. I've got Jackie here with me. Christopher Levine is on the way, and I need you here, as well."

"What's going on?" he asked, more intrigued than alarmed.

But Rayna had already hung up.

Quickly, he signaled for the check and paid, leaving a generous tip. After cleaning off Theo's face and hands with a baby wipe, Eli lifted him out of the booster seat and carried him inside.

The instant he stepped into the sheriff's office, the receptionist waved him past. He hurried through the open area, back to Rayna's office. When he arrived, he knocked on her closed door.

"Come in," she said.

Inside, Rayna sat behind her desk. Jackie sat in one of the visitor chairs, while Christopher Levine sat in the other.

"About time you got here," the jeweler muttered, eyeing Eli with a sour expression.

As for Jackie, she wouldn't meet his eyes. Judging by her tightly crossed arms and her defensive body language, she wasn't happy with whatever news Rayna had shared.

"This came today," Rayna said, handing him a photocopy of a letter. He recognized Charla's swirly handwriting immediately.

Only then did he realize that both Jackie and Christopher also held copies.

Reading it quickly, when he got to the end, he shook his head. "This is not true. At all."

Now Christopher smirked at him. "That's exactly what I said. Why would I kill her before I got back what she stole from me? I think she's setting us up."

"You may be right." Judging from Rayna's noncommittal tone, she'd set up this meeting just to see what bringing them all together might shake out.

Jackie spoke up for the first time. "Actually, you both have motive. Charla stole from you, Christopher. And Eli, she took your son away."

When Eli opened his mouth to reply, Jackie held up her hand. "I'm not finished. Personally, the more I've come to learn about my sister, the more I've come to realize she wasn't a very nice person. One thing I do know for sure is I don't think there's any way in hell the two of you would work together since I know Charla had an affair with you, Christopher, while she was still married to Eli."

Though Christopher flushed, he didn't deny her observation. How could he, when it was true?

"Then what could be Charla's motive?" Rayna asked, her gaze briefly settling on each of them in turn.

"Faking her death to disappear with my money," Christopher replied. "Come on. It's pretty damn obvious."

Though his comment earned a scowl from Jackie, she didn't dispute his statement.

"That's one possibility," Rayna chimed in, once again the voice of reason. "The other, though doubtful, is that Charla really has met some sort of serious harm."

No one responded to this, though Jackie sighed.

"Does anyone have any other suggestions?" Rayna asked. "Because after looking over the records Mr. Levine has provided, due to the amount of money missing, this is a felony."

"Does that mean you'll be calling in the FBI or the Texas Rangers?" Jackie asked.

"No." Rayna smiled. "Those agencies are busy with other larger crimes. They don't like to deal with business crimes. Embezzlement is much more common than you realize."

Christopher opened his mouth as if to protest, and then closed it.

"However, since Mr. Levine has pressed charges, I've been able to put out an APB on Charla. This will help get other state police departments on alert. If they see her, she will be arrested."

Jackie turned to face Christopher. "If you don't mind me asking, exactly how much money did Charla steal?"

He swallowed hard. "Over the last three years, it's half a million dollars."

Shocked despite himself, Eli glanced at Jackie.

Jackie sat back in her chair. "I…" she began. "I don't know what to say."

"Yeah," Christopher said, glum-voiced. "I trusted her. I really trusted her. I still haven't told Kim."

His wife. Eli wondered if Kim knew about the affair. Since it wasn't his business, he decided not to ask.

"Does Kim know about you and Charla?" Jackie asked, evidently feeling no such constraint.

Christopher blanched. "No. And I'd like to keep it that way. Charla and I ended things and we were just employer/employee for a good while. When she returned to work after having her son, one thing led to another and..." He shook his head. "Looking back on it now, I think she used that to distract me so I didn't notice her stealing from the company."

"Any other suggestions?" Rayna asked, clearly trying to bring the discussion back on track. "I've already spoken with Delia and asked her to provide me a list of places Charla might have talked about visiting. I'd like the three of you to do the same. In the meantime, I have friends who work for the Houston Police Department. They have contacts in Galveston and Corpus, in case Charla might have fled to the coast."

"Do you really think she's still in the country?" Eli had to ask. "Because it seems to me more likely she might have taken off for somewhere like the Bahamas or Grand Cayman. It'd be much easier to disappear, especially with that much cash."

Though Rayna nodded, Jackie stubbornly shook her head. "Even though you're running with the theory that my sister cut and ran, promise me you're still looking into the chance she might have come to harm. Between the text message, her friend Natalie and this note, it seems to me that's still a very real possibility."

"Of course." Rayna nodded. "One thing I've learned

since beginning work in law enforcement is never to close my mind to any scenario."

Eli felt compelled to speak. "One thing I can say for certain is that I didn't harm Charla in any way."

"Me neither," Christopher seconded. "I just want my money and my missing gemstones back."

Looking from one man to the other, Jackie didn't speak.

"All right," Rayna said, pushing to her feet. "I've got to get back to work. I'll keep you all posted if I learn anything."

Waiting while they all filed out, Rayna held out her arms to Theo. "Come see Auntie Rayna," she crooned.

Eyeing her with suspicion, Theo squinted at her. Then, either remembering her or just deciding he liked her, he giggled and leaned toward her. Eli passed him over, conscious of Jackie standing behind him and quietly watching.

"Let me walk you out to your truck," Rayna said, still bouncing Theo. "You, too, Jackie."

Jackie nodded. "Sounds good."

"Where's Christopher?" Looking around, Eli realized the other man must have already gone.

"He took off the second I ended our meeting," Rayna responded. "I'll definitely be keeping an eye on him."

Once they were outside, Rayna continued to hold Theo while Eli unlocked his truck. She then handed him over, watching while Eli buckled him into his car seat. "Jackie, wait," she called out. "Come here for just a second. I have something to say to Eli and I think you need to hear it."

Though her reluctance shone in her face, Jackie complied.

"I want you to know I'm not only going to be watching Mr. Levine," she said. "I'll be keeping an eye on this one, too. But honestly, I truly don't think Charla is in any danger. My best guess would be that she took the money and ran. I wouldn't be surprised if she hasn't left the country already." Looking from Eli to Jackie, she nodded. "Either way, we will find your sister. You can count on that."

"Thanks." Jackie nodded. "I appreciate that. Have you mentioned this latest letter to Delia yet?"

"Not yet."

"I'd appreciate if you'd hold off," Jackie asked. "I understand if you feel you can't do that, but Delia is already out for blood. Charla can do no wrong as far as she's concerned. I'm afraid something like this might send her over the edge."

Rayna nodded. "I figured. I'll keep this to myself for a while longer. Y'all have a good rest of your day, all right?" With that, she turned and went back inside.

Without looking at him, Jackie also took off, high-tailing it to her rental car. Eli thought about calling to her and decided against it. They'd all had a bit of a shock this afternoon. Each of them had their own way of dealing with things. He'd leave Jackie alone and let her figure this out on her own. After all, she knew how to reach him.

Chapter 11

Driving through downtown Getaway, sleepy and quiet in the sunshine, Jackie didn't know what to think or how to feel. This was absolutely insane. Everything she'd thought she knew or believed about her sister had been turned upside down. On the one hand, she'd much rather believe Charla to be safe somewhere, maybe lounging on a beach, even if she'd stolen a huge amount of money and abandoned her son. On the other, she couldn't quite discount the possibility that her sister might have actually come to some harm.

The letter had been the tipping point, at least for her. It was complete and utter nonsense. No way would Eli and Christopher Levine have worked together against Charla. If Charla truly thought anyone would believe such a thing, she'd guessed wrong. The only person

Jackie could think of who might would be Delia. Which was why Jackie had asked Rayna not to share it with her yet. All they needed was Delia going off on another frenzy.

The only thing Charla's letter had accomplished, as far as Jackie was concerned, was that she actually felt sorry for both Eli and Christopher Levine. While she couldn't deny that the jewelry store owner had done wrong by having an affair with his employee, he didn't deserve to lose half a million dollars.

And Eli, poor Eli. From the various clues she'd been picking up ever since she'd met him, he'd at first been blinded by Charla's beauty and her fake charm and had never seen the true Charla coming. She managed to completely upend his life, leaving a trail of destruction behind her like an EF4 tornado.

She made it back to the motel and let herself into her room. Housekeeping had already made the room up, which meant she wouldn't have to worry about being disturbed.

Head pounding, she decided to try and take a nap. She hadn't slept well in Eli's guest bed and there'd been too much emotional drama in the past twenty-four hours. She'd barely crawled between the sheets when her phone rang. Fumbling in the dark room, when she saw Eli's name come up on caller ID, she declined the call. She didn't really feel up to talking to him right now. She needed both time and space to clear her head.

An instant later her phone chimed, indicating a voice mail. She debated, but in the end decided to go ahead and listen. "I need your help. Your mother is here. She's demanding I hand over my son and is refusing to leave until I do, which isn't happening. I thought I'd try you before I called Rayna. I guess I have no choice."

Muttering a curse word, she hit Redial. Eli answered immediately. "I stupidly let her into my house because she apologized and seemed normal. She is Theo's grandmother after all, and I felt like she has a right to see him. But then she went into his bedroom and started packing him a bag. She got loud and hostile, which scared my son. He's crying, I'm trying to calm him down and she's refusing to leave without him. I can tell you right now, that isn't happening."

"I'm so sorry," Jackie said, her headache intensifying. In the background, she could hear Theo wailing and her mother ranting and raving. "I'm on my way. But since I doubt she'll listen to me, go ahead and call Rayna." After ending the call, she grabbed the car keys and ran to her car.

Though she drove as fast as she dared, by the time she pulled up to Eli's ranch house, a sheriff's department cruiser was already parked next to her mother's red Camaro.

With a dread settling in her chest, she got out and climbed the steps to the front porch. While she still grappled with her feelings for Eli, in the end he was Theo's father, and Delia had no right to try and take his son from him. Her mother appeared to have completely gone off the rails.

As she raised her hand to ring the doorbell, she heard Delia shouting inside. Jackie tried the knob and finding the door unlocked, simply walked into the house. Immediately, she saw the sheriff, back to her, facing off with Delia. Eli and Theo must have gone to another room.

Rayna turned, relief flashing across her face. "There you are," she said. "Maybe you can talk some sense into your mother before I have to arrest her."

"For what?" Delia bellowed. "I haven't done anything wrong. In fact, I seem to be the only one here who hasn't lost their damn mind. I want to save my grandson's life. How can anyone deny me a chance to do that?"

"Mom." Jackie moved forward. "You've got to stop this. We have no proof that Eli did anything to Charla. He's Theo's father, so he has every right in this situation. You don't."

"Traitor," Delia sneered, her lip curling. "You've always thought you were so smart, such an intellectual, looking down on me and your sister. Now that man has you wrapped around his finger, blind of anything but how badly you want to—"

"Stop." Eli entered the room, cutting off Delia. "I'm going to ask you nicely once again to leave. If you refuse, I will press charges for trespassing and ask the sheriff to arrest you."

"You can't do that," Delia protested. Her gaze swung to Rayna's. "Can he?"

"Yes. And since I sure hate the idea of you riding to the jail in the back of my patrol car and all the gossip that will come from that, I'd suggest you do as Mr. Pitts asks and leave."

"Right now," Eli added for emphasis. "I finally got Theo calmed down. I don't need you riling him up again."

Looking from one to the other, at first Delia didn't move. Glancing from Eli to Jackie to Rayna, she appeared to be weighing her options. For a second, Jackie feared her mother might make a mad dash toward Eli's room in an attempt to snatch him up and run.

Finally, Delia shook her head. Muttering under her breath, she marched toward the door. When she reached Jackie, she stopped and looked her older daughter in the face. "I think you should take a long, hard look at how you're acting here. You need to be thinking more about helping your sister and less about yourself."

Then, head held high, Delia sailed away.

A moment later they heard her car rumble to life. Spinning her tires in the gravel in a final show of defiance, she took off.

Jackie let her shoulders sag with relief.

"That was intense," Eli said, his expression troubled. "I know Delia tends to be dramatic, but that was bizarre even for her."

"She's worried sick about her daughter," Rayna pointed out gently. "I think she feels like she should be doing something, anything. In her mind she honestly feels there's a very real possibility you might have harmed Charla. She told me this. She even said she could hardly blame you, after the way Charla treated you."

"Delia spoke to you about her feelings?" Jackie asked, hardly able to believe it. "When?"

"She stopped by my office bright and early this morning." Rayna met Jackie's gaze before doing the same with Eli. "And for the record, I had to show her that letter from Charla. I couldn't lie to her. She broke down and wept."

"That's what set her off." Eli dragged his hand over his chin. "Considering I went through hell just getting Theo from her last night, I couldn't figure out why she was already back at it this morning."

Rayna grimaced. "She told me she was going home. That she was going to go by Jackie's room at the Landshark so they could talk, maybe work out a plan of action. I take it she didn't come by there?"

Feeling like a deer caught in the headlights, Jackie shook her head. "Not while I was there, at least." She hoped Rayna didn't ask her to elaborate, because even though her overnight stay at Eli's place had been innocent, she doubted anyone would believe that.

Luckily for her, Rayna didn't press. Instead, she told them to let her know if they needed anything else and left.

Drained, Jackie turned to do the same.

"Wait," Eli said, touching her arm, his gaze pleading. "Can we talk? Please? I put Theo down for a nap and I'm thinking we might need to clear the air after all that."

Slowly, she nodded. "Look, Eli, I'll be up-front with you. I feel as if you are being put in an awful position here and you don't deserve that. Right now, I wish my sister would just show up and admit to what she's done wrong and get some help. But I think we both know that's not going to happen."

Cautiously, he agreed.

"That said, until she can see and talk to Charla, my mother is going to think the worst of you. I'm not sure why, as she's known you longer than I have, but that's clearly how it's going to be."

His expression darkened. "I can't have her upsetting my son. Theo's been through enough in the last couple weeks. He needs stability and calmness. All that shouting and screaming had him shaking and sucking his thumb. That's not acceptable at all."

Her heart squeezed at the idea of that precious little boy quaking in terror of his own grandmother. "I agree," she said. "Once she's had time to calm down, I plan to have a word with my mother, though clearly she thinks I've gone over to side with the enemy."

Gaze locked on hers, Eli nodded. When he looked at her like that, with his heart in his eyes, she couldn't think, never mind speak a coherent sentence.

"You're probably right," he said, his voice dejected. "I'm sorry you got dragged into the middle of all this, Jackie."

Stunned, she eyed him. "The fact that you're apologizing to me seems like almost a bitter irony. Especially since it's my sister and my mother causing all this."

"I have Theo back," he told her. "The rest of this is a fresh hell, but none of it matters now that my son is safe."

Did that mean he was washing his hands of everything else?

"Are you still going to help me search for my sister?" she asked. "Since you have Theo back and all, I wouldn't blame you if you decided you were done."

"Of course I am." His chin came up, his gaze steady. "I have to clear my name. Now that she's thrown around all these false accusations, I want to find her more than anything."

"Fair enough." She actually managed to smile at him.

For one awkward moment they stood there, separated only by a few feet, breathing the same air. She had the sense that one move toward him on her part and she'd find herself wrapped up tight in his arms.

The sound of car tires on gravel jerked them back to reality. Eli went to the window and swore. "She's back. Your mother. I'm not going to answer the door." He pulled out his phone. "Should I call Rayna? This is ridiculous."

"Not yet." Rolling her shoulders to try to relieve some of the tension, Jackie took a deep breath. "Let me go outside and talk to her. Maybe I can convince her that this is a huge mistake."

"I'll go with you," he decided. "I won't hesitate to call Rayna if Delia tries to start more trouble."

"Let me try to handle this alone first," she insisted. "I'll call you if I need you." Not giving him a chance to argue, she slipped out the front door and waited for her mother on the porch, heart pounding.

As Delia slowly got out of her car, Jackie debated whether to go down and intercept her on neutral ground. In the end, she decided to stay where she was, ready for anything. For all she knew, her mother might have decided to resort to physical violence. She hoped not.

"Are you still here?" Delia asked, seemingly surprised, though so far her tone sounded reasonable.

Instead of answering, Jackie gave her mother a stern look. "What are you doing, Mom? There's no sense in stirring up more trouble. I know Rayna doesn't want to arrest you, but she will if she has to."

"I came to apologize to Eli," Delia responded. "And since you're here, to you. I'm out of my mind with worry. I don't know how I'll go on living if Charla is dead." Her voice shook. Then, covering her face with her hands, she started sobbing. Loudly and noisily.

Now Jackie left the porch to put her arms around her mother's shaking shoulders. "She's fine, Mom. I truly believe she's fine. I still intend to find her."

The front door opened and Eli stepped outside, just in time to hear Delia's last statement.

"Me, too," Eli said, the sympathy in his deep voice bringing tears to Jackie's eyes.

Delia looked up, still crying. "I'm sorry for how I treated you, Eli. You didn't deserve that. Neither did Theo. When Rayna showed me that letter Charla had mailed, I lost my mind."

"I understand." Eli didn't move. "But you cannot ever do that to Theo again. He's very uncertain due to all the changes he's been through. You coming here and screaming and cursing made him shake and cry. I had a tough time getting him settled back down. I can't allow you to be around him at all if you can't act like a responsible adult and a loving grandmother. Do you understand?"

Wiping away her tears, Delia nodded. "I'm sorry. It won't happen again, I promise."

Though he didn't appear convinced, Eli finally nodded. "What about your other daughter?" he asked, nodding toward Jackie. "You owe her an apology, too."

Delia's jaw tightened, making Jackie realize for

whatever reason, her mother found saying she was sorry to Jackie more difficult. "I shouldn't have said what I did," Delia admitted. "You've always been so smart, so accomplished. Charla and I always felt somehow less around you."

Stunned, Jackie wasn't sure how to respond. She'd never ever treated either her mother or her sister as if she considered herself better than them. In fact, she'd always secretly envied the close bond they'd shared, their vivaciousness and blond good looks.

When she said this out loud, Delia appeared shocked. "Honey, I had no idea." She reached out and pulled Jackie in for another hug. Not a social hug, or a for-appearances'-sake hug, but a genuine let-me-offer-comfort hug. For the first time since Jackie could remember, she allowed herself to lean in and hug back. It felt pretty darn good.

Delia then stepped back and looked at Eli. "Since we're admitting truths, I should tell you that I had high hopes when Charla married you and got pregnant. I figured if anyone could help that wild child settle down, it would be you. Don't think I didn't see how she treated you."

He opened his mouth to respond, but Delia held up a hand. "I'm not finished. Despite all that Charla put you through, I noticed how you responded. You never once raised your voice or your hand to my daughter. That's why I know you wouldn't have hurt her, no matter what her letter says."

Eli smiled wryly. "Thanks, but like any married couple, we argued. I'm sure I might have yelled once or twice. But the other, no. I was raised to understand that a man never hits a woman."

Nodding, Delia turned to face Jackie. "Your sister is up to something," she said. "I understand she might have stolen a lot of money from Levine's. It's been all over town. People are speculating that she might have escaped to the Caribbean, but I know for a fact that Charla never got around to getting her passport. That makes her leaving the country highly unlikely."

Fascinated, Jackie tried to understand her mother's mercurial change of heart. She wasn't entirely sure Delia was sincere. "How are you so certain that Charla is okay?" she asked. "Barely an hour ago you were convinced Eli had done something to her."

Delia lifted her chin, looking from Jackie to Eli and back again. "Because I know my daughter. Charla was always into those true crime television shows. I think she's trying to make people think she's dead so she can get away with stealing that money. And sadly, she's trying to make either Eli or Christopher Levine take the fall."

Struggling to process this, Jackie shook her head. "To do that, she'd need a body. They'd have to match the DNA to hers. How on earth would she pull something like that off?"

"There are a lot of ways." Suddenly the expert, Delia spoke with more confidence. "She and I used to discuss this all the time. Like I said, she was fascinated by the subject. Her personal favorite was an explosion with fire on board a yacht in the ocean. As long as there was enough proof she'd been on board, she wouldn't need a body."

Frowning, Eli shook his head. "That sounds complicated. That'd be a lot of work. I don't think Charla could manage that alone."

"That's just it," Delia replied. "She wouldn't be alone. I didn't mention this to anyone before because quite frankly, it didn't occur to me, but Charla had met a man online. I'm not sure where he lives, but I remember her saying it was on the coast."

"There's a lot of coast," Jackie said slowly. "Gulf coast, east coast, west. Is there any way you can narrow it down?"

"I can." Voice triumphant, Delia nodded. "It has to be the Texas coast. Charla always said she'd never date anyone but a Texan."

Stepping out of the room, Eli phoned Rayna and filled her in. "There's a lot of coast in Texas," he said. "I wish we could have more specifics, like which city."

"We need access to Charla's online dating profile," Rayna said. "There are a ton of different services, so it would help if Delia can narrow it down to one or two." She paused for a moment, clearly thinking. "It'd be even better if we had access to Charla's computer. Now that Mr. Levine has pressed charges, we'll get a warrant to search her apartment. Hopefully, she'll have left something behind."

"Sounds good. What, if anything, can I do to help you?"

"Just sit tight," Rayna responded. "I promise I'll keep you posted. One more thing. I probably don't have to say this, but watch out for that Delia. She's not stable. The wild mood swings have me worried."

He glanced back toward the house. "Right now all is quiet, but I get your point."

The front door opened just as he ended the call. He shoved his phone into his pocket as Delia hurried out. She stopped short, obviously surprised to see him. "I'd wondered where you'd gotten to," she said, smiling. "I hope you won't hold my hysterics earlier against me. I'd like to see my grandson again. Jackie said he was sleeping and she didn't want me to wake him, but will you bring him by my house sometime?"

"Sure." He dipped his chin, thinking not any time soon. He had no idea what Delia might be up to, but he didn't entirely trust her. As Rayna had mentioned, Delia wasn't stable.

"That was weird," Jackie said as soon as he walked inside. "At first, I so wanted to believe her. The little kid in me, I guess, still craving her mother's love." She took a deep breath. "But this feels off."

"I agree." Walking to the back, he checked on Theo, still sound asleep. When he returned, he motioned for Jackie to follow him into the kitchen, so he could fill her in on his conversation with Rayna.

"I think it's important we continue to play along with your mother," he continued. "Maybe you can call her and ask her if she knows what dating services Charla used."

"I can do that," Jackie replied. "One thing, though. I don't think you should allow Delia anywhere near Theo until Charla is found. I know she might have seemed sincere in her regret and all, but I have no idea what might set her off again. She might suddenly decide you shouldn't be raising your son and cause another big scene."

"Agreed." Unable to resist, he crossed the room and pulled her into his arms. She wrapped her arms around him, and they stood that way, each silently drawing on each other's strength.

"This is one big cluster," she murmured, her face pressed into his chest. She felt good, nestled against him, her soft curves molded into his.

Inhaling the sweet scent of her hair, he agreed. At least he had her, at least for now. Jackie in his life might be only temporary, but she was the best thing that had ever happened to him, other than his son.

In fact, he knew he'd fallen hard for her. His ex-wife's sister, who happened to live all the way across the country. Talk about poor choices. He grimaced. As if he'd had a choice. The instant he'd seen Jackie, standing on his doorstep with fire in her eyes, he'd been lost.

When she finally moved out of his arms, her expression looked as bleak as he felt inside. "I'm sorry about all of this," she said softly. "It seems my entire family has gone off the deep end."

He tried to lighten the mood. "Unfortunately, we don't get to choose our relatives."

"Truth," she replied, though she didn't smile. "I'd better be going. I want to see if Rayna would let me help look at Charla's computer, if they find one. I'm a bit of a computer nerd and I think my skills might be helpful."

He had some horse training and barn cleaning to do. He usually just set up a playpen and put Theo in it where he could keep an eye on the toddler. But lately, at least according to Charla, Theo had been climbing out of the playpen on his own. This wouldn't be good around horses.

He eyed Jackie, wondering. "I need a favor first," he said. "If it's not imposing too much. It'll probably take Rayna a bit to get a judge to sign off on that search warrant. I'm wondering if you'd mind watching Theo while I work the two horses I have here to train. I also need to clean out a couple of stalls."

"I can do that," she said. "How long are you thinking?"

"Maybe three hours, four tops." Bracing himself for her to decline, he exhaled in relief when she nodded. He couldn't really afford to slack off with his work. Though he'd been paid a retainer, he wouldn't receive the balance until he had these two horses trained.

Thanking her again, he hurried out the door, intent on getting right to it. He saddled up the first horse, a beautiful palomino gelding the owner had nicknamed Johnny, and rode out to the outdoor arena.

The work went well, with Johnny responsive and seemingly eager to learn. Once Eli had removed the saddle and put the horse on the electric walker, he went to retrieve Ro, the other gelding. He rode Ro back into the arena and began to put the animal through his paces. Ro had a different personality than Johnny, more skittish and a bit antsy, though still responsive and willing to learn.

Movement over by the railing had Ro sidestepping, showing the whites of his eyes. Eli glanced over, surprised to see Jackie standing there with Theo in her arms, pointing out his daddy on top of the horse.

For an instant, just one flash of time, Eli could picture a future where this scenario was a regular part of the day. Doing what he loved to do, working a horse, with Jackie and his son looking on.

Even knowing damn well that such a thing wasn't realistic didn't stop the rush of yearning for it to be.

When Eli finished with Ro, he unsaddled him and put him on the automatic walker, while he took Johnny to brush down. By the time he'd taken care of both horses, Jackie and Eli had returned to the house.

He rushed through mucking out the stalls, something he usually had one of his part-time helpers do. When he'd finished, he walked back to the house, dirty and sweaty and in need of a quick shower.

Smiling, Jackie agreed. After a quick, restorative shower and some clean clothes, he returned to find her in the kitchen, feeding Theo macaroni and cheese in his high chair.

"There's more on the stove if you're hungry," she said, the warmth in her gaze letting him know she liked the way he'd cleaned up. Naturally, his body responded immediately.

Grabbing a bowl, he helped himself to some cheesy carbs and sat down next to his son. Theo grinned, clearly happy to see him, and began talking his particular brand of toddler gibberish, punctuated every now and then by an actual word.

Jackie stood for a moment, watching them, and then checked her watch. "I've really got to go."

"Of course." Looking down to give himself time to mask his disappointment, Eli stood. He debated kissing her goodbye, but ended up thanking her politely instead. For a second he thought he saw a flash of disappointment cross her face before she nodded and smiled.

"No problem," she replied. "I enjoyed hanging out with Theo and getting to know him."

As if he understood exactly what she'd said, Theo waved his arms and chortled, making Jackie laugh. Her laughter, joyful and unaffected, made him happy. Hell, just breathing the same air as she did brought him joy. Sometimes, the thought of how much she'd come to mean to him so quickly terrified him. Right now, he wished he could preserve this moment forever.

She caught her breath. "Eli? Are you all right?"

Blinking, he nodded. "Yes. Why do you ask?"

"I don't know." She shrugged. "Maybe because you seemed a thousand miles away."

"I..." Deciding to be honest, he took a step closer to her. "I was wishing this could be a regular thing. You, me and Theo. I know, I know." Grimacing, he held up a hand. "Can't blame a guy for wishing."

This time her smile seemed tinged with a bit of sadness. "I get that. Spending time here today with you and Theo made me—" She stopped, shaking her head. "I'd better get going."

Reaching out, he touched her arm. "Made you what?" he asked.

"Made me long for something that isn't possible," she whispered, her eyes huge.

He kissed her then, crushing her to him and taking her mouth as if this might be the last kiss they ever shared. She opened to him, her small tongue driving him wild. Only the sound of Theo chortling in the background kept him from deepening the kiss.

They both were breathing hard when they broke apart. Blindly, Eli turned away, desperate to hide his massive arousal. When he did, Jackie slipped from the room. A moment later the front door opened and closed. Bereft, he gripped the sides of the counter and tried to regain his composure.

"Dada?" Theo's hesitant voice came from behind him. "Dada?"

Instantly, Eli turned to his son, pushing away his own issues and focusing on Theo. "I'm right here, Theo," he said, making his voice both gentle and reassuring. "Do you want some more macaroni and cheese?"

After Theo finished his lunch, Eli watched him play for a little bit before he noticed Theo's eyes drooping. "Time for a nap, little man," he said, scooping the toddler up and carrying him to his room. Once there Eli changed his diaper, helped him get settled in his bed with his favorite stuffed animal and kissed his soft, chubby cheek. As Eli turned out the light, he caught himself wondering once again how Charla could bear to leave their son. As long as he lived, such a thing would be beyond his comprehension.

What would happen once Charla returned? He knew she'd be arrested and in the end, would most likely serve time for her crimes. His heart ached at the thought of possibly having to take Theo to visit his mother in prison, but then again, maybe Charla wouldn't want to see him.

No matter how this ended up shaking out, Eli would

never understand how Charla could abandon her son. He might not have agreed with her lifestyle choices, but he'd never in a million years have guessed she'd be a thief and a fugitive.

At least his son was safe. That was what was important here. He knew he needed to focus on the positive. After all, no matter how much love he might offer Jackie, he couldn't make her stay. She had to choose Getaway—and him—for herself.

Chapter 12

After leaving Eli's, with her insides a jangled mess of raw emotion, Jackie drove around town for a bit. Now that downtown had been almost fully restored, Main Street had a homey, welcoming feel. For a moment she could see herself staying there, making a life in Getaway, with Eli and Theo at her side.

And then she thought of her mother and Charla's return, and that particular fantasy came crashing down. While New York and her life there seemed light-years away, she loved it there. If she kept herself busy to ward off the occasional loneliness, she didn't think that was unusual. She adored her job, her tiny apartment, the hustle and bustle and how she could always find a new place to eat just by taking a random walk. Where at first she'd found the crowds intimidating, she'd gotten used to moving effortlessly among them. She no longer heard the constant cacophony of horns and vehicles. In short, she'd adapted.

Then why did returning to Getaway feel so much like she'd come home? She had a feeling the real reason might be Eli. The more time she spent with him, the more she wondered how she'd survive without him.

Passing Serenity's, the metaphysical bookstore that had fascinated her when she'd been a teen, she made an impulsive U-turn and parked across the street. Ever since she'd talked to Charla's coworkers at the café, she'd meant to stop by and see if the store's proprietor, a self-proclaimed psychic named Serenity Rune, might be able to help with figuring out where Charla might be. Not only did everyone in town go to Serenity for help with various personal problems, but Serenity had also always been kind to a much younger Jackie, so she knew asking wouldn't be a problem.

Stepping through the front door with its jingling set of bells, Jackie inhaled the strong scent of incense and looked around. The place looked pretty much the same as it had back in the day.

"Welcome," a rich, feminine voice drawled, coming out from a back room. A moment later, Serenity came into view. Her eyes widened as she caught sight of her visitor. "Jackie? Jackie Burkholdt, is that you?"

"Serenity!" Smiling, Jackie walked into the other woman's hug. In her flowing, colorful caftan, bracelets jingling and dangly earrings swaying, Serenity didn't appear to have aged a single year.

"I heard you were back in town and I wondered when you'd stop by." Serenity grinned, her eyes sparkling. "Come into the back room with me. I just made a pot of tea and we can catch up."

"I can't stay long, but I'd love to." Following the older woman, she found herself in a crowded stock room of sorts, with a table and chairs, a small refrigerator and a microwave.

"My home away from home," Serenity chirped. "Have you heard anything from that sister of yours?"

"Not a thing." Settling into one of the chairs, Jackie watched as Serenity loaded up a silver-plated tray with a ceramic teapot and two matching mugs.

"Earl Grey all right with you?" Serenity asked as she poured.

"Yes, thanks." Never having asked for anything psychic related, Jackie wasn't sure how to begin, or even if she wanted to.

Once Serenity had filled two cups, she offered Jackie a small bowl with packets of both sugar and artificial sweetener.

"None for me, thank you." Picking up her steaming mug, Jackie blew on it, inhaling the distinctive scent of the tea. "I wanted to ask you if you've *seen* anything?" she asked, feeling slightly foolish. "Psychically, I mean."

Serenity eyed her over the rim of her own cup before taking a small sip. "I see you're on the verge of finding the joy you were always meant to have," she said. "Your sister has gone in pursuit of the opposite kind of joy. I'm not sure her choice will make her happy."

Though her face felt on fire, Jackie nodded. "Are you able to see where Charla might be?"

Closing her eyes, Serenity took one more drink before setting the cup on the table. She kept her eyes closed, swaying slightly from side to side, humming some sort of off-key, esoteric melody under her breath.

Jackie shifted uncomfortably in her chair, not sure what she should do, if anything. Apparently, this was what Serenity did when she wanted to have a vision or whatever she called it.

Sipping on her tea, Jackie began regretting her impulsive decision to stop by.

After a minute Serenity stopped humming and opened her eyes. "Your sister is near a beach," she said, frowning. "There are palm trees and those exotic drinks with umbrellas in them. I can't see who she's with, but I didn't get the sense it was a man."

Heart skipping a beat, Jackie leaned closer. "So Charla is alive and unharmed?"

"Yes, she is." Serenity appeared surprised at the question. "She seems pretty relaxed, without a care in the world."

"Seriously?" Jackie asked. "You've probably heard by now what she's been accused of doing."

"I have." Picking up her tea, Serenity took another sip. "I don't understand why she would steal from her job, but more importantly how she could leave her own child."

"I don't get it, either."

Serenity sighed. "The things people do constantly amaze me. How is her little son holding up?"

Again, Jackie blushed, for no reason that she could tell. "He seems good. I watched him for a little bit this morning while his father worked on the ranch. I don't know much about toddlers, but he appears to be a happy little thing."

"And how is Eli doing?"

Face on fire, Jackie pretended a sudden interest in her tea. "He seems good, too."

Serenity sighed. "Be careful what you throw away, my dear. A career won't keep you warm at night."

Jackie snapped her head up. How had she known? Maybe there really was something to this psychic stuff.

Suddenly, desperately, she wanted to ask the older woman for more advice, but she wasn't sure what to say. "I barely know Eli," she began. "But it feels as if we've been together forever."

"That's good, isn't it?" Serenity asked. "Rare, even."

"Maybe. I don't know." Miserable, she met Serenity's serene gaze. "He's my sister's ex-husband. When I came here, I'd convinced myself that he'd hurt or killed her. I couldn't have been more wrong."

"Then what's the issue?" Serenity's tone was gentle. "From what I can tell, your sister doesn't give a rat's ass about what happens to him."

The choice of words made Jackie smile. "Maybe not, though my mother has made it clear she highly disapproves."

Serenity snorted. "Delia has no room to talk. She hasn't entirely treated you well over the years."

Not sure how to respond, Jackie simply shrugged.

"Do you really care what your mother thinks? No judgment here, I promise. But if you're still trying to win her approval now, as an accomplished grown adult, I think that ship has sailed."

This comment made Jackie smile. Serenity's no-

nonsense advice combined with her uncanny psychic abilities was one of the reasons so many people supported her business.

"It's not only that," Jackie admitted. "I live in New York. I have to return when all of this is over."

"Oh." For the first time, Serenity appeared troubled. "I'm sorry. I don't see that. I don't see that at all."

A bit nonplussed herself, Jackie frowned. "What do you mean? You don't see me going back to my life on the east coast?"

The lines in Serenity's face smoothed. "You know what, dear? We all have our own choices to make, our unique paths to follow. Sometimes, my visions are foggy and unclear and I must interpret them as best I can."

Though Jackie wasn't sure what to make of that explanation, she also believed in free will. No matter what anyone said, she made her own choices.

She just wished sometimes they weren't so damn hard to make.

Checking her watch, she was surprised to realize a half hour had passed. "I've got to go," she said, genuinely regretful. "I need to run by the sheriff's office and talk with Rayna."

"I understand." Serenity got up with her and walked her to the door. "Please don't be a stranger. Stop by again."

Promising she would, Jackie got into her rental car and drove the few short blocks to the sheriff's department.

This time no one manned the front desk. Jackie waited a few minutes and then took herself into the back and toward Rayna's office. Since the door stood open, Jackie tapped lightly.

"Jackie!" Rayna looked up from her computer. "What brings you here?"

"I thought I'd check to see if you'd had any success getting a search warrant for Charla's apartment," Jackie said.

"I did. I have people over there right now."

Disappointed, Jackie nodded. "You're not handling this yourself?"

Rayna's gaze sharpened. "I can assure you that my deputies are well trained and well qualified. They'll bring back any evidence they find for me to review."

"I'm sorry. I'm sure they are more than capable." Jackie dropped into one of the chairs. "It's just that I was hoping to go along with you when you searched her place. If my sister left a computer behind, I'd like to offer my assistance at going through it. I'm pretty skilled at that sort of thing. Even if Charla thinks she wiped it clean, I can find whatever she might be trying to hide."

"Really?" Rayna cocked her head, appearing interested. "That's not something anyone in my department can do. If we happened to locate one, I was going to have to send the CPU over to the FBI, which, as you might be aware, could take some time."

"Which we might not have."

"Very true." Considering, Rayna finally nodded. "Let me call and check with my guys. If they did locate a computer, once they've brought it here, I'll give you a call."

"Thanks." Jackie jumped to her feet, disappointed

Rayna hadn't offered to let her meet her people at Charla's. Maybe doing so would compromise the investigation. "I'm hoping we can find Charla before I run out of vacation time. I only had two weeks. I had to buy a round-trip ticket, so I fly back home on Sunday."

Rayna's brows rose. "That's not all that far away. Any chance you can ask for an extension?"

"I might have to try." Jackie thought for a moment. "Even if it's unpaid. My boss is really understanding. But you can see why I seem in a bit of a rush to help. The sooner my sister is located, the better." Even though inside, she truly wanted more time with Eli.

"Completely understandable." Rayna picked up her phone. "Let me call. If Charla did leave a computer behind, I'll have Bill run it over here right now."

Still standing, Jackie thanked her. Listening to Rayna's side of the conversation, it sure sounded as if Charla had left behind a desktop computer. Which was slightly disappointing, since most people these days tended to use their laptop for just about everything. Jackie said as much to Rayna once the sheriff had finished with the call.

"I know. But it's all we have. The rest of the apartment seemed pretty clean. No receipts, no credit card statements, though we haven't had a chance to check her mailbox. She didn't leave behind any jewelry, though she left most of her clothes. I think she was trying to make it look as if she was grabbed, which would go along with the scenario she appears to be attempting to set up."

Jackie nodded. "What will happen once we find her?" she asked.

"She'll be arrested and charged. Depending on how good of an attorney she retains, she'll probably post bail, if a judge allows bail to be set. That might not happen, since certainly, she's a flight risk."

How odd to be speaking of her sister as if she were a criminal. Though technically, she sort of was.

"What kind of prison sentence will she get if she's convicted?"

Rayna shrugged. "That depends on the judge. She's a first-time offender, but the amount of money is astronomical, so there's no way to know. I'd guess at least five years, maybe longer."

Five years. "I can't even picture Charla making it in prison."

"She's a charmer," Rayna responded. "People with her type of personality tend to do well." She indicated the chair Jackie had just vacated. "You might as well sit. It's going to take a few minutes before Bill gets that computer back here. There's a pot of coffee on in the break room if you want some, though I can't guarantee how fresh it might be."

"Thanks, but I'll pass." Jackie grimaced. "I had enough caffeine over at Eli's earlier. I watched Theo for him so he could get some work done. I wonder what he's going to do for a sitter once I'm gone."

Rayna glanced up, her sharp gaze missing nothing. "You two seem to have become close in the short time you've been here."

Not trusting herself to speak, Jackie slowly nodded.

"Eli Pitts is a good man," Rayna continued. "Your sister did a number on him, but he behaved honorably, trying to do what was best for his boy. That's why I never believed, not for one minute, that he'd ever do something to hurt Charla. With all the things she put him through, if he was going to snap, he would have done it long ago."

Not sure how to respond, Jackie looked down at her hands instead.

"Are you okay?" Rayna asked, her voice soft. "I know this entire situation has been stressful. Your mother's behavior hasn't helped, either."

Jackie raised her head. "It has been stressful," she admitted. "Though not because of my mother. She's always been dramatic and distant." Not sure how much more to divulge, she sighed. She liked Rayna and in other circumstances, believed they could be friends. "Things have gotten complicated."

"Because of Eli?"

"You're very perceptive," Jackie said.

"It kind of goes along with the job," Rayna relayed. "Does he feel the same way?"

"I think so." Shaking her head, Jackie corrected. "Actually, I *know* so."

Sitting back in her chair, Rayna regarded her. "What are you going to do?"

"Now, that, I don't know. I'm hoping I'll figure it out soon."

"I'm sure you will." Rayna's phone rang. "Just a second. I need to take this." Answering, she listened for a moment. "Sounds good. I'm on my way."

Hanging up, she pushed to her feet. "I'm sorry, but I have to run out to Charla's apartment. Bill can't bring the computer right now. Something else came up."

Alarmed, Jackie stood, too. "What is it? Can I go with you?"

"Not this time," Rayna responded. "This is an official investigation. I can't let a civilian, never mind a relative, contaminate any possible evidence."

"*Evidence?* As in of another crime?"

"Exactly." Ushering Jackie toward the door, Rayna pursed her lips. "I'll fill you in when I can, but I can't discuss this yet. And when we do get that computer over here, I'll give you a call."

With Theo napping, Eli did a few loads of laundry and some housecleaning. He didn't want to run the vacuum and take the chance of waking his son, but he dusted and swept and mopped the kitchen and bathroom. There were still a million other things he could be doing outside, but he couldn't leave his son unattended. Instead, he went online and ordered a toilet training potty and some toddler training underwear. Might as well make plans to start Theo on that and wean him away from diapers.

Even though Jackie hadn't been gone long, Eli already missed her like crazy. He fought the impulse to call her just to hear her voice, wondering how he'd managed to fall so crazily deep in such a short period of time.

He had it bad.

Filling in time, he passed the rest of the day with other household chores and playing with his son. Theo always woke up grouchy and could only be mollified with fruit or cereal. After he had his snack, his mood always improved.

Eli loved taking care of his boy. He'd actually missed Theo far more than he'd missed Charla when they'd split up. He'd begged her not to take Theo with her when she left, having already gleaned an idea of how she felt about motherhood. But like Delia, Charla was all about appearances, and she knew leaving her son would generate a lot of gossip in town. Now, clearly, that no longer mattered to her.

That evening, as he made dinner, again he considered calling Jackie to see if she wanted to come share the meal. In the end, not wanting to impose any more than he already had, he didn't.

Once the dishes had been done, Theo played in his playpen while Eli watched TV. As soon as Theo started nodding off while still sitting, Eli got him into the bathroom and helped him brush his teeth before changing him into his pajamas. Though he usually bathed the toddler before bed, he decided this time he'd do that in the morning.

Kissing his sleepy son on the cheek, he turned out the lights and went back to the TV. A couple hours later he turned off all the lights and went to bed.

A weird sound, likely a creak in the floorboards or a tree branch scraping the side of the house in the wind, woke him sometime in the middle of the night. He sat up, listening, trying to decide if he could go back to sleep or if there truly might be a cause for alarm.

He really should get a dog, he thought, his thoughts still fuzzy from sleep. A dog would bark, warning him if there was anything actually wrong.

His bedside alarm clock showed 2:13 a.m. Yawning, he waited for the sound to come again. The fact that it didn't alarmed him more than it should. Better go check on Theo, just in case.

He threw back the covers and barefoot, padded down the hall toward his son's room. The past couple of nights, Theo had experienced a few nightmares and woken crying for his mother. Eli had comforted him and ended up letting him sleep in Eli's bed, which seemed to help.

But tonight his son was quiet. Maybe the out-of-place sound he'd heard had been his own imagination.

A rustle of clothing, a movement, made Eli freeze just outside his son's door.

"Gamma?" Theo's high-pitched voice, thick with sleep. And then someone else, whispering, telling his son to be quiet.

What the actual hell? Heart pounding, Eli rushed into the room and flicked on the light. Eyes wide and looking like a deer caught in headlights, Delia stood in front of him, holding Theo protectively in her arms. She glanced left, then right, at the window and back at Eli.

Luckily, he stood between her and the door. Not wanting to alarm his son, Eli kept his voice calm and reasonable.

"What are you doing, Delia? How did you get into my house?"

Instead of appearing sheepish or even ashamed, Delia raised her chin, her expression belligerent. "Charla gave me her key. It's your own fault for not changing the locks."

Carefully moving toward her, Eli lifted his boy out of her arms. He half expected her to resist or try to move away, but she surprisingly released Theo without any fuss.

"I don't want any trouble," Delia said, backing away, her hands raised. Then she shoved past him and sprinted for the door and down the hall. A moment later he heard the sound of her Camaro starting up and realized she'd parked it a bit down the drive, so the noise wouldn't wake him. Stunned, he tried to process what had just happened.

Delia had actually tried to kidnap his son.

Theo made a sound, both bewildered and sleepy. "Gamma?" he asked, gazing up at Eli with his eyes at half-mast. "Dada?"

"I'm right here, Theo," Eli said softly. "Your gamma went home. Are you okay?"

Yawning, Theo appeared to be trying to go back to sleep. Eli gently placed him in his bed, drawing the blanket over him. With a sleepy and trusting smile, Theo closed his eyes all the way. In an instant he'd drifted off.

Eli stood for a moment just watching him, trying to slow his heart rate. Multiple emotions crashed through him—fear and disbelief, but most of all, anger. Undoubtedly, everything Delia had done earlier had been an act. So she could let herself into his house, steal his son and then what? No way would she have been able to keep Theo undetected.

Leaving the room, Eli locked the front door and then braced a kitchen chair up against it for good measure. He'd call a locksmith in the morning. Deliberating a moment, he heaved a sigh and phoned Jackie.

"Hello?" she rasped, obviously, barely awake.

He filled her in on what had just happened. "I wanted to let you know before I called Rayna. Delia's going to be arrested. She went too far this time."

Silence while Jackie digested this. "I agree," she finally said. "But a thought occurs to me. Hear me out and run it by Rayna and see what she thinks. What if Delia was trying to grab Theo and take him to Charla?"

At first, the possibility made no sense. After all, Charla had been the one to run off without her son. He said as much to Jackie.

"Maybe she regrets that," she responded. "It's entirely possible that Charla didn't realize how much she'd miss Theo."

"Possible, but unlikely. He'd put a serious crimp in her style."

"Not if she had a built-in babysitter," Jackie said.

"Delia." Everything clicked into place. "And all that sincerity and love she exhibited earlier was just a show."

"Are you surprised?" Jackie didn't even sound bitter, just certain. "It would have been extremely naive to think my mother could change her entire personality just like that. Yet, we both fell for it, hook, line and sinker."

He ached to be able to hold her. Though she put on a brave front, her mother's continued rejection had to wear at her.

"Go call Rayna," Jackie said. "Though I'm sure she won't be overjoyed to be woken up with this news, she needs to arrest my mother before Delia skips town. Even though she wasn't successful at grabbing Theo, she most likely will still go to Charla."

"I have a better idea," he said slowly. "Delia could lead us to Charla. Maybe Rayna could follow her at a safe distance."

"Or we could." Jackie sounded wide-awake now. "Don't call Rayna. My mother doesn't know what kind of rental car I'm driving. Throw some clothes and stuff in a bag and get Theo ready. I'll swing by and pick you up."

"What if she's already gone?"

"Then we're out of luck. But I have a feeling she went back home to regroup and let Charla know she couldn't get Theo. She'll probably head out soon, though, just in case you send Rayna to arrest her, so we need to hurry."

Though he couldn't help but wonder if this would turn out to be another wild-goose chase like their Big Bend trek, he had to admit Jackie's theory had a certain kind of logic to it. He grabbed enough clothes for a couple days, packed the same amount for Theo, plus diapers. On an afterthought, he packed a few more of the latter. He really needed to start getting Theo potty trained. Carrying the bags to his front door, he went out to his truck and removed the car seat. If they were taking Jackie's vehicle, he'd need to install it in her back seat.

A few minutes later he checked the front window, relieved to see headlights making their way up his drive. She pulled up, got out and gave him a quick hug and then popped her trunk so he could load his bags.

He got the car seat installed and then returned for his boy.

Theo stirred groggily when Eli lifted him from his

bed, but he barely woke, even when Eli strapped him in his car seat. "Do you want to drive first?" she asked. "I thought we could take shifts."

Surprised, he shrugged. "You sound as if you have an idea where we might be going."

"Don't you?" She pushed back her long dark hair with a graceful gesture. "Even if my mother was lying yesterday, I have a feeling she might have been truthful about Charla heading to the Gulf Coast. And while she might have gone to another state, I'm thinking she'd stay in Texas. Now, that could be anywhere, South Padre, Galveston, who knows. I'm sure that's what Charla would be counting on, being able to disappear seamlessly in one of the tourist locales."

"What about Mexico?" he asked. "You don't think she'd look for an opportunity to vanish in a foreign country?"

"Maybe, but not only does she not speak Spanish, but she'd stand out more there. That's why letting Delia lead us to her is our only real hope of finding her."

"That's a lot riding on a hunch," he said. "I still think we should tell Rayna and see what she thinks."

"Fine, call her on the way. We're running out of time. Here." She tossed him the car keys. "You drive first. Let's cruise over to her house. If we're lucky, she's still there."

Getting in her car, he started the engine. He wasn't sure why he believed her scenario. Common sense said Delia would have hit the road the second she'd grabbed Theo. Otherwise, she'd run the risk of having the sheriff's department descend on her to get the toddler back. Either way, an Amber alert would have been issued, and there wouldn't be any place Delia could hide once that went out.

When he said as much to Jackie, she nodded. "I'm sure she and Charla had something planned to deal with such a contingency."

"Maybe, or it's entirely possible that Charla didn't know Delia planned to snatch Theo. That makes more sense. After all, Charla made it clear she was done being a mother." As soon as he voiced the thought, he knew he was right.

"Are you serious?" Jackie stared at him.

"Yes. In fact, I'm positive. Delia acted on her own when she tried to grab my son."

Though she shook her head, Jackie didn't argue the point. He supposed by now, nothing her mother did surprised her.

They pulled up on Delia's street.

"Now what?" he asked, slowing. "Do I kill the lights and park somewhere? Or do you just want to drive by?"

"Just cruise past," she said. "We need to at least get an idea if she's home or not."

To his surprise, though the house appeared dark, Delia's beloved Camaro sat parked in the driveway. He slowed and then parked, killing his headlights but not his engine.

"She is using another car," Jackie insisted, her voice flat. "That customized paint job she has is too darn recognizable. Plus, I know for a fact she always keeps that Camaro parked in her garage. If she left it out, it's because she wants people to think she's home. She's already gone."

"That's a lot of speculation," he pointed out. "Don't you think we should at least make sure?"

"Maybe." She fidgeted in her seat. "But how do we do that? Oh, wait. It's a long shot, but she always used to keep a spare key under that gnome statue in her flower bed, in case she accidentally got locked out. Since she felt free to break into your house, she shouldn't mind if I do the same with hers."

Uneasy, he considered. "I don't like it. I don't want you to put yourself in danger."

"Danger?" she scoffed. "She might be a pain, but she's still my mother. Plus, if she's in there, she won't have any idea that I know what she did. I can come up with some other BS reason for being there."

And then, without waiting for him to agree, Jackie slipped out of the car and strode up the front sidewalk toward Delia's house.

Chapter 13

Though Jackie had pretended to be cool, calm and collected, in reality her heart was tripping in her chest like a mini jackhammer. Delia wouldn't take too kindly to her intrusion if Jackie happened to be wrong.

Luckily, the streetlight helped illuminate parts of the front yard. She located the little stone gnome she remembered from her childhood and lifted it. Sure enough, a spare key sat in the dirt underneath.

Turning, she flashed Eli the thumbs-up sign and then went to the front door. As a precaution, she went ahead and rang the doorbell, listening as the chimes echoed through the small house.

Then, before using the key, she took out her phone and called her mother. The call went straight to voice mail and she left a message. "Hey, Mom. Just wanting to touch base with you. I couldn't sleep, and I thought you might be up worrying, too. Call me when you can."

That done, she used the key, unlocked the front door and slipped inside.

Though she tried to move as quietly as possible, her footsteps seemed to echo in the too-silent house. She went from room to room, moving slowly but carefully, saving her mother's bedroom for last.

As she'd suspected, the house was empty. In her mother's room, the bed sat neatly made, though the closet door stood open. Checking that, Jackie saw evidence of missing clothing, items grabbed off hangers that now hung askew.

She'd been right. Delia had switched cars and run. Jackie's quick surge of triumph was followed by the crushing knowledge that she'd been too late.

After locking up, she replaced the key under the gnome and returned to Eli and Theo. A quick glance revealed the baby still slept. Keeping her voice low, she recounted everything she'd seen.

"Time to let Rayna know," Eli said, already pulling out his phone. "Though I hate to wake her, this is something she definitely needs to be aware of."

Jackie listened as he filled Rayna in. By the time he'd finished with the fact that they were sitting outside Delia's house, Jackie figured the sheriff had to be wide-awake.

"Sure. We can do that," Eli said, ending the call. He turned to Jackie, grimacing. "She wants us to meet her at the sheriff's department in twenty minutes."

This made Jackie perk up. "I wonder if she finally

got Charla's computer. She promised to let me have a crack at it."

"In the middle of the night?" Eli asked.

"Sure, why not? I mean, she probably intended to call me in the morning, but with everything that's happened so far, it couldn't hurt. At least we might be able to get an idea where they might have gone."

Hearing herself, Jackie couldn't help but marvel at how quickly things had changed. She'd returned to Getaway thinking her sister's life was in danger. Now that same sister was on the run from the law.

"One thing still doesn't add up," she said out loud. "Why did Charla send me that text? She didn't want anything to do with me for the last three years. Why involve me now?"

Shifting into Drive, he kept his foot on the brake. "Because she was trying to engineer an elaborate setup to make it appear as if she'd been murdered. She figured your presence in town would help push that story along."

They pulled out onto the street, driving past the town's only all-night gas station and mini-mart. Jackie glanced over, spotting one customer in the blinding lights, walking from the building to her black pickup truck parked at the gas pumps.

Her heart skipped a beat. "Eli," she said, still low voiced, "I just saw Delia getting gas back there. She's driving a black pickup. You need to pull a slow U-turn so we can see which way she goes."

Eli immediately complied, without asking a single question. They were almost at the station when she spotted the pickup pulling out, luckily traveling in the same direction they were now heading.

"There." She pointed. "I wonder where she got that truck. I hope she doesn't notice us. It's not like there's a lot of other traffic out this time of the morning."

Intent on driving, he kept a fair amount of distance between them and Delia. "That'll change once we get to the interstate. I think she'll take I-20 east and then some of the smaller routes south, most likely US87 if I remember right. Either way she's got to go through San Antonio. Once she gets there, it'll depend where on the coast she's headed as to what route she chooses."

True to his prediction, Delia took the entrance ramp onto I-20. They followed. Jackie was glad to see the increase in traffic, even though it mostly seemed to be eighteen-wheelers.

They'd gone about five miles when Eli cursed under his breath. "We forgot about Rayna."

"I'll call her really quick and tell her what's going on," Jackie volunteered. "Once we get a better feel for where Delia's headed, maybe Rayna can call the police there and give them a heads-up."

"Maybe." Eli glanced at her, still keeping a fair amount of distance between them and the black pickup. "But I'm thinking Rayna's not going to be happy about this."

"You might be right, but I don't see what else we could have done," Jackie argued. "If we'd gone to meet Rayna, we would have missed the opportunity to follow Delia. At the very least, we know what kind of vehicle she's driving."

"I agree," Eli finally said. "Though Rayna might not see it the same way."

"Probably not." Jackie considered. "But the end result is what really matters, right?"

"Maybe. Except we don't work in law enforcement. That's going to be Rayna's big sticking point."

Turning her phone over in her hands, Jackie shrugged. "Right now all we're doing is following my mother. We're not committing a crime."

"True. You're stalling. Why?"

With a sigh, she admitted the truth. "I want to make sure we're far enough out that Rayna can't catch up to us. If Delia were to get one hint that anyone—especially the sheriff—was onto her, there's no way she's going anywhere near Charla."

This made him laugh. A startled bark of laughter, but not the reaction she'd expected. "What?" she asked. "What's so funny?"

"You think of everything." He changed lanes, passing a slow-moving semi before dropping back into the middle lane, keeping a couple of vehicles between them and Delia. "I never once considered that Rayna might want to follow us or take over the pursuit."

For whatever reason, this observation pleased her. "I edit a lot of romantic-suspense novels," she said. "I guess I kind of have a feel for how this sort of thing works."

Again, he laughed, the rich, masculine sound making her smile.

"Go ahead and call Rayna," he said. "By now she's probably wondering where the hell we are."

As if on cue, his phone rang. Keeping his eyes on

the road, he passed it over to Jackie. "Looks like she saved you the trouble."

Making a face, she answered.

"Where are you?" Rayna demanded. "I'm not a fan of coming into work in the middle of the night unless absolutely necessary."

"Following Delia," Jackie replied. "We were on the way to meet you when we happened to spot her at the Quick Gas station. She's driving a black pickup. I have no idea where she got it or who it belongs to."

Rayna went silent, clearly processing this. "Why?" she finally asked. "What are you hoping to learn?"

"We think she's going to lead us to Charla."

"But she didn't get the baby," Rayna said. "Why would Delia go to Charla since she failed?"

Jackie explained Eli's theory that Delia had acted on her own, trying to grab Theo.

"That makes more sense," Rayna agreed. "Since Charla clearly doesn't want her son."

For whatever reason, Jackie felt compelled to defend her sister. "She could have changed her mind, you never know."

Eli shook his head at that, but didn't comment.

"Anyway," Jackie continued, "we think Delia is headed to the coast. Where exactly, we don't know. But we're hoping she's going to join Charla."

Eli chimed in here. "We'll know more depending on which direction she goes once we reach San Antonio. I agree with Jackie. Delia is going to join Charla."

"Either that, or she decided to take a quick vacation after what she did," Rayna said. "Though that's unlikely, it's entirely possible. Just don't let her see you and stay safe. Keep me posted."

Jackie agreed and ended the call. She looked out the window, realizing sunrise was still several hours away. Glancing at Eli, concentrating on the road and maintaining a respectable distance between them and Delia, she felt a rush of emotion and immediately tamped it down.

"Whichever way Delia chooses, it's going to be a long drive," Jackie commented. "I hope you packed accordingly."

"I can always buy more if we need it," he responded. "There never seems to be enough diapers, so I figured I'd need to get more at some point."

"Like if we need a potty break?" Jackie asked.

He grimaced. "That's the thing. Since she left in the middle of the night, I figure Delia intends to complete the drive without stopping much to rest. But I'm thinking she'll have to stop sometime to use the restroom."

"True." Jackie nodded.

"She'll have to refuel at some point," he continued. "And so will we. That's going to be the tricky part. We can't use the same station to fill up since we'll run the risk of her seeing us. And if we use another place, there's always a chance we could lose her."

Jackie sighed. "We'll have to be careful," she agreed. "But if she uses one of those super stations, we could be at one end with her at the other and she'd never see us."

They made good time, reaching San Antonio shortly after seven, which meant they'd get through before rush hour got fully underway. Once they hit the loop, she took I-10 toward Houston.

"At least we'll miss the worst part of morning traffic," Eli said. "We should get to Houston around ten or ten thirty. Though traffic is going to be bad no matter what."

"She's going to Galveston," Jackie speculated. "It's a straight shot down from Houston."

"What are we going to do once we get there?" he asked quietly. "We aren't cops, so we can't just bust in wherever Delia is holed up and arrest her. And since Theo is with us, there's no way I'm letting her get anywhere near him."

"Good question," Jackie replied. "I'm thinking we call Rayna and have her alert Galveston PD. It's too convoluted a story for us to try and explain it to them."

Shortly after they reached Houston and heavy traffic, her boss called. Jackie answered with more than a little trepidation.

"Just checking in with you," Prudence said. "Your two-week vacation is almost over and I thought I'd see how things were going."

"We still haven't found my sister," Jackie admitted. "But we're getting really close." She took a deep breath and then decided she might as well bring it up now. "In fact, I might need to extend my time off. I'll need another week, though two would be optimal. I would be using up my vacation and personal days. After that, I could take a leave of absence if necessary. Or I can work remotely, if you'd allow that. But I really don't want to leave until Charla is located and everything is settled here."

Eli glanced at her when she said that. She made a face at him and waited to hear what her boss would say.

Prudence's extended silence sent a prickle of unease up Jackie's spine. "I'm not sure that's going to be possible, though we'll definitely try to figure it out," Prudence finally said. "I'll check with Lennon and get his thoughts, but with those two big book series coming up, we need all hands on deck, so to speak. Our department is already shorthanded, as you know. And it's unfair to shift your workload off to another editor who is already overloaded." She sighed. "You know we'll do our best to help you out. I hope you sister is found soon."

Heart pounding, Jackie tried to think of something to say. As senior editor, Prudence Jones had been the one to hire her. She'd been a great mentor and boss and completely understood how badly Jackie had wanted this job.

Still wanted it, right? Of course she did. Except suddenly, she wasn't sure. Head spinning, she reminded herself she didn't need to make a major decision right this instant.

"Thank you," Jackie replied quietly. "I've still got a few more days left on my vacation. Hopefully, my sister will be found before then."

"Agreed. But if she's not? What will you do then?"

Jackie didn't want to lie. "I'm not sure. But I promise, I'll let you know. In the meantime, send me some work. I'll get as much done as possible."

"I appreciate that." Prudence paused. "I'll need your decision as soon as possible."

After ending the call, Jackie tried not to hyperventilate. She was about to lose her job. Her *dream* job. She still had time left on her leased shared apartment, a tiny bedroom full of her own furniture and a life she loved back in New York City.

While here… She closed her eyes. She could honestly see herself making a life with Eli and Theo on his ranch. Assuming he wanted that, too.

But what would she do for a job? She'd worked hard to get her degree, and she'd set her sights on eventually getting promoted from assistant editor to editor. She knew if she continued to excel, she'd eventually get it.

And what about Charla? Jackie's sole reason for even being here in Getaway. Her head spun. Her sister had turned out to be someone utterly different from the person Jackie remembered. From all appearances, she'd not only lied to her husband, mother and friends, but also abandoned her son, stolen from her employer and was now what? Planning to fake her own death so she could disappear with her stolen money? How crazy was that?

Her stomach churned. She was about to find her sister, end this crazy charade. Then she'd have some hard decisions to make. She didn't want to give up her job, but conversely, how could she say goodbye to Eli?

Conscious of him quietly sitting beside her as he drove, she felt lucky he didn't press her with questions. She appreciated him giving her space. Since he'd heard her side of the conversation, she figured he had a pretty good idea what the call had been about.

Turning her face to look out the window, she felt too stressed to even cry. This—the search for Charla, the reason she'd come back to Getaway in the first place—was almost over. Before nightfall she guessed her sister would be arrested, maybe her mother, too, depending on if Eli pressed charges.

And then what? Shake hands with Eli and return to her former life, trying to pretend nothing had happened, that this man hadn't upended her world as she knew it?

What were her options here? Go home and work and fly back on the weekends to try and spend time with him? She didn't really have the funds for that kind of thing. She suspected he didn't, either.

"Are you all right?" Eli asked quietly.

Without looking at him, she nodded. "I'm fine," she replied. It was the first and only time she'd ever outright lied to him.

One thing Eli knew for a fact was that Jackie was *not* fine, no matter what she said. Though she tried to hide it, the sudden stiffness to her posture, the way she kept her face averted and the odd hitch to her breathing told him she struggled to keep her emotions under control.

Judging by what he could hear of the phone call she'd taken, she'd been told to either return to her job or lose it. What he couldn't figure out was why that upset her. It wasn't as if such news could have come as a surprise. And as far as timing went, it would appear as if that had worked out, as well.

Undeniably, this thing with Charla was about to wrap up. Her sister would be located unharmed, and handed over into police custody. He hadn't decided yet whether or not he wanted to press charges against Delia for breaking into his house and attempting to kidnap his son, but he probably would. That woman, like her daughter Charla, needed to understand there were consequences to her actions. He only hoped Jackie could understand and accept his decision. Because even if he never saw her again, he cared about her and how she regarded him.

A quick glance in his rearview mirror showed Theo still slept. Riding in the car always lulled him to sleep, though Eli was surprised he remained that way for so long.

Jackie caught him watching his son and smiled. "He's a good little traveler," she said. "You're so lucky."

Right now, in this instant, this moment in time, he felt lucky. The two people he cared the most about were with him in this car, his ranch had begun to be successful and life truly appeared to be looking up. If only Jackie wasn't going to be leaving soon.

The instant he caught himself longing for something he couldn't have, he pushed the thought away. He had no choice but to take this time with her as it came and try to let her go without regrets. Charla's mysterious disappearance was about to be solved, and soon he could resume his life. With Theo, but without Jackie.

As they drove across the causeway that took them to Galveston Island, he eyed the bright blue water, wondering why he didn't feel more of a sense of closure.

Glancing at the beautiful, kind and sexy woman who continued to gaze out the window, lost in her thoughts, he knew he had to let himself acknowledge that the thing that had developed between them had likely come to an end, as well. She'd be gone by the time the weekend ended, and most likely would never look back.

The aching sense of loss such a thought brought felt staggering. The idea of never seeing Jackie again, hearing her voice, seemed unfathomable. Yet, she either had to return to New York or lose her job. He already knew which one she'd choose. She'd made no bones about that from the first moment they'd gotten together. He just hadn't expected it to hurt this much.

Briefly, he entertained the idea of following her to New York, though he had no idea what he'd do there. Plus, he didn't want to raise his son in the hustle and bustle of a northern city. Theo had been born a Texan and would be raised a Texan. Just like Eli had been, and his father before him.

Focus, he reminded himself. Focus on the present. There were still two cars between Delia's truck and theirs. So far she'd given no indication that she knew she was being followed.

As they entered Galveston proper, instead of going to one of the many motels, hotels or condos, Delia drove to a large restaurant and bar located on Seawall Boulevard called The Spot. The impressive building with lots of glass and wood had open-air seating and views of the gulf. The lunch crowd had just started arriving, and the parking lot was not yet crowded, though he suspected it would be soon.

Delia parked her truck, got out and disappeared inside the restaurant.

"Odd," Jackie mused. "I would have thought they'd meet up at Charla's hotel room."

"I'm guessing Delia is hungry," Eli replied. "She didn't eat much on the drive down."

Her stomach chose that moment to growl, reminding them both that they hadn't eaten, either.

The sound made Eli chuckle, breaking up the gravity of the moment. And now that they were no longer driving, Theo woke up and began crying.

"He probably needs a diaper change," Eli said. "For right now let me give him some juice and a snack." He rummaged in his pack, locating both and passed them back to his son. Then, while Theo contentedly ate and drank, Eli turned back to Jackie.

"You're so good with him," she couldn't help but comment.

This appeared to surprise him. "He's my son," he replied.

"As if that explains everything," she said.

"Doesn't it?"

A slow smile spread across her face. "You know what? In a way, I suppose it does."

He wanted to kiss her then, but he resisted. Neither of them needed any distractions right now, and he knew how quickly a simple press of their mouths together could fan the flames. Would he ever get used to this constant ache for her? He wondered how long it would take to abate once she left.

"What do we do now?" she asked, gesturing toward the restaurant, clearly unaware of his thoughts. "Obviously, we can't stroll on in there and grab a bite to eat."

"Sit tight and let me call Rayna. She'll let us know how she wants us to proceed."

She nodded. "Okay."

Eli put the phone on speaker and made the call. When Rayna came on the line, she sounded both tired and relieved. He quickly filled her in.

"Do not go inside the restaurant," Rayna ordered, once he'd finished talking. "I'll notify Galveston PD, but you need to let them handle it. We don't even know for sure that Charla is inside. And if she is, they generally prefer not to make arrests in crowded public places."

"Then maybe we should wait to call them," Jackie interjected. "A large police presence will definitely scare Charla off."

"How about this?" Rayna suggested. "I alert them and we'll see how they want to handle things. I don't want you two getting any further involved. I'll call you back and keep you posted."

After Rayna had ended the call, he and Jackie exchanged looks.

"How about you sit here and watch for them and I'll go get us something to eat," she said.

"Where?" Looking up and down Seawall Boulevard, he didn't see any other restaurants within a quick walking distance.

"In there." She pointed to The Spot. "The place is packed now. Surely, they have a take-out counter or something. If not, I can always go into the bar and order something to go."

"No." He immediately discounted that plan. "It's too risky. Delia or Charla might see you."

"I'll be careful," she said. "Really. Aren't you starving?"

"I am, but not enough to risk everything. I packed a bunch of snacks for Theo. How about we eat something from there? It should be enough to hold us over until we can grab a real meal."

She sighed, but finally gave a reluctant nod. He reached into the back seat and grabbed his backpack, extracting a box of assorted breakfast bars. "Chocolate chip or strawberry?"

"Chocolate chip please."

They munched on those, plus a handful of trail mix he'd brought. He'd even had the foresight to pack several plastic bottles of water, though they weren't ice-cold.

"Wow. You thought of everything," she said, smiling.

A police cruiser pulled into the parking lot. Swearing under his breath, Eli froze. "I was hoping they'd wait."

"Me, too." Jackie shook her head. "I'm thinking it might be okay. When they walk into the restaurant, neither Delia nor Charla will have an idea they've come for them. I mean, police officers eat lunch, too."

Watching as the police cruiser parked, Eli shook his head. "I wonder if they're going to make the arrest inside. If so, I really wish we could see it."

"Me, too," she said. "I'm half-tempted to slip inside and watch for myself. I know, I know." This as he started to speak. "I won't. For all we know, those officers might be here to eat lunch."

A few minutes after the first two officers went inside, a second police car pulled into the parking lot.

"Either this place is popular with law enforcement for lunch, or they called for backup."

In the back seat, Theo had grown restless. Squirming and asking to be out of the car seat. Eli found one of Theo's favorite games on his tablet and handed it to him. He didn't like to let his son spend too much time playing with electronics, but if ever a situation called for a distraction, this one did.

When the second pair of police officers got out of their car, they didn't go inside. Instead, they stood near the entrance, one on either side. They didn't have their weapons drawn or anything, but they appeared intent.

"Waiting there in case someone tries to make a run for it?" Jackie ventured.

He shrugged. "Maybe. Who knows?"

Watching and waiting for something to happen felt anticlimactic. While he knew the takedown probably wouldn't be dramatic, like something from a TV show, he'd definitely expected things to move a little faster.

Finally, after what seemed like a long time, the first two officers emerged and conferred with the second pair.

"Where's Delia?" Jackie asked. "And Charla? I figured they'd come out with those two in custody."

Confused and more than a little concerned, he shook his head. "No idea. Maybe the first two officers really did just go there to eat. Is it possible they have no idea Charla and Delia are inside?"

Chapter 14

Jackie had never been a patient sort of person. It took every ounce of self-control she had to keep herself from getting out of the car and striding over to question the police officers. But she knew if they were waiting for Charla and Delia to emerge, the sight of her would definitely jeopardize the actual arrest. This entire situation felt surreal. Sitting in a rental car in a seaside parking lot, the cheerful sounds of a toddler's game playing in the back seat, waiting for her sister and her mother to be arrested.

"The suspense is killing me," she mused out loud. "Are the police really going to just stand around and wait for them to come out?"

Arm on the back of the seat, Eli faced her. "It looks that way. They probably don't want to cause a huge disruption inside the restaurant, so they're planning to nab them when they leave. And if you think about it, they haven't been in there long enough to have a meal."

He had a point. Especially since Charla and her mother had a lot of catching up to do. Not surprisingly, she felt a twinge of pain at the thought. On the flight west from La Guardia, she'd envisioned an eventual joyful reunion between her sister and her. To be fair, she'd also seen herself in the same role she'd always played, swooping in to save Charla. Now she'd gradually come to realize that her baby sister had become an adult and had to bear responsibility for her poor choices. It just wasn't easy to watch.

Theo made a sound from the back. She turned and realized he was still intent on his game. Such a cutie, his curly blond hair and bright blue eyes fixed on the tablet, his little tongue peeking out one corner of his mouth.

"How could she leave him?" she wondered softly. "I just don't understand it."

"I don't, either," Eli admitted. "She fought me for custody, claiming he belonged with his mother. When she won, I watched her as she continued to party every single weekend, even the ones where she had him. It just about killed me. My only consolation was that she seemed to love him. At least in front of me, she doted on him."

Heartbreaking.

"Look." Eli pointed, his voice hushed. "Something is happening."

The first two officers stepped in front of two people while the second pair slipped in behind them. Though

Jackie sat up straight and tried to see, due to all the movement, she couldn't make out either her mother or sister.

"They're arresting them." Pain tinged Eli's deep voice.

Just then, the police moved enough for her to see he was right. Charla and Delia stood, expressions shocked, unresisting while they were handcuffed. Jackie assumed they were also being read their rights.

"What do we do now?" she finally asked, not bothering to hide how shaken all of this made her.

"I'm calling Rayna." Eli already had his phone out. "She wanted to be updated."

Numb, she watched while her sister and mother were marched over to two separate police cars and loaded inside. Meanwhile, Eli told Rayna everything that had happened.

"Ask her if I'm allowed to go see Charla," Jackie interjected. "I'd like to talk to her now if possible." Damned if she wanted to go back to Getaway with no idea of how long it would be before Charla made it back. Especially since Jackie had a plane to catch this coming weekend.

"Thanks, Rayna." Eli ended the call. "She says to go by the Galveston police station and ask. They might make you wait until she's been booked in and transferred to the jail, but at least you'll know."

Tears inexplicably stinging her eyes, she nodded. "Thanks. I really don't want to leave Galveston without seeing her."

Gently, he squeezed her shoulder. "I understand. If

it's going to be a few hours, I really want to show Theo the beach and the ocean."

When the two squad cars pulled out of the parking lot, Eli swung into place behind them, following them to the police station. Once there, they parked and watched as once again Charla and Delia, still cuffed, were led inside.

Jackie got out of the car slowly, her heart beating rapidly. She had no idea what to expect, seeing her sister for the first time in three years, under such circumstances. She suspected she knew how her mother would react, and then realized she really didn't care. She'd come back to Getaway for her sister, and now they'd finally get the chance to talk.

"Are you ready for this?" Eli asked, lifting Theo from the car seat. "Oh, wait. I need to change him." He laid his son on the back seat and made quick work of changing the diaper.

Once again, Jackie found herself awed by his quiet competence. Something of her thoughts must have shown on her face, because when he glanced at her, her shook his head and grinned. "Single dads have to learn how to do this stuff, you know," he said. "It's really not a big deal."

Now that Theo had been changed, Eli hoisted him up on one hip. "Though I really want to ask her why she was setting me up in her fake murder thing, I think I'm going to wait with Theo in the waiting area. I'm not sure how I feel about him seeing Charla and then having to be taken away from her."

Though she nodded, because she got it, she really did, another part of her ached for her little nephew and what he was going through. Theo had no idea what his mother had done. He loved her, the way all innocents did, and would no doubt cry for her if he caught sight of her. "No sense in putting him through that," she agreed quietly. "Especially since he wouldn't even begin to understand why he had to leave her again."

Surprise flickered across his expression, though he hid it quickly. She guessed he hadn't been expecting her to agree with him. Once, she wouldn't have. Now she was no longer on Charla's side.

Walking inside, Jackie resisted the urge to clutch Eli's hand. Little Theo looked around him with interest, his bright blue gaze inquisitive. "Mama?" he asked, his high voice hopeful. "Mama."

Eli cursed under his breath. The shattered look on his face matched the way hearing her nephew's plaintive voice made her feel. Once again, she found herself wondering how her sister could do this to her own child.

Shaking off her emotions, she marched over to the front desk and let the woman know why she'd come.

"This is highly unusual," the older woman said with a frown. "But I'll let them know. Why don't you have a seat and someone will be with you shortly."

After thanking her, Jackie returned to Eli and Theo. "Hopefully, they'll let me see her," she said.

"I think they will," he replied. "If not, you can always call Rayna and ask her to intervene."

She nodded. The idea of having come all this way, gone through all she had in her search for her sister and then having to fly back to New York without seeing or talking to her seemed unthinkable.

"Ms. Burkholdt?" A uniformed officer called her name. "You can come on back with me. Since your sister is going to be here until transport arrives to take her back to your local jurisdiction, I see no reason why you can't speak with her and your mother. Your sheriff explained your particular circumstances." With that, the officer glanced at Eli and Theo.

"We'll wait here," Eli said. "I really have nothing to say to either of them."

"I really just need to see my sister," Jackie said. "If that's all right with you."

"Certainly. You were going to have to see one at a time anyway as we're keeping them separated."

Following the officer, Jackie took deep breaths, trying to maintain some semblance of composure. Three years had passed since her sister had cut her out of her life, and surely, the person Charla had become bore no resemblance to the baby sister Jackie remembered. She still loved her fiercely, of course—love didn't die simply because of someone's bad choices. She just wasn't sure what to expect.

"You're going to have to speak with her with glass separating you," the officer said, stopping outside a heavy-duty door with a card key lock. "A guard will be present with her at all times and your visit will be limited to twenty minutes. There are phones you can use to communicate. Do you have any questions?"

Taking a deep breath, Jackie shook her head. She waited while the guard unlocked the door and stepped back, motioning her into the room.

A single plastic chair sat in front of a battered Formica counter, with a dirty glass partition that went all the way to the ceiling. Charla sat on the other side, unsmiling.

Still standing, Jackie took in her baby sister. She still looked the same, though she'd evidently spent a lot of time in the sun, judging by the rich tan color of her skin. She stared at Jackie, her blue eyes cold.

Picking up the phone, not sure what to say, Jackie dropped into the chair. She waited until her sister did the same. "Charla. I'm glad you're all right."

"Are you?" Voice dripping with disdain, Charla scrunched her face exactly the way she used to do as a child. "From what Mom's been telling me, you've taken up with Eli. Is that true? Are you sleeping with my ex?"

"I got your text," Jackie said softly instead of answering. "I dropped everything, took my vacation and flew home. I was worried sick about you—and your son. I demanded the sheriff's department open an investigation, interviewed your friends and coworkers and accused Eli of hurting you."

"That's exactly what you were supposed to do," Charla said, sneering. "What went wrong? My saintly ex-husband couldn't keep it in his pants?"

Again, Jackie ignored her. "Then I learn you were not only having an affair with Mr. Levine, but you embezzled and stole from his store."

Expression unchanged, Charla shrugged. "Your point?"

"Why?"

Now Charla leaned forward, her voice fierce. "Christopher owed me that money. For years, starting when I was too young to know better, he took advantage of me. He kept promising he'd leave his wife, and I believed him. It wasn't until I wised up and told him it had to stop that I started taking money. A little here, a little there."

"Half a million dollars, Charla. That's a lot."

Charla's mouth twisted. "Listen to you, Miss Holier-Than-Thou. You got out. You got away. And you left me there to rot in that Podunk little town."

Shocked, Jackie gripped the phone. She wasn't even sure how to respond to that. She'd urged her sister to finish high school, go to college, in short, to follow a similar path as she had.

"I knew you'd show up when I sent you the text," Charla continued. "The guilt over abandoning me must have been eating you alive. So imagine my surprise when Mom told me you've been fooling around with Eli."

"Your ex-husband," Jackie pointed out, still reeling from Charla's earlier comment. "The one you tried to set up for your fake murder."

"He deserved that," Charla said, lifting her chin. "He broke his promise to me. When we married, he swore to stay by my side no matter what."

Not sure how to react to that, Jackie sighed. "I thought you were the one who asked for the divorce since you didn't want to be married anymore. Plus, you had all these guys on the side…"

"That was all a test of his loyalty."

It began to dawn on Jackie that her sister had become a complete narcissist. Heck, she'd probably been that way all along and Jackie had been too blind to see. "I understand. What about Theo? How could you just leave your son like that?"

Charla shrugged. "Motherhood isn't really for me. I don't have the time or the patience to deal with a kid."

"Then why did you fight for custody?"

"I had a couple of reasons," Charla replied, her lip curling. "One, I wanted to keep Eli under my thumb. I knew he really took being a father seriously. The other was Getaway itself. You know how people gossip in that town. It would have looked terrible if I'd given up custody of my own child. They would have turned up their noses at me."

In Charla's world, everything was about her.

"What about stealing from Levine's? You know Mr. Levine pressed charges for both the money and the diamonds. You know you'll probably go to prison for that, right?"

"Prison?" Charla laughed, amazingly carefree. "That's all a misunderstanding. Christopher and I were in on this together, so it wasn't stealing. He was going to leave his wife and meet me in the Bahamas. Setting it up to make it look as if I was a thief was all his idea."

"I hope you have proof," Jackie pointed out. "Because that sounds weak even to me."

Charla shrugged. "It'll all work out in the end for me. It always does."

"Mom's in trouble, too, you know. She tried to snatch Theo out of his bedroom at Eli's house. Eli walked in on her and stopped her."

For the first time Charla appeared surprised. "What? Why would she do that? I certainly didn't ask her to."

"I don't know. Maybe because she loves her grandson." Though in all probability, Delia had felt Theo needed to be with his mother.

"Mom is a fool." Charla shook her head. "She's more like you than I realized." With that, she hung up the phone on her side of the partition, indicating to the guard that she wanted her visit to be over.

Still holding her own phone, Jackie sat frozen and watched as her sister was escorted out.

"Ms. Burkholdt?" One of the guards had opened the door. "Are you all right?"

Slowly, Jackie replaced the phone in its cradle and got to her feet. "I'm fine," she answered, though in reality she still tried to make sense of the entire conversation she'd just had.

Following the guard back to the waiting area, her chest tight, she tried to force a smile for Eli though she knew he'd see right through her.

As she approached, he stood, shifting Theo from his lap back to his hip. "Come on," he said, taking her arm. "Let's get out of here. I think it's time to grab something to eat and then take a walk on the beach. Let's show Theo the ocean and see what he thinks."

Eli kept up a steady stream of chatter as he walked out to Jackie's rental car. She hadn't been able to hide her shock and devastation, though she'd clearly tried. He waited until they were in the car and driving to find a parking spot on the seawall near a restaurant before he brought up what had just happened.

"Are you okay?" he asked, checking on Theo in the rearview.

Jackie shrugged. "I never really understood that my sister was a textbook narcissist. Everything is about her.

She honestly thinks she can get out of the embezzlement and theft charges with more lies. I wish her luck."

Ahead, a small sports car pulled out. Feeling lucky, Eli got the space. "Here we are," he said. "This isn't as crowded as it would be if we went to one of the beaches. There's just enough sand and waves for us to walk."

"Do you mind if we eat first?" Jackie asked. "That restaurant is close."

"Food, then beach," he replied. "Sounds good."

Clearly still lost in thought, Jackie nodded and got out. He wanted to ask what Charla had said to her, but figured if she wanted him to know, she'd say so. He got Theo out of the car seat and carrying him, walked with Jackie over to the restaurant, a place called Miller's Seawall Grill. Since it was in between the lunch and dinner rush, they didn't have to wait and were shown to a table on the outdoor patio with a view of the sea.

The ocean looked peaceful, perfect waves rolling gently in, the bright sunlight making the blue water sparkle. Jackie appeared to notice none of it, still mulling over her conversation from back in the jail.

"Don't let her get in your head," he said instead. "You came all this way to help her. Nothing she says can take that away from you."

"I know." Blinking, she smiled at him. "I hope the food is good here. I'm seriously starving."

The waitress came over, bringing menus. "Do you have good burgers?" Jackie asked without even opening hers.

"We do," the young woman answered, smiling.

"I'll have a cheeseburger and fries." Eyeing Eli,

who'd grabbed the menu, looking for the kid section, she smiled. "Do you have hot dogs on the kids' menu?"

"We do. They come with fries or macaroni and cheese."

"Fries," Eli put in. "And I'll have the bacon cheese-burger."

They also ordered tea. Once the waitress moved away, Eli shook his head and laughed. "You're a little impatient there, aren't you?"

Appearing not the least bit contrite, she made a face, wrinkling her cute nose. "I'm sorry. It's been forever since I've eaten and I'm a little bit cranky. I get like that if I let it go too long between meals."

"I'll have to remember to keep that in mind," he said before he thought better of it. He found himself wondering if this would be the last meal he shared with her before she left. Surely not. Though now that she'd seen her sister, she really had no more reason to stay.

"Did Charla ask about her son?" he asked, pretty sure he already knew the answer.

Glancing from him to Theo, Jackie slowly shook her head. "Everything was a means to an end as far as she's concerned. A baby becomes a bargaining tool in her world. And from what I could tell, she expected you to be her doting sidekick no matter what she did. She even went so far as to blame me for her own poor choices. She regards me leaving town as the ultimate betrayal, which is why she hadn't spoken to me ever since I left."

He hated seeing the raw pain in her eyes. "Unfortunately, none of that comes as the slightest surprise to me," he said.

Jackie leaned forward, her gaze intense. "If you knew what she was like, why'd you marry her? Did you think you could change her?"

The waitress brought their drinks, promising their food would be out soon, and then left.

Eli gave Jackie's question the careful consideration it deserved. "I've wondered that myself recently," he admitted. "You know that old saying *love is blind*? I thought I loved her and I really believed she loved me back. Clearly, I ignored the warning signs that were there in the beginning. When she got pregnant with Theo, honestly, I was really happy. I figured a baby might just be what she needed to finally settle down. I was wrong."

Jackie's troubled gaze met his. "How do you know when love is real?" she asked quietly. "It might all be smoke and mirrors. You could be risking your heart. So how do you know, Eli? How can you be sure you won't make that same mistake again?"

This might be the most important question she'd ever asked him. He needed to think carefully on how to frame his response.

Except he didn't want to. Instead, he answered from the heart. "Sometimes you just have to take that chance. We all have our own ideas about what love is, but for me it's more than physical. It's when you're attracted to more than just that person's brain, or their beauty, and when all you want to do is make them happy."

Her eyes got huge as she stared at him.

Aware he might have just revealed far too much about his feelings, he looked down. Luckily, the waitress chose that moment to arrive with their food.

Theo seemed thrilled to see his hot dog, refusing to allow Eli to help him eat. He did a good job of dipping his fries in ketchup, though more of it seemed to end up on his face and hands than in his mouth.

Smiling, Jackie leaned over and wiped Theo's little face with her napkin, making him grin as he happily continued to eat.

Only then did Jackie dig in to her own meal.

It struck him then that this was the sort of thing parents did—put their child's needs ahead of their own. Jackie was only Theo's aunt, but she cared enough to take care of Theo first. Eli recognized that he did that instinctively on a regular basis but Charla never had. Everything in dealing with her son appeared to irritate or inconvenience her. How could one sister be so different from the other?

As he slowly ate his burger and watched Jackie alternate between devouring hers and helping Theo, he realized he truly loved her. Not the superficial infatuation he'd felt for Charla, but a deep and certain love.

That love was the reason he wouldn't tell her how he felt. He knew how badly she wanted to return to New York, how happy her job and her life there made her. Loving someone meant not being selfish, but wanting the best for them even if it meant letting her go and breaking his own heart.

They finished the meal, Theo eating most of his hot dog and half his fries. The waitress cleared the table and left the check. Heart aching, Eli watched as Jackie cleaned his little boy's face and dropped a quick kiss on the top of Theo's head.

Somehow, he forced himself to smile. After leaving cash on the table to cover the bill and the tip, he reached for his son. But Theo leaned away, holding up his arms to Jackie.

Jackie laughed, unbuckling him from the child seat and lifting him in her arms. "Do you mind?" she asked, meeting Eli's gaze and making him wonder if something had shown on his face.

"Of course not," he said. "But let me know if he gets too heavy."

It turned out to be a moot point. In the fickle way of toddlers, they'd walked halfway to the door before Theo squirmed in Jackie's arms, crying out for his daddy.

As Jackie handed over his son, Eli shook his head. Together, the three of them walked out into the bright sunshine, a little family that could never be. He vowed Jackie would never know she'd broken his heart.

As they took the concrete steps down to the sand, Jackie looked at him and smiled. She took out her phone and snapped a few photos. "With the wind in your hair and the sea in the background, I want to always remember this day," she said.

Spoken like someone who would soon be leaving. Which she would. He knew better than to hope she'd stay.

"Let Theo walk in the sand and see what he thinks," Jackie suggested. "Maybe we can even take him in at the edge of the waves."

Since he figured the sand might be hot, he left Theo's sneakers on as he lowered him to the ground. He took one hand and Jackie took another since Theo was apt to take off running. This new situation appeared to confound him. Small brow furrowed, Theo looked from the sand to the water and back to Eli. As they approached the water, Theo pointed, his attention riveted on the waves. "Go there," he said, clear as day.

"I wish we had flip-flops," Jackie mused. "We either have to take off our shoes or get them wet."

"Or not walk in the water," he added, wondering how they'd clean all the sand off before getting in the car.

She shot him a look of patent disbelief. "We drove hours to reach the ocean. You have to let Theo feel the water on his bare feet. How about we all take our shoes off and leave them up on the sand."

Not entirely convinced, he decided to let his son decide. Once he'd stepped out of his shoes and removed his socks, he helped get Theo out of his. Jackie grinned at him and did the same.

"Ah," she exclaimed. "Nothing like the feeling of toes in warm sand."

Though Eli disagreed, her excitement was contagious and he found himself smiling back. "Let's do this," he said, motioning for her to grab Eli's other hand again. Together, they lifted him up, to his giggling delight, and walked over to the edge of the surf.

When they lowered him down, still holding tight to his hands, his little feet were in the frothy water. Not much—just enough to cover his toes, but he let out such a loud squeal full of joy that Eli found himself laughing. "Come on," Eli said, encouraging his boy to take a step on his own. "It's the ocean."

Theo tried to tug his hand away, clearly wanting the freedom to play in the water, but Eli held on tight. Jackie didn't. She let him go, bending down to show him how to splash in the waves, laughing as he crouched down and mimicked her. In one quick movement, he spun and splashed his daddy's leg.

Though Eli continued his grip on Theo's hand, by the time they were ready to leave, Theo's entire outfit had gotten soaked, as well as Eli's jeans. Somehow, Jackie had managed to remain mostly dry.

Watching her frolic in the water with his son, Eli couldn't help but notice the way the tension seemed to melt off her. With sunlight making copper fire in her dark hair, the shocked look vanished from her eyes. She laughed and splashed and Theo ate it all up. In that moment Eli had never loved her more.

Another family came over, setting down beach towels and an umbrella, turning their radio on and playing loud country music. Eli and Jackie exchanged looks, silently agreeing their own respite should end.

They collected their socks and shoes and walked barefoot back to the seawall. Depositing Theo on a bench, Eli asked Jackie to look after him while he went to fetch some baby wipes, a fresh diaper and a change of clothes.

It didn't take long for Eli to get his son cleaned up. He and Jackie used the wipes to get as much sand off their own feet as possible before slipping their socks and shoes back on.

"What about your wet jeans?" Jackie asked, her eyes still shining, her hair wild from the wind.

"They'll dry," he told her, still aching with the love he felt for her. His reply made her laugh again; her entire face lit up.

"The ocean was good for you," he said as they got back into the car.

"It was. I might be a west Texas girl at heart, but I sure do love the sand and the sea."

A west Texas girl. Not a New York girl. Not sure what to make of that comment, he pulled out into the road and headed back toward home.

"What about you?" she asked, marveling at all the fully restored mansions as they drove up Broadway. "I see all that playing in the sun and sea spray wore little Theo out, but did getting out there near the gulf help you at all?"

"*You* helped me," he told her, deciding to be honest. "Through all of this, you've been your sister's fiercest champion, but your support of me and now my son, never wavered. I don't know how I ever can repay you, but it meant the world to me. Thank you for that."

Glancing at her as he spoke, he couldn't decipher the emotion that flickered across her expressive face.

"You're welcome," she replied quietly, averting her face, but not before he saw the sheen of what looked like tears in her eyes. Since he had no idea if something he'd said had hurt her feelings, he decided it'd be better to be quiet, so he turned up the radio and concentrated on his driving.

Chapter 15

Though Jackie knew he'd meant it as a compliment, Eli's words had gutted her. Nothing romantic about them, he'd more or less complimented her for being a good friend.

Was that how he regarded her? A female friend with whom he'd shared occasional benefits? This knowledge made her feel even more foolish for even considering staying.

Except for one unalterable and certain fact. She loved him. With every fiber of her being, with all that she was. She loved him. This didn't feel like a passing infatuation, but a deep and certain love, the kind upon which futures could be built. Watching him with his son today had cemented it, erasing any lingering doubts she might have had. She loved Eli Pitts. And his adorable little son, Theo, her nephew.

She might only have known Eli two weeks, but she felt as if she'd been hit by a lightning bolt. Cupid's arrow. The thought made her smile. Cheesy, maybe. But a feeling this strong and sure was definitely worth exploring and seeing where it could go.

Maybe even forever.

Such a thought stunned her. She'd been in love before, or thought so at the time. But she'd never met someone with whom she could imagine spending the rest of her life. Even here in Getaway, in the town where she'd grown up.

Except she wasn't sure Eli felt the same way. Which should make her decision all that much easier.

Her head began to hurt as much as her heart. Too much sun, most likely. Eli had gone silent, so she decided she would, too.

For the next several hours she alternated between dozing and trying to figure out her future. When they stopped for gas in San Antonio, she offered to drive since Eli had driven the entire way down, but he'd insisted he did better when he had something to do. So with her head throbbing and exhaustion coloring the edges of her vision, she let him, turning her face to the window.

Amazing how in such a short time, her outlook on life had changed. Her once beloved New York no longer held as much appeal as it had before. Glancing at him through her lashes, she eyed the ruggedly handsome man behind the wheel, turned to view the adorable toddler sound asleep in the back seat. She couldn't imagine leaving them. The idea made her feel as if she'd be ripping her heart clean out of her chest.

She honestly didn't know how the hell she would be able to do it.

However, Eli hadn't asked her to stay. He hadn't even hinted. When he'd given her his thoughts on what love meant to him, she'd nearly swooned right there at the table. Luckily, their food had arrived and she'd been able to focus on devouring her hamburger.

Then, at the beach, she'd felt part of a sweet little family of three. Something she'd never even realized she'd wanted, never mind the brief flash of longing to have her own baby. Until then, after practically raising Charla, she hadn't been certain she even wanted children.

New York, with its constant activity, rushing from one thing to another, now seemed as if it belonged to another person. She could imagine how wonderful it would be if she had someone like Eli to share that life with, but she knew he wouldn't flourish in the city. He belonged in Getaway, in dusty west Texas, with his horses and his ranch. She wasn't even sure where she'd fit in his world. Or if he even wanted her to. After being burned by her sister, she couldn't blame him for being gun-shy. Especially since they'd only known each other a couple of weeks.

Again, she peeked at him. Strong jaw clenched, he appeared to be concentrating on driving.

Summoning up her courage, she almost asked him if he could ever imagine her having a place in his life. But saying that not only felt presumptuous, but made her feel raw and exposed, too, so she didn't. Something like that couldn't be prompted or forced. If he truly wanted her to hang around, he'd have to say so of his own free will.

Sometime between San Antonio and Abilene, she actually managed to fall asleep. And naturally, she dreamed of Eli, holding her close and professing his love. In her dream she asked him if it wasn't too soon and he responded by telling her he'd known the first moment he'd seen her. When you know, you know.

She woke with that phrase echoing in her head. Dream Eli had been right. Too bad real Eli didn't feel the same.

"Hey there." Eli smiled at her. "Did you enjoy your nap?"

Covering her mouth to stifle a yawn, she sat up straight. "I think so. Wow. I've never been able to sleep in cars or planes. It's so weird that I did."

"You must be really tired. I know he is." He used his head to let her know to check the back seat. When she turned, she saw little Theo, still fast asleep in his car seat.

"I am. Finding my sister sure didn't end like I hoped it would. Instead of becoming close, she made sure to burn all remaining bridges."

He nodded. "What about your mother? I know you didn't actually speak with Delia while we were in Galveston, but are you going to be upset with me if I press charges over what she did?"

"No." She didn't even have to think about her answer. "She and Charla are much more alike than I realized. They both need to understand there are consequences for their actions."

"I can't even imagine going through that hell again

if she'd succeeded in snatching my son," he told her. "When he was missing before..."

Reaching out, she placed her hand on his shoulder and squeezed. "I can't imagine. I'm so sorry my sister put you through that."

When he turned to look at her, the raw need in his face made her catch her breath. "Will you stay with me at my ranch for the rest of the time you're here, Jackie? I know you're planning on leaving this weekend."

Her heart, which had leaped at the first sentence, stuttered at the rest. "Of course," she replied, wondering how she'd endure the heartbreak. "I wouldn't have it any other way."

By the time they pulled off the highway, taking the exit that would lead them to Main Street, the entire town had shut down. Though the streetlights were lit, all the store windows were dark and the parking lots empty, except for the Rattlesnake Pub. "Does that place they called The Bar get a pretty good crowd on weeknights?" she asked, curious.

He shrugged. "I don't know. It's not like I do a lot of bar hopping these days. And I'm more of a Pub type of guy."

As they pulled up in front of the Landshark Motel, parking under a streetlight, her weariness threatened to overwhelm her. "I'll wait here while you grab your stuff," he said. "Theo is still asleep."

On the verge of asking if she could wait until morning to stay at his place, she realized they were in her car and if he went home without her, she'd be left here without a vehicle.

With her back stiff, she got out and went inside to

collect her belongings. The melancholy affecting her had to be due to the long day. She didn't want it to ruin what little remaining time she had with Eli and Theo.

It only took her a few minutes to throw everything into her suitcase. She cleaned out her toiletries, too, deciding she'd check out in the morning. Once she'd done a complete sweep of the room to ensure she hadn't left anything behind, she took a deep breath, straightened her shoulders and went back out to the car.

Catching sight of her, Eli grinned, the streetlight illuminating his face. She felt the power of that smile all the way to her toes. He popped the trunk and she stowed her luggage there, closing it quietly and carefully. Climbing into the car, she glanced into the back seat where Theo still slept; she gave Eli a quick thumbs-up before securing her seat belt.

Once they reached the ranch, she grabbed her bags while Eli carried his boy inside. Waiting in the living room, she wondered if she'd be sleeping in the guest bedroom or with Eli. She stretched out on the couch to wait and closed her eyes, intending to merely rest them for a moment.

She must have fallen asleep again, because she woke with Eli nuzzling her neck as he murmured her name. Smiling, she pulled him down to her, kissing him with as much sleepy passion as she could summon.

"Your choice," he said, mouth against hers. "You can sleep here, or in the guest bedroom, or with me."

"As if there's even a choice," she scoffed, holding his gaze. "I want to be with you."

Still kissing, stumbling toward the bedroom like a pair of punch-drunk lovers, they fell onto his bed, passion flaring hot, heavy and all-consuming. He had enough self-restraint to grab a condom, but once he'd done that, he was insatiable.

Finally, that particular hunger slaked, he cleaned up and then returning to bed, wrapped himself around her to sleep.

The next morning, waking up in his arms, Jackie gazed at the sleeping man beside her and sighed, her heart full. She didn't want to move, didn't want to do anything to disturb this blissful moment.

"Mornin'," he said softly, opening his impossibly blue eyes. He twisted slightly, nudging her with his fully aroused body, which made her melt.

After he grabbed a condom from his nightstand, they made love again, slowly instead of the rushed, passionate frenzy of the night before. They explored each other's bodies as if they had all the time in the world. The thought made Jackie's heart ache, even as she arched her back, her pleasure coming in waves as she found release. Eli followed an instant after, and then they simply held each other. No words were necessary or wanted.

Jackie wished they could stay that way forever.

In his bedroom, little Theo started calling for his daddy. Eli hollered that he'd be right there, kissed Jackie and got out of bed. "Let's have breakfast at the café this morning," he said. "I'm going to clean up really quick and get Eli ready. While I'm doing that, why don't you go shower and we'll meet in the kitchen."

Stretching lazily, she gave him a sleepy smile. "Sounds perfect." She couldn't resist eyeing his sexy butt as he headed toward the bathroom.

Later, craving a cup of strong coffee, she hurried into the kitchen. The sight of Eli, sitting on the floor, playing trucks with his son, stole her breath away. This man, this handsome, ridiculously sexy cowboy, had so much tender patience and love inside him and he wasn't afraid to show it.

He looked up when she entered, his blue gaze warm. "There she is," he told Theo. "Your aunt Jackie. You ready to go get some breakfast?"

Theo nodded vigorously. He pushed to his feet, a little wobbly, but strong. Gaining momentum, he barreled toward Jackie in what looked like a drunken run. Just as he reached her, she scooped him up and swung him around, which made him squeal with glee.

As usual, the Tumbleweed Café parking lot had very few empty spaces. Eli found a spot and they all got out. For some inexplicable reason, Jackie felt nervous, as if people could look at her and know exactly what she and Eli had been doing.

They lucked out and were shown to a booth near the front window, with a view of the parking lot and Main Street. All around them, conversation hummed. Several people greeted Eli by name and a couple of older ladies stopped by and cooed over Theo, eyeing Jackie with open curiosity. Eli introduced her as Charla's sister, which inevitably led to Charla's disappearance. Eli informed everyone that Charla had been found and that Rayna or one of her deputies would be bringing her back to Getaway. The two women rushed away, as if they could hardly wait to start spreading the gossip.

"That's why you wanted to come here, wasn't it?" Jackie asked.

"Partly," Eli admitted. "I wanted to clear my name, and the fastest way to spread news around Getaway is tell people here at the café. A few well-placed words and everyone in town will know before nightfall."

During their breakfast a few other people stopped by the table and each time, Eli managed to work something into the conversation about Charla. By the time the waitress dropped off the check, Jackie figured he'd accomplished what he'd set out to do.

Rayna walked in just as Eli was paying the check. She headed straight for their table. "I've already had three phone calls asking me if it's true that Charla and Delia are in jail down in Galveston," she said. "I'm guessing that's why you're here?"

Eli grinned. "You caught me. I wanted to clear my name and fast. Plus, we needed a great breakfast after the day we had yesterday."

"Brilliant strategy," Rayna agreed, laughing. Her gaze slid to meet Jackie's. "Hey, just in case I don't see you before you leave, I wanted to tell you goodbye. I hate to see you go. I really wish you were here permanently."

Again, Jackie felt that twist in her heart, though she took care to hide it. "Me, too," she replied, jumping to her feet to hug the sheriff as she threw out a hint to Eli. "Take care."

Rayna moved on, heading toward the takeout counter, evidently to pick up her own breakfast.

"Are you ready?" Eli asked, wiping off Theo's face before lifting him out of the booster seat.

Jackie nodded, taking one last look around the packed restaurant. She found it strange how three years ago she couldn't wait to see the last of this town. Now she found herself dreading leaving.

As they walked outside to Eli's truck, she wondered if she should go back to her motel room for her last two nights. Maybe making a clean break would hurt less than dragging it out.

But as she buckled herself in, she looked at the man she now knew she loved and shook her head. No point in trying to fool herself. She wanted to spend every minute she had left with Eli and Theo. No matter how much harder it would be to go.

"We need to swing by the motel," she said. "Since I'm staying at your place, I need to check out. There's no point in paying for the room when I won't be using it."

At the Landshark, Eli and Theo waited in the car while she took care of checking out. When she returned, feeling somehow lighter now that she'd finished that final chore, she impulsively leaned over and gave Eli a kiss.

"What do you want to do today?" he asked. "We can do anything you want, just name it."

"Are you not working?" she countered. "I can watch Theo if you need to work around the ranch."

Expression incredulous, he eyed her. "That wouldn't be fair. I'd feel like I'd be taking advantage of you."

"Not at all," she replied, meaning it. "I enjoy spending time with Theo and I love helping you. Go ahead and get your work done." She couldn't bear to ask him what he'd do for childcare once she'd gone.

Pulling into the ranch drive, he shook his head.

"Work can wait. I want to spend the rest of the time you're here with you."

Once again, like a fool, she caught herself waiting for him to say more. Almost as if she held herself still enough, he might actually ask her to stay.

But he didn't and she knew she'd need some time to regroup and get her emotions under control. "I appreciate that," she finally managed to say. "But a couple of hours of work won't hurt anyone. Go get it done. I promise I'll be here waiting when you get back."

Walking toward the barn and leaving Theo with Jackie, Eli tried to settle his mind so he could think. Jackie filled his thoughts. Jackie smiling, her eyes shining as she gazed at him. Kind, tenderhearted Jackie, so strong and brave and beautiful. She'd befriended him, her sister's ex, supported and helped him and even shared her body with him. Despite the intensity of the heat that flared between them, she'd made no bones about her leaving, honest and up-front about everything. Unlike her sister, Jackie was real.

It might only be wishful thinking, but part of him couldn't shake the feeling that she might actually be willing to stay. The other, more rational side of him figured he thought that because he wanted it so badly. She'd lose her job if she did, and he couldn't bear the thought of her giving up everything she'd worked so hard for.

Either way, he planned to sound her out about it at dinner that night. There had to be a solution, some sort of compromise, if they both wanted it enough. This thought gave him hope. He might only have known

Jackie a short time, but he couldn't imagine life without her.

He worked the two horses and then did a rushed clean-out of their stalls. His part-time worker would be there tomorrow, so he'd have help with some of the grunt work, but he'd need to find someone who could look after Theo at least part-time.

Rayna called just as he was finishing up. "I've sent Sam down to Galveston to bring Charla and Delia back," she said. "I thought you might want to be the one to tell Jackie."

"Thanks."

"How's she doing?" Rayna asked. "It's got to be rough, learning both your sister and your mother are under arrest and possibly going to serve time."

"She seems okay," he replied. "That meeting she had with Charla really opened her eyes. As for Delia, that woman has apparently always treated Jackie like dirt."

"Still," Rayna persisted, "she is her mother."

"Is this your way of hinting I need to think about dropping the charges?" he asked. "Because even Jackie feels her mother needs to learn there are consequences for her actions."

"I agree. And no, I'm not hinting about anything. I'm just throwing that out there in case Jackie might be having trouble dealing with all this. It's a lot."

"I agree. I'll take care of her. She's staying with me at the ranch until she leaves." Just saying the words made his heart ache.

"Good. Oh, and I do have other, nonrelated news." Rayna's deliberate tone warned him she'd carefully considered her next words. "Normally, I try to mind my own business. But even I can see the connection you and Jackie have. So I thought I'd pass along that Myrna Maples is looking for a ghost writer and editor. Not only does she want to hire someone to take over writing her advice column, but she wants to write a memoir. Since Jackie is an editor at a book publisher, I immediately thought of her."

Myrna Maples, the syndicated advice columnist, was the most famous person in Getaway. She'd almost died at the hands of her serial killer son, though Rayna had saved her. The two women had become friends after that.

"I can put in a word with Myrna for her, if she'd like," Rayna continued.

Hope flared, though he quickly extinguished it. "Thanks for letting me know," he said quietly. "I plan to talk to her tonight to explore what options we have of continuing this relationship."

"At least you can let her know she might have a job here."

"True. And thank you," he said. "I'll have Jackie contact you if she's interested."

After ending the call, he mulled over what Rayna had said. While he knew Jackie was a book editor, he had no way of knowing whether or not she'd be interested in working for Myrna Maples. He'd have to figure out a way to ask her without putting pressure on her to stay.

Back inside the house he headed directly to the shower to wash off the smells of horse and barn. When he emerged, hair still damp, he followed the infectious sound of Theo's laughter to the kitchen, where he found

Jackie sitting at the table playing with Play-Doh. They'd made all kinds of interesting things, from snowmen to what appeared to be horses.

The moment Theo caught sight of his dad, he lifted up whatever he'd been making and squeezed it in his little hand, crushing it. "Come see," he said, startling Eli. His son hadn't spoken much yet and despite his urging Charla to have him tested, she'd never done so. Eli figured he'd get that done, too.

"What do you have there?" Eli asked, crouching down next to Theo. "It looks like a big dog."

Theo shook his head. "Horse," he said clearly, beaming.

Amazed again, Eli glanced at Jackie. She grinned, noticeably proud.

"Have you been coaching him?" Eli asked, his heart full.

"A little," she admitted. "Right, Theo?"

At that, Theo laughed, a boisterous, joyous sound that made Eli smile. Jackie leaned close, her mouth to Eli's ear. "I think he's been starved for attention. He'll flourish now that he has you."

And you, he wanted to say. But he didn't. She'd be leaving soon, so it wouldn't be true. She got up and moved away, back to her chair.

"What would you two like me to make for dinner?" he asked, jumping to his feet. "Let me look and see what I've got to work with."

"No need," Jackie interjected. "I took out some chicken legs and used the microwave to defrost them. I was going to make oven-fried chicken."

"You don't have to cook for me," he said.

"I know that. Maybe I want to." She got up, moving gracefully. "Why don't you sit and play with your son and let me get the meal prepared."

Slowly, he nodded. Smiling at Theo, he reached out and grabbed a piece of the soft clay. "I'm going to make a horse," he announced.

Meanwhile, Jackie bustled around the kitchen. Once she'd put the chicken in the oven, she came back to sit at the table. "Chicken and roasted veggies," she announced.

"Sounds great," Eli responded. "But next time I want to cook for you."

She grinned. "That sounds like a plan."

When the meal was ready, they all sat at the table and ate like a family. More than anything, Eli found himself wishing they were.

For the rest of the afternoon and evening, Eli allowed himself to wallow in the comfortable feeling of family, even though he doubted Jackie even knew she brought it. Things had never felt so cozy and domestic, not even during his brief marriage to Charla. Jackie hummed to herself as she worked, slightly off-key, and a soft sort of happiness radiated from her. All smiles, Theo clearly picked up on it, too.

Damn, he could get used to having her around. Especially with the sexual tension running just underneath the surface, heating his blood and making him envision what he wanted to do to her once they went to bed.

Assuming she wanted to share his bed.

Later, after he'd bathed Theo, read him a bedtime story and tucked him in, he rejoined Jackie in the living room. She'd poured herself a glass of wine from the bottle they'd opened to have with dinner, and he grabbed a beer before taking a seat on the couch next to her.

"Hey there," she said softly. "It's been a really nice day. Thank you for inviting me into your life."

"Are you still planning on going back to New York?" he asked, inwardly wincing at his bluntness. He'd meant to try and ease into the subject, be casual. Instead, he'd blurted it out without warning.

Her head snapped up, her gaze flying to his. "I'm not sure," she said, choosing her words carefully. "Do you not want me to?"

"I want you to do whatever makes you happy," he said. The flash of disappointment that crossed her face made him wonder if he was going about this all wrong. He decided to say what was in his heart. "I want to be with you, Jackie. To see where *this*, whatever this is, takes us. I'm in love with you. But I can't ask you to give up your job, your life, just for me."

Slowly, gaze locked on his, she nodded. "I get that. I want to be with you, too, Eli. I'm in love with you, too."

He froze. Opened his mouth, tried to speak and failed. This gift he hadn't even dared to hope for filled him with wonder and joy, and a rush of desire so strong he could scarcely think.

He wanted to pull her into his arms, crush her to him and kiss her senseless. But that would all have to wait until later. This moment was too damn important to both of them to be rushed or turned into something else.

Looking down at her hands, she took a deep breath. When she raised her head again, he saw determination in her face, that strong and steady will that he'd come to love. "I never in a million years expected something like this to happen. Knowing you has changed my life. It's a difficult choice."

"It doesn't have to be." He took a deep breath, suddenly certain. "I'll do whatever it takes to work this out. If you can't stay, I want to go with you. I'll sell the ranch, move to New York and find work there."

Clearly shocked, she slowly shook her head. "No, Eli. I can't ask you to do that. This ranch is your life," she said, her voice as fierce as her expression. "You belong here, Eli. In Getaway. Not in New York."

Though he knew she was right, he meant what he'd said. Life with her, wherever that might be, was infinitely preferable to the bleakness of imagining a life without her.

"Then help me figure out a compromise," he replied, reaching for her hand. "Help me figure out a way to stay together."

"I want to be with you," she told him, lacing her fingers through his. "And part of your life here, on this ranch, in this town. Theo deserves the chance to grow up in Getaway. He belongs here as much as you do. And honestly, I can actually see myself living here with the two of you. Maybe even someday we can have one or two babies of our own." She blushed, though she kept her steady gaze locked on his.

He grinned. "I'd like that very much." And then he kissed her, a deep, sensuous kiss that left no doubt how he felt about her.

When they finally broke apart, he eyed her swollen, soft mouth and dazed expression, aching. "I love you so damn much."

Her smile bloomed, lighting up her face. "Right back atcha, Eli Pitts. I'm going to call my boss tomorrow and give my two-week notice. I'll have to go back and work those weeks, box up my things and see if I can get out of my lease."

"That's understandable." And who knew, but maybe her boss would cut her loose before the two weeks was up.

"Once all those details are taken care of," she continued, "I'm going to need to figure out what kind of job I could find here. Except for retail or food service work, it's always been kind of slim pickings in Getaway."

"I think Rayna might know something you'd like to do," he said, and then passed along all the info Rayna had given him earlier.

"Wow." After sipping her wine, Jackie shook her head. "Like everyone else who grew up here, I've always been in awe of Ms. Maples. I even wrote to her once, when my mother made me wear these awful patent leather shoes to the first day of middle school. While she didn't use my problem in her column, she did write back."

"What did she say?" he asked.

"She was very nice. Sympathetic. She said something about how my mother just wanted me to look pretty. I let that one slide, because she didn't know my mother." Jackie shook her head. "She bought Charla the expensive, name-brand sneakers that everyone else was wearing. I got stuck with the cheap patent leather because Charla lied and told her I wanted them."

Shaking his head, he took her wineglass from her and placed it on the coffee table. Then he pulled her into his arms and proceeded to try and make her forget about the past. They had an entire future to look forward to together. Everything else would simply fall into place.

* * * * *

Don't miss out on other exciting suspenseful reads from Karen Whiddon:

Texas Rancher's Hidden Danger
The Widow's Bodyguard
Snowbound Targets
Texas Ranch Justice
The Texas Soldier's Son

Available now wherever
Harlequin Romantic Suspense books
and ebooks are sold!

WE HOPE YOU ENJOYED
THIS BOOK FROM

HARLEQUIN
ROMANTIC SUSPENSE

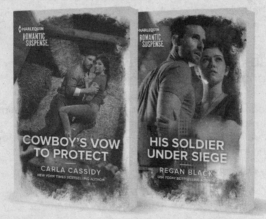

Danger. Passion. Drama.

These heart-racing page-turners will keep you guessing to the very end. Experience the thrill of unexpected plot twists and irresistible chemistry.

4 NEW BOOKS AVAILABLE EVERY MONTH!

She lunged forward, slamming him against the brick wall
at his back, her forearm against his throat. "Who are you?"
she snarled.

Stunned, he didn't resist her. Clearly, Rachel had some
serious self-defense training, which only furthered his
certainty that this was a woman who believed herself to be
in mortal danger.

"I told you," he rasped past her forearm. "I'm Marcus Tate."

"That's your name. Who are you?"

"I don't understand—"

"How did you follow me without me spotting you? How
do you know I look in shop windows to check my six? For
that matter, why are you here? Why did you think you could
take down some bad guy who might be following me?"

Ah. He didn't usually talk about his job, and certainly not
with civilians. But this situation was not usual in any way.
"I'm a soldier," he gasped.

All of a sudden, the pressure from her arm was so heavy he couldn't breathe, and he abruptly feared she might actually crush his larynx. Urgently needing to breathe, he reached up in reflex and pinched the pressure point in her hand between her thumb and fingers.

She yelped and jumped back from him, settling into a fighting stance with her hands in front of her and her weight lightly balanced on the balls of her feet.

"I mean you no harm, I swear," he said desperately. "You were just cutting off all my air."

"Who. Are. You," she bit out.

"Lieutenant Marcus Tate, US navy SEAL."

She hissed in sharply at that. Welp, she knew who the SEALs were. More to the point, she wasn't thrilled he was one. Which was weird as heck. Most people would be jumping up and down for joy that a SEAL had their back.

He continued doggedly. "I messed up my shoulder a couple of months ago. Had surgery on it a few weeks ago, and I'm here in Sunny Creek to rehab it. I'm staying with my old teammate, Brett Morgan, at Runaway Ranch. He'll vouch for me and everything I've just told you."

Speaking of which, his shoulder was screaming in protest at all the exertion he'd just put it through.

"If you don't mind," he said carefully, "I'd like to walk back to my truck and get some ice for my shoulder. It hurts like a sonofa—" He broke off. "It hurts a lot."

"You can walk in front of me. I'll follow behind you," she said grimly.

Don't miss
Her SEAL Bodyguard *by Cindy Dees,*
available May 2022 wherever
Harlequin Romantic Suspense books and ebooks are sold.

Harlequin.com

Love Harlequin romance?

DISCOVER.

Be the first to find out about promotions,
news and exclusive content!

Facebook.com/HarlequinBooks

Twitter.com/HarlequinBooks

Instagram.com/HarlequinBooks

Pinterest.com/HarlequinBooks

YouTube.com/HarlequinBooks

ReaderService.com

EXPLORE.

Sign up for the Harlequin e-newsletter and
download a free book from any series at
TryHarlequin.com

CONNECT.

Join our Harlequin community to
share your thoughts and connect
with other romance readers!
Facebook.com/groups/HarlequinConnection

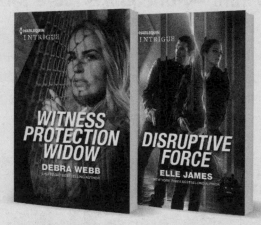